Completely Captivated

A.D. JUSTICE

COMPLETELY CAPTIVATED.

PROLOGUE

The End...Or Not

July, Present Day

This is the story of two very different men who are in love with the same woman. To grasp the full impact one person has on another's life, I'm starting at what seems to be the end of the story. But don't be deceived by appearances. I'll just be getting started with my plans for them by the time you catch up with me.

Who gets the girl and lives happily ever after is yet to be seen. My part in this story will be made clear soon enough. Until then, I'd like to introduce you to Christa, Aaron, and Jared. How they started. Where they fell apart. Then you and I will see how they end up—together. This is their past. Their future is still to come.

Buckle up, buttercup. We're all going for a ride.

Christa and Aaron walked hand in hand into the ultrachic, urbanely modern downtown office building. She was still reeling from their whirlwind weekend. Reality hadn't yet set in, leaving her to question if she'd hallucinated everything that had happened. A beautiful, life-changing, dream-come-true hallucination.

If I am, don't ever let me wake up, she thought.

As they crossed the marble floor of the lobby, she glanced over at Aaron for the hundredth time, convinced she was dreaming it all. A recurring unease ran through her mind repeatedly and plagued her thoughts. She was desperate to ask if he felt as shocked with their new life as she did. Part of her wanted to know if the extreme mixture of excitement, fear, and exhilaration, immediately followed by sheer terror, overwhelmed him as much as it did her. But she didn't want to be *that* girl—the needy, clingy, "*What are you thinking?*" type of girl.

Her thoughts drifted to how different everything she'd ever known was compared to just a few short months ago before she'd met Aaron. Even at her young age of twenty-two, she'd learned firsthand how life wasn't fair. Her parents had made sure to teach her that valuable lesson.

She'd also accepted she'd never be lucky in anything. She'd been unlucky in having the big, loving family she'd dreamed of her entire childhood. As the only child of a deadbeat dad and a neglectful mother, the only people she could lean on were friends she'd made along the way. The Miller family had all but adopted her, giving her the only stability throughout her childhood.

Luck in money had escaped her, since she had scraped by on her very last dime for anything she'd ever had. She'd worked tirelessly to start her own business, rising early in the morning and remaining in her shop until late at night to get her café off the ground.

Finally, she'd most decidedly been unlucky in finding love. The few men she'd made time to date turned out to be less stellar than she'd initially thought. Or dared to hope. But after the last three days, she was finally convinced her luck had changed for the better, that true love could happen, that happiness could last.

As they walked into the posh office building, nausea washed over her in repetitive waves when she realized she was completely out of place and notably underdressed. Elegant, professional women clicked by in their stiletto heels, with their hair perfectly coiffed and their nails fashionably manicured, wearing their expensive designer business clothes. Unlike everyone else, she was dressed in faded jeans, off-brand Ugg-type boots, and a generic name sweater. Her long, straight blond hair usually refused to cooperate, preferring to hang loosely on her shoulders.

She was grateful Aaron held her hand tightly in his, paying no attention to the beautiful women surrounding them. His strength flowed into her through their connected hands, giving her the courage to face whatever awaited them.

The security guard noticed her first and stood as though to stop her. The moment he realized she was with Aaron, his demeanor changed. "Good morning, Mr. Rivers."

"Good morning, Ty." Aaron dismissed the guard with a nod.

Aaron pushed the up button, and they were soon joined by several other people in the morning rush to their posh offices. Neither spoke as the elevator climbed to the twenty-sixth floor, where he led Christa to an expansive corner office.

The space was professionally decorated, with pictures and sculptures arranged to be both visually pleasing and modernly chic. The large, dark cherry wood desk was strategically placed in the corner, facing the door but not obstructing the impressive view of the city from the floor-to-ceiling windows on each side. Her back was to the door, staring out at the sights, until the angry male voice behind her caught her attention.

"Hold all my calls, Barbara." His command

resembled an irritable growl when he entered the office and all but slammed the door shut behind him.

He cut his gaze to Aaron and sighed heavily without even attempting to disguise his disgust and disapproval. She watched the wordless exchange between the two men, observed as Aaron quickly averted his eyes from the heavy glare of the other man. She had a quick and powerful urge to come to Aaron's defense and put the other man in his place. The obvious question was why he'd be so disappointed in Aaron in the first place.

"Hello, I don't believe we've met before. I'm Christa." She extended her hand to offer a handshake.

"Yes, I know who you are, *Christa Lanes*. I'm Lance Rivers, Aaron's older brother." His reply was curt and brash as he blatantly ignored her proffered hand.

She immediately noticed he didn't say it was nice to meet her, and a sickening feeling about this impromptu, early morning meeting settled into her gut.

Lance's stare darted between Aaron and Christa, throwing daggers in their direction. "Have a seat." He motioned at a small conference table close to the window then jerked the chair out for himself.

Aaron took the farthest seat, putting his back to the window. Christa sat directly across from Aaron.

Lance sat at the head of the small table and waited for them to settle before he began. He opened the manila folder he'd brought with him and pushed a neatly stacked collection of papers in front of Christa. He then clicked his pen and laid it directly on top of the papers.

"Ms. Lanes, let's cut to the chase, shall we? My brother, Aaron, is quite impetuous—that means he doesn't always think through his decisions as thoroughly as he should." Lance's tone was extremely condescending.

"Yes, I know what 'impetuous' means, Lance. What are you trying to say?" Christa's hackles were immediately raised, her tone rife with indignation over his assumption she was ignorant.

Lance smiled, but his eyes lacked any humor or warmth. "Everything I need to say is right there in those papers in front of you, Ms. Lanes."

Christa looked down at the papers, and her world came to a crashing halt. She couldn't breathe and couldn't form a coherent thought. The words jumped off the page at her, but in her panicked state, they were in no discernable order. Her mind raced and her heart throbbed, rendering her unable to comprehend the meaning of the words. Everything was a jumbled mess. But there was one lone word that resonated and reverberated throughout the echoes of her mind.

Divorce.

"I don't—I don't understand. Wh-what is this?" Christa demanded of Aaron when she finally found her voice. She searched his face intently, but it was void of any emotion. He deliberately masked his feelings, retreated inside himself, and blocked out the unpleasantness around him.

"It is exactly what it says it is." Lance spat out his sarcastic response. "Ms. Lanes, you and my brother do not have a real marriage. This fiasco never should've happened. We need to rectify this situation as soon as possible. As Aaron's lawyer, I've drawn up these papers to handle the procedures speedily."

She gripped the armrests of her chair, trying to focus on a single spot while a vortex of blackness threatened to erase her very existence. Her entire world stopped spinning and hung precariously on its axis, of that much she was sure. But the room she sat in was spinning fast enough to draw the air from her lungs, making it harder and harder for her to maintain her composure.

"Aaron. *Why?*" Desperation gripped her like a heavy vise and spilled over into her voice—forcing the pleading tone that was obvious even to her. She struggled to maintain her dignity and poise over the despair that suffused her. Everything she'd ever wanted in life was within her grasp, and she felt it slipping away, like tiny grains of sand sliding through her fingers. She was powerless to stop it.

"Ms. Lanes, surely you didn't think your relationship with Aaron was anything more than a passing fling. That's all Aaron *ever* has—just a quick fling, a one-night stand, and then he's through with them," Lance retorted, disdain dripping from his every word.

Christa heard a low growl emanate from Aaron's chest, but he didn't dispute Lance's mean-spirited words. He also didn't disagree with Lance's assessment of their relationship. She knew that was Aaron's life before her, but *they* were different. *He* was different with her. They were a couple now.

"Aaron—tell him that's not true. Tell him it's different with us," Christa pleaded.

Lance continued as if her world wasn't disintegrating all around her. Like the very person she loved the most wasn't being ripped from her life. Like her heart wasn't being cut out of her chest.

"Ms. Lanes, as you can see, Aaron is offering you a very generous settlement. You will be given ten million dollars, a house, and a vehicle of your choice, and you may keep any gifts Aaron has given you. This is the *only* time you will be offered this generous settlement." Lance's heartless words and matter-of-fact tone matched the sneer on his face.

"*What?* Ten million dollars? What are you talking about?" Unable to stay seated a second longer, Christa rose and quickly stepped around the table to sit beside Aaron. She was close enough to touch him, to feel the heat of his body, and to inhale the faint smell of his cologne. She watched him lower his head and stare down into his lap before she spoke softly to him.

"Aaron, please look at me," she requested. She watched as his Adam's apple bobbed up and down when he swallowed hard before slowly raising his chin. He turned his head toward her, his eyes indulging in a slow perusal of her body. When their gazes finally collided, she saw his emotions in the stark blue pools of his eyes before he quickly masked his feelings and his eyes became hard as nails again.

"Aaron, what's going on? Why are you doing this to us?" Christa asked softly.

She desperately wished Lance wasn't in the room so they could talk alone, and she could at least try to understand what was happening. She laid her outstretched hand on Aaron's arm and lovingly stroked his skin with her delicate fingers.

"I don't understand. I don't know why you're doing this. But it doesn't have to be this way. We don't have to do this. We can just leave now and go home *together.*"

"Let's be frank, shall we? You know who Aaron is.

You and he married without a prenuptial agreement. You may have fooled him for a short time, but no judge will ever give you more than what we're offering you right now when you've only been married a few days. You are not entitled to half of everything he owns. If you want to fight us over it, rest assured we have the resources to keep you tied up in litigation for *years,* and you will not see one penny the whole time. Take the offer. Live comfortably. Move on with your life," Lance barked.

Pain and confusion were etched on her face. *I know who he is? What does he mean by that?* So many questions flew through her mind at lightning speed, too many to even try to vocalize. The only coherent thought she could latch on to was *those were divorce papers.*

Didn't we just walk in here holding hands? He brought me here to serve me with divorce papers, but I don't understand why. What's happening? The questions kept coming. They flooded her mind and made it impossible for her to make a logical decision on her own. When she sat motionless and silent for a moment too long, Lance continued.

"Ms. Lanes, it is my belief that you drugged my brother to get him to agree to marry you, and that you have continued drugging him to keep him with you for the last three days. Now that he can think clearly again, he's agreed not to press charges against you, provided you agree to this deal," Lance concluded.

"Drugged him? Press charges? I haven't done anything wrong! I don't use drugs, and I'd certainly never drug him. I wouldn't even know *where* to go to get drugs, or even *what* to get." Her gaze darted between the two brothers, waiting for one of them to speak words that made any sense to her. Her lips parted, her chest rose and fell in rapid succession, and her hands shook. Her mind was reeling, and she couldn't reconcile how Aaron could think so poorly of her.

"Aaron." The tears glistened in her eyes, spilled over her bottom lids, and poured like a torrent over her beautiful, porcelain cheeks. "You know that's not true. You know I'd never do that to you."

"Aaron doesn't remember getting married. He doesn't remember anything about the last few days with you, Ms. Lanes. These are very serious charges—you could possibly even be charged with attempted murder, if the right information was given to the police." Lance raised his eyebrows, and his tone hinted he was considering the idea of calling the police.

"You don't remember anything?" Christa barely spoke the words aloud. Lance opened his mouth to speak yet again, but she cut him off. "*Aaron*—please say something."

"No, I don't remember anything about the past three

days. I don't know how we got married. How you ended up moving in with me. Nothing." Aaron's smooth, sexy voice finally found its place in the conversation.

Christa inhaled sharply, and her hand flew to her chest, covering her heart. She searched his eyes for any indication that this was some cruel, sick joke, but she found no humor in them. Nothing was there but what appeared to be contempt for her.

"You don't remember asking me to marry you, Aaron?" Christa whispered to him.

"No."

This can't be happening, she chanted silently.

"Is this what *you* want?" she asked, inclining her head toward the divorce papers.

"Yes."

She took his big hands and placed them on either side of her face, forcing him to turn in his chair to fully face her.

"When you proposed to me, you held my face like this. You said, *'Christa, you are more beautiful to me than the purest diamond. You are more precious to me than the rarest jewel. I want to be this happy every day of my life. Will you marry me?'*

"You were so loving and so sweet to me, Aaron. Even

though it was already late at night, you said you were going to make Bellasara's open so we could pick out our rings and get married immediately. You said you wanted to make me yours before anyone could come along and steal me from you. I laughed because I thought you were just being funny—acting out the scenes like in the movies.

"But when we pulled up outside of Bellasara's and the door opened for us to enter, I was shocked beyond words. We searched through every bridal set before you found the exact ones you wanted me to have. Don't you remember that?"

Aaron didn't answer audibly. He only slightly shook his head to indicate *no*. He listened intently as Christa continued recanting their story through her tears. The tears that were now soaking Aaron's hands as they held her face. Her eyes, pleading with him, held his gaze steadfast, and he briefly wondered if she could read his thoughts. Without a conscious decision, Aaron's thumb lightly grazed across her face and wiped away one tear as it fell from her eyes. It was quickly replaced by another.

"You picked out my rings—the diamond engagement ring and the diamond-circled wedding band. When you found them, you told me to always remember one thing." Christa stopped talking for a second to try to control the sob that was threatening to break free.

Aaron furrowed his brow, his eyes pinched together in the corners, silently asking her what that one thing was while he continued to watch her with rapt attention. He allowed some small amount of emotion to shine through his eyes.

Pity. He pities me. If that's what it takes to get through to him, I can endure pity for a short time.

"You said," she started and stopped to swallow a sob. "You said if I ever gave these rings back to you, it meant I was giving your love back. You said if I did that, I'd never get your love back again. You told me to hold on no matter what happened—to hold on to our love and never give it back."

Aaron's jaw muscle ticked from the hard grit he held. His breaths were quick and shallow, uncertainty and mistrust marring his handsome face. But he couldn't remove his hands from her face. Despite the terrible thoughts flying through his mind, he couldn't break the connection with her once he touched her. Everything about her had been his weakness. Her purity. Her innocence. Her admiration of him. *Had it all been a lie?* His eyes could no longer conceal the upsurge of emotion that flowed through him.

When she noticed the change in his demeanor, a seed of hope blossomed in her chest that she was getting through to him. Perhaps he did remember but suddenly had cold feet when the weekend ended and reality hit him. One thought after another swirled through Christa's mind while she tried to make sense of it all.

Did he have a change of heart?

Did he think getting married was a huge mistake?

Am I not good enough for him?

"Is this what *you* want, Aaron? You honestly don't want to be married to me? You don't want me at all?" Christa asked, leaving the tears to flow freely and her love for him to shine in her eyes.

Aaron maintained eye contact with her—gazing deeply into her eyes, looking for something, before his eyes followed the trail of her tears to where his hands cradled her face. He looked hard at the moisture gathered there. His gut told him one thing. *This was no act—no one could cry that hard, that much, and be faking her feelings. It wasn't possible.*

"I think it's best for both of us to end it now," he finally answered on a whisper.

He noted that her tears increased after his declaration, and the warm glow that shone in her eyes was slowly extinguished. He watched in slow motion as she reached up, wrapped her small fingers around his large ones, and dragged his hands off her face. The immediate emptiness slammed into him, driving deep into his core. He was losing her, losing his love, possibly even losing his destiny. *Something* vitally important was gone instantaneously, something he feared he'd never feel again.

Life had been hard for Christa, but she was no shrinking violet. She'd never felt such pain and despair. She had no doubt it would take her a lifetime to heal from the blow he'd dealt, but she didn't have it in her to roll over and give up. She reined in the minor breakdown Aaron and Lance had already witnessed, swallowed the broken heart that now resided in her throat, and straightened her spine.

"I'm not signing those papers," Christa stated with firmness but was quickly interrupted by Lance's angry growl before she could finish her sentence.

"We will see you in court in a couple of years, then!" Lance bellowed.

"I wasn't finished!" Christa yelled back before returning her gaze to Aaron, instantly softening, but maintaining her inner determination.

"As I was saying, I'm not signing those papers. Draw up a new agreement. I don't want anything from Aaron. I don't want his *money*. I don't want a *house* or a *car* or his *gifts*. I will agree to the divorce when you've taken all that out."

Looking down at her hands, she stared at the beautiful wedding rings for what felt like an eternity. She was still close enough to him that she could feel the weight of Aaron's stare on her like an iron anvil resting on her shoulders. From the corner of her eye, she knew he was also looking at her rings—the rings he chose for her. She mustered all the courage she could find as her right hand found her left ring finger. Her hands visibly trembled when she deliberately removed the beautiful diamond rings that symbolized their union.

Christa took Aaron's hand in hers, turned it over, and placed the rings in the center of his palm.

"I'm not giving your love back to you, Aaron. You're taking your love away from me. All your money, your houses, and your cars—they're all just worthless junk to me without *this*," she said as she closed his fist over "*his love*," her wedding rings. "I won't fight you over the divorce. If you don't want me, don't love me, there's nothing to fight for." For all the boldness she tried to project, inside she only felt defeated and crushed beyond repair.

Christa rose from her chair, and Aaron's eyes followed her every movement. She wiped the remaining tears from her face and dried her hands on her jeans. Looking at Lance, she spoke clearly. "I assume you'll contact me when you have the new papers ready for me to sign?"

Lance cleared his throat, obviously surprised by this odd turn of events. "Yes. Yes, I'll be in contact. It'll probably take about a week, though, because I have previous obligations to attend to first. I'd really prefer that we get something in writing from you today."

Christa quickly picked up the pen, drew lines through the settlement portion of the legal papers, put a big, fat zero in its place, and scribbled her initials beside it.

"Will that be good enough for now?"

Lance simply nodded, stunned, and for once in his life, speechless.

"If you honestly believe he's been drugged for the last three days, you should get him to the hospital to be tested. He may need medication to counteract any further effects." Christa's remarks were made to Lance, but she couldn't keep the true concern for Aaron out of her voice. "If he was drugged, it wasn't by my hand. I would never hurt him."

Aaron couldn't stop watching her every move. He was completely mesmerized by her, but he knew he had to break the spell. She had more natural beauty in one little pinky than all the professional models he'd *dated* combined. Her long, thick blond hair draped loosely over her shoulders—her shoulders that stood proud even when she wanted to break down.

Her petite frame and stature were dwarfed by his, but somehow, she had fit perfectly into his side. Her hand fit his like it was made for him and him alone. Her expressive brown eyes held nothing back, and she gave her love to him freely. Even at that moment, when she was hurt beyond measure, he had no doubt if he asked for forgiveness, she'd give it without question.

She was more honest, giving, and loving than anyone in his life, but he was pushing her away. She was the light in his dark, dreary world, and he was extinguishing her flame. He couldn't shake the feeling that she was the epitome of all that was good and pure, and he was the exact opposite. The sins of his past wouldn't let him forget what he'd done. When it came to personal relationships, his judgment had been clouded, his heart jaded. He couldn't trust his decisions or feelings, and he'd learned to bury them over the years. Regardless of the emotions she evoked, he couldn't allow himself to give in.

Christa wiped her face again, reeled in her emotions, and stepped toward the door. She was only a few feet away from Aaron, but it may as well have been miles. Christa was simply trying to keep her composure until she could get back to her small apartment and have a total breakdown in private. She didn't want the workers in the pretentious office to see the telltale signs of her ugly crying—red-rimmed, puffy, bloodshot eyes, red nose, and tear-streaked cheeks. Her sole focus now was to get to the elevators as quickly as possible, but Lance's next comment stopped her dead in her tracks.

"Ms. Lanes, there's one more delicate subject we need to discuss before you leave." Lance was almost hesitant, and he nervously cleared his throat. Christa knew whatever was coming next couldn't be good.

"And what's that? What more could you possibly want from me?" she asked incredulously as she whirled around to fully face him.

Lance cleared his throat again, something she noticed he did when he wasn't comfortable. "I need you to list anyone with whom you've ever had sexual relations. In the event you try to claim that you're pregnant before this divorce is final, I assure you we will require a vast measure of tests to be performed to confirm paternity."

Lance knew demanding that information was a far stretch if it came down to a fight in a court of law. She didn't have legal representation present, and they didn't have a prenuptial agreement. He knew he didn't have a valid reason for requesting this information at this point, but he was banking on the fact that she had no legal knowledge or training.

She didn't know the wicked ways in which he could use this information against her if she later changed her mind and pursued the path to gain a full half of Aaron's considerable assets. But he needed to make sure his brother and their fortune were safe and secure from any gold-digging harlots.

Lance pushed a blank sheet of paper across the table in her direction. She looked from Lance to Aaron, clearly unsure of what she should do, and silently praying that Aaron would come to her rescue. But he sat stone silent, patiently waiting for her to complete the embarrassing and humiliating task Lance had asked of her.

Christa stepped to the table and scribbled a couple of words before shoving the paper back at Lance. He balked when he read the paper. "Ms. Lanes, I need you to list *everyone*."

"I did," she responded indignantly, then turned her head to look Aaron squarely in the eye.

Unable to contain his curiosity of what the paper held any longer, Aaron grabbed the paper from Lance's grip. He couldn't believe his eyes. He looked from the paper to Christa's face, closely examining her while he tried to come to terms with what he saw.

"It only has my name on this paper," Aaron stuttered disbelievingly.

"I know. I was waiting for the right man. I told you that on our wedding night," she said as the blush crept up her face. If Aaron had to guess, he would say she was clearly remembering their first night together. The night he couldn't remember at all. He suddenly wished he could remember that night more than any other night he'd ever spent in a woman's arms.

Aaron stared back down at his name on the paper. The shame and guilt immediately started building in his chest. He knew people—he could read them like a book. He knew in his gut that she was telling the truth. She was still so young at twenty-two, mostly isolated and completely introverted, and didn't engage with anyone outside her small circle before he came along and charmed her. She'd been a virgin until he took that away from her. On top of ruining her life, he was divorcing her after not even remembering marrying her.

Aren't I quite the catch? he thought to himself. *She'll be better off without me.*

When he finally looked up, he noticed the door to Lance's office was standing wide open, and Christa was gone. Her rings were still in one of his clutched fists, and the paper that contained only his name was in the other.

And Aaron was completely alone.

CHAPTER ONE

Table for Two

April

"Christa, the delivery man is here. Can you watch the front while I handle our delivery?" Allie asked.

"Sure, Allie. I got it," Christa responded.

Allie Barker was Christa's best friend and only employee at her coffee shop and bakery, The Sweet Spot, but somehow, they made it work together day after day. When the small shop in the high-rent district of an influential San Francisco neighborhood became available at an amazingly affordable price, Christa took it as a sign that it was meant for her. The fact that it had a ready-to-use gourmet chef kitchen was an additional bonus.

She thought if she could get her business going with fast and easy treats first, the kitchen would be perfect for catering larger events later. She had a five-year plan and was determined to see every last detail through to fruition. She was so involved in her thoughts about those plans, and how her business was performing, she didn't hear the bell over the door chime when the next customers walked in.

When she looked up, she was pulled into the deepest, most delicious sea of blue ever to grace a man's face. He was more than handsome—he was drop-dead gorgeous. His blue eyes sparkled with mischief, his smile was warm and contagious. She felt her own cheeks lifting in response.

His dark black hair was naturally messy and sexy, perfect for the obligatory finger-gripping during wild, swinging-from-the-rafters sex. His face was covered in just the right amount of five-o'clock shadow. He was tall, with broad shoulders, a narrow waist, and had a finely sculpted chest, if the shirt stretched tight across his shoulders was any indication. He had just the right amount of muscular build to be athletic.

Unfortunately, he'd walked in with an equally beautiful woman by his side.

As if I had a chance with him anyway, Christa thought to herself.

She pasted her best hostess smile on her face and greeted her new customers, mentally reminding herself she needed the clientele more than she needed a date.

"Hello. Welcome to The Sweet Spot. What can I get you?" she asked cheerfully.

"Hello." The sexy, baritone voice was like smooth velvet to her ears. "Can we get a large regular coffee and a medium skinny white chocolate mocha, please?"

"Sure. Just have a seat, and I'll bring it out to you. Anything from the pastry case?" Christa offered, practicing her salesperson skills.

The tall stick figure that accompanied the Adonis standing before her replied with disdain dripping from her lips. "Oh, those things have a million carbs. Keep them away from me."

As if on cue, the handsome man responded with the opposite. "They look delicious. How about one of those croissants—toasted, with plenty of butter on the side?"

Christa wasn't certain, but she would've sworn he ordered the pastry just to antagonize his date. She rang up the sale, quickly filled the coffee cups, and delivered the order to their table.

"Aaron, really, did you have to get the croissant? It's the biggest pastry in the case," the stick figure whined.

Aaron picked up the pastry and sank his teeth in. "Oh my God!"

Christa had turned her back to him the second before she heard his exclamation. She whirled around, placed her hand on his shoulder, and leaned in close to him. "What's wrong?"

He almost laughed at the concern on her face. "Absolutely nothing is wrong. This is *the best* croissant I've ever had. Where do you buy these?"

He watched her beautiful face turn the loveliest shade of pink as her embarrassment set in. She quickly snatched her hand from his shoulder and straightened her back. "Umm, I don't buy them. I make them here."

"I'm impressed—honestly. This is heaven. It literally melts in my mouth."

"I'm glad to hear that." Her reply was as warm and honest as her returned smile.

"I'll have to come here every day now," he said with a playful wink and a knowing smile. A smile that said he knew affected her and he knew she wished she could hide her reaction from him.

He'd always had the same effect on the ladies, and he'd frequently used his good looks to his advantage. He'd learned to read the signs; he knew when they were interested in him, and what they wanted from him. He'd give them a good time for a night or so, but no one ever held his interest for too long.

As he watched her walk away, he contemplated how he wouldn't mind that little lady being next on his list. He was well-known in the influential celebrity and business circuits and often dated high-profile models. *Dated* was a generous term. He wined, dined, and sixty-nined them, then sent them on their way. His work had him hip-deep in models on a daily basis. Models that were long-legged, skinny, and wouldn't eat more than a couple of pieces of dry lettuce to avoid gaining an ounce.

But everything about her seemed to contradict his normal type. Her name tag read *Christa*. She couldn't have been over five foot three barefoot. She didn't have long legs like his current companion, the one whose name he'd already forgotten. Christa had curves in all the right places, like a real woman should. Her breasts were small but perky, her legs were short but sleek and muscular, and her perfectly round ass—he could feast on it all day.

Her hair was long and blond, but it was her amazing brown eyes that held the magic. They captivated him, reached out and physically touched him, holding him as her hostage. For the first time in his adult life, he decided he'd gladly give full control over to someone else. The term *love at first sight* had always been a cliché to him. He'd argued there was no way a person could fall in love when they first met. But the feeling that stirred in his chest told him this pure, natural beauty was a threat to his one-night-only rule.

He watched her as she returned to the counter, took

a few orders, and gave every customer her personal touch as she filled their orders. He was amazed at how she made each person feel like a welcome guest in her home, and they were all glad to be there. His eyes followed as she continued to move around the room, talking to her patrons as if they were long-lost friends. She adjusted pastries in the case and refilled the carafe with hot coffee with ease and care.

She returned to his table a few minutes later. "Can I warm you up?"

His lips curled into a slow, sensual smile. He intentionally misinterpreted her offer and his playful eyes danced with mischief. "I wasn't aware that was a menu choice."

When she realized her choice of words, he watched with amusement as the red crept up her neck and face.

"Your *coffee*," she clarified with a laugh, thankful that his date was on the phone and completely oblivious to their conversation.

"I'm good," he responded, lifting one eyebrow and deliberately leaving his response open to interpretation. Christa's face suddenly looked like she had a sunburn, and he was completely enamored with her. "Keep blushing like that, and I might start to think you like me."

She laughed nervously and straightened imaginary

wrinkles from her clothes. "We can't have you thinking that, can we?"

The next day, Aaron showed up with a different girl—same build, same attitude, but his attention was transfixed on Christa. They continued their playful banter, with Aaron making comments to ensure Christa knew he was more than interested in her. Her natural shyness around men was evident, but that was part of his intense attraction to her and the foremost reason why he tamed his approach. She wasn't seeking attention, fame, or fortune. She was genuinely a beautiful person, inside and out, and he wanted to get to know her and see where their mutual attraction took them.

"Hi, Christa. Did you save any of your delicious, mouthwatering croissants for me?" Aaron asked in his smooth as silk, sexy bedroom voice as he strolled up to the counter.

Christa smiled through her awkwardness. "I might have one or two left."

"Feel free to save me one every day. I'll have to add some extra time to my work-out schedule to make up for it, but it's so worth it," he joked, patting his already muscular stomach.

Over the following week, Aaron came in alone and ordered his usual. Their witty dialogue increased daily along with their comfort level. When he couldn't wait any longer, he decided to make his move when Christa delivered his order to his table. He put on his best smile and held out his hand. "I haven't introduced myself. I'm Aaron Rivers."

"Christa Lanes," she replied as she accepted his hand.

"I'd really like to have breakfast with you, Christa."

Confusion shrouded her face. "Umm, right now?"

He nodded, his genuine smile covering his face, and gestured to the empty chair. "Right now would be perfect."

Christa looked around her café and decided Allie had everything under control. "One minute." She scurried behind the counter and grabbed her cup of coffee and a caramel croissant, a brand-new menu item she had just perfected the night before. She hurried back to his table and slid into the chair across from him.

His eyes bugged out at the sight of Christa's pastry. She giggled as he looked back and forth at their plates, trying to figure out the difference between the flaky pastries.

"What is *that*?" he asked spiritedly, while never taking his eyes off the deliciousness on her plate.

"It's something new I'm trying out to see how customers like it. It's a caramel croissant. My own concoction." She finished speaking as she raised her fork to cut off a bite. Before the tines touched her pastry, Aaron snatched her plate away and replaced it with his own.

"Let me be your guinea pig." He vigorously dove into the baked bliss, licking his lips while never taking his eyes off it. Christa watched his facial expressions for his reaction, her teeth leaving their imprint on her bottom lip in anticipation. She didn't have to wait long to know exactly what he thought about it.

"Fuck. This is incredible, Christa. This is the best thing I've ever eaten. It almost tastes better than sex feels." Then, as if it suddenly hit him, his expression turned serious as he continued. "I can't believe you gave me the plain one and took the caramel one for yourself."

She laughed heartily as she explained her duplicity. "Honestly, I had a feeling you'd take this one away from me as soon as I brought it out. It actually took you a little longer than I thought it would. I almost got a bite of it. You were a little slow on the uptake. Maybe I gave you too much credit, after all."

They settled into a playful banter, enjoying the company throughout the rest of their breakfast. With the pair feeling at ease with each other, their conversation moved easily from one topic to another, questions and answers freely shared as they became better acquainted. When the coffee and croissants were finished, Aaron reluctantly rose from the table.

"I have to get to work now. Can we do this again tomorrow morning?"

Christa was in awe of his confidence. He was so sure of himself, and he had no fear of rejection. *Then again*, she thought, *why would he?* He was beautiful, and she was…well, she didn't feel like she was in his league. But he made it a point to come into her establishment, ask to have breakfast with her, and he wanted to do it again. Those had to be positive signs.

Christa rose from the table and smiled as she nodded. "I'd like that."

She watched him leave while she picked up their plates and began preparing for the lunch crowd. Allie slid up beside her, smiling broadly while she watched Christa watching Aaron.

"You like him."

"He's funny. But I'm definitely not his type." Christa sighed to herself, refusing to get caught up in the "I wish" world she could easily lose herself in. She'd wished her childhood away. That sentiment had gotten her nowhere. Her new focus was "I will," and she only focused on the goals she knew she could attain.

Aaron Rivers wasn't one of those attainable goals.

"He may be funny, but he's not the only one. You're funny if you think I can't see through you, Christa Lanes. You definitely like him, and he seems to be into you too. Now, if you'd just let him *get into* you...if you know what I mean."

Christa lowered her head and covered her forehead with her hand. She shook her head and chuckled at her best friend. "Did you defrost the meat for lunch like I asked you to?"

"You know, C, you should've asked that hunk about lunch meat before he left."

"This is why I can't have anything nice."

CHAPTER TWO

Take A Chance

May

"I really hate my job." Aaron checked his calendar for the day and instantly wanted to throw his laptop out the high-rise window. A meeting with his brother and a potential client covered most of his day. Since the client was a major player in the fashion industry, Lance would be even more overbearing and demanding than usual.

Every attempt to concentrate on the headshots in front of him resulted in more frustration. None of them met his expectations. The problem, he realized, was he couldn't focus on anything remotely work related. His mind was on a certain beautiful young lady who'd captured his eye and wouldn't get out of his mind.

Over the past four weeks, he'd spent every weekday morning and evening in The Sweet Spot, working his way into her life before he officially asked her for a date. She'd greeted him with a welcoming smile every time he walked through the door. Their flirty banter increased with every visit, giving him hope she wouldn't turn him down flat.

That morning, he'd arrived earlier than usual and stayed longer than he should have.

"Here, take this with you." She'd approached him with a large coffee in a to-go cup. "You look like you could use an extra dose of energy this morning."

"Thank you, gorgeous. More energy would be great, but I'd love it even more if you'd find a way to get me out of work today. Care to play hooky with me?"

"So tempting."

"Say the word, and I'm all yours."

"Just like that?"

"Just like that."

She pulled her bottom lip between her teeth, trying to hide the smile threatening to claim her face. "While I'd love to play hooky with you, I have a lot of work to do today myself. Rain check?"

"Rain check. Sunny day check. Cloudy day check. Twenty-four-hour check. Whatever you want." He opened the door and took a step outside the shop before turning back to her. "I'll be back for more energy later this evening,"

"You know where to find me."

His only thought as he left, already running late for work, was she was worth the time, the shit his brother would give him, and anything else he had to endure. Those few minutes with her had become the highlight of his days.

She was a breath of fresh, genuine air in his world of fake, plastic cover models. When he first became an agent, he was all about wining and dining the "hopeful ones," as he'd dubbed them. The women who were encouraged by family and friends to take that leap into the big world of professional modeling, but when compared with a real model, they had no chance of ever gracing the cover of anything.

But giving them just a glimmer of hope made them more pliable, like putty in his hands, and he could do whatever he wanted with them. They were all too willing to use sex to get ahead, and he was all too willing to oblige them. With the sex, that is—not with getting ahead in the modeling world. He had his own reputation to uphold. He brought the best talent to the table, and that skill earned his company more contracts and more money.

His lady-killer reputation preceded him, and he'd made no attempts to hide it. By this way of thinking, the "hopeful ones" knew what they were getting into and knew the gamble they were taking. As with any risk, there were winners, and there were losers. He had been one of the definite winners in that industry, hustling to make his business name one that was instantly recognized.

But Christa was completely different from any of the women he'd ever been around. Spending time with her had been the most fun he'd had with a woman in many years, and he hated to end it. He thoroughly enjoyed their conversations and how well they got along. Just the thought of being stuck in his office all day turned his stomach.

Being a multimillionaire had once been his ultimate life goal. He'd attained that and so much more. But, he started questioning whether one could have a midlife crisis at the ripe old age of twenty-seven.

Working with his older brother, four years his senior, was wise financially, but had turned out to be a terrible decision on a personal level. Aaron's every move was closely scrutinized. Lance criticized him every chance he got, especially about all the models he'd slept with, and how Aaron was going to screw up one day and get one of them pregnant. Aaron felt trapped in a world he was no longer interested in—dating and representing models, working with his brother, and doing the nine-to-five grind. He'd gained nothing from it but a terrible reputation, a long line of "hopeful ones" he had no interest in, and the uneasy feeling that the light at the end of the tunnel was actually a speeding locomotive bearing down on him.

The buzzing of his phone signaled yet another

meeting he had to attend, another client in which he had no interest in helping. A meeting with yet another account that needed a specific look, a specific body type, and a specific edge to make the marketing ads stand out from the rest of the industry. They'd expect his undivided attention, just like every other client did. He'd personally sort through hundreds of headshots to find that exquisite needle in a haystack. It didn't matter who this meeting was with, how much they paid, or what they were looking for—every damn meeting was the same.

"Aaron, Lance wanted me to remind you that you have an eleven o'clock meeting in his office," Barbara, Lance's secretary, said over Aaron's office intercom.

It wasn't Barbara's fault that Lance was such an asshole. Aaron tempered his reply so he didn't come across curt with her.

"Thanks for the reminder, Barbara. On my way now." Aaron stood from behind his desk and grabbed his jacket from the back of his leather chair.

He arrived in Lance's office at 11:01 and was considered late by his brother. He could see the disdain on Lance's face the second he stepped into the room.

"I apologize for my tardiness. I had an urgent matter that couldn't wait, but I am all yours now." Aaron smoothly eased any tension in the room. The ad executives around the table nodded in understanding, and Aaron started his sales pitch.

After three hours of giving the same spiel he'd given countless times, and the same sleazy smiles to entice and cajole, the client was clearly impressed and wanted to sign Rivers Forte to handle their talent acquisition needs. Lance was ecstatic because it obviously meant a lot more money to line their pockets. Aaron kept his business face in place, but he felt himself die a little more inside with every deal. He also knew as soon as that meeting was over, he'd be locked in another fight with his damn overbearing brother over something asinine and unimportant.

Taking the only chance he could hope to have, he offered to escort their clients out of the building, and they graciously accepted. Aaron's actions were transparent, and he knew Lance saw right through him, but he didn't give a shit what Lance thought. After he parted with their new client, Aaron made his quick exit to his car and didn't even pretend not to know exactly where he was going.

To The Sweet Spot.

To Christa.

Changed into his well-worn jeans and a formfitting Polo shirt, Aaron parked outside Christa's café and watched her through the large picture window for several minutes. The café was unusually busy for this time of the late afternoon, but she moved with ease from table to table, checking on her patrons with her easygoing smile and mannerisms. Aaron realized a permanent smile had been plastered on his face the entire time he'd been watching her.

He grabbed the bundle on the seat next to him and slid out of his sleek, dark silver Jaguar F-Type R coupe with his natural ease and prowess. He was a confident man, and his gait demonstrated his self-confidence as he swaggered toward the door. The same self-confidence had bled over into his business life and helped make him and his brother übersuccessful in their endeavors.

But right then, at that very moment, he wasn't as cocky as he normally portrayed. Inside, if he admitted it, he was afraid the petite, beautiful woman who'd invaded his mind would reject him for no other reason than he wasn't good enough for her. He knew he wasn't. He knew so much of his past was not one to be proud of by any means—the models, the rumors, that one incident that forever changed him. None of that stopped his fascination with her, though.

Aaron froze midstep when Christa glanced up and saw him through the front window of her café. Shock and surprise registered on her face first, then her cheeks rose, and Aaron was rewarded with her gorgeous smile. It was warm, inviting, and showed she was genuinely glad to see him. For just a second, she stood still, watching him as his smile matched hers.

He regained his stride and moved to open the door as Christa met him there. "Hi, Aaron. You must've played hooky, after all. I've never seen you in casual clothes on a workday before."

He produced the bundle from behind his back and was instantly thankful for the hours of chick-flick torture he'd endured at the hands of his dates. Her eyes held a look of pure adoration at first then a quick flash of insecurity.

"Are these...for *me*?" she asked tentatively, and she reached to take the huge bouquet of beautiful flowers from him.

Accustomed to reading people from his numerous interactions as an agent and, ultimately, a salesman dealing in the commodity of people, faces, and beauty, he surmised attention wasn't something she was comfortable with. From her unsure tone, he didn't need a degree in psychology to deduce she lacked confidence in herself, in her overall worth, and in her striking beauty. The very fact that she questioned the gift, when the flowers were presented directly to her by his own hand, told him others had often taken her for granted or taken advantage of her good nature.

He stared at her, in awe of the natural radiant beauty that rivaled the sun's brilliance. A thousand different emotions flooded him, and without warning, he became the unsure one. If she doubted herself, what right did he have to be confident at all?

When he looked at the petite, beautiful young woman before him, he saw an innate genuineness in her that others in his life lacked. He saw someone who was truly happy with the person she was. She wasn't focused on what she wanted the world to think she was. If she agreed to go out with him, it would be because she wanted to be with *him*, not his persona or what she could gain from him.

The most prevalent emotion he locked on to during his unexpected inner montage was the dire, carnal need to shelter and protect her. Aaron, immediately intrigued, vowed to be the one to remove that uncertainty from her. In their few encounters, she'd taken root in his mind, and he was surprised to find he liked having her there.

He consciously avoided using his *"close-the-deal smile,"* while lowering his voice. He stepped in closer to deliver his personal message with all the sincerity he could muster.

"Yes, these are for *you*, Christa. I thought they were beautiful when I first saw them, and they reminded me of you. But I was so wrong. Compared to you, they're just...*plain.*"

The pink tinge started at her neckline and worked its way up to color her cheeks. She looked down sheepishly, burying her nose in the flowers and inhaling deeply.

"You shouldn't tease like that, Aaron," she replied softly. She lifted her gaze to meet his and pulled the flowers into her chest. "They're *gorgeous*. I don't know what to say. *Thank you* so much. How did you know Stargazer lilies are my favorite flower?"

Aaron casually chuckled. "I didn't, but thanks for the tip. I just thought that roses were...too common...to fit you."

The heat in her cheeks escalated to scorching, and she fidgeted nervously. She inwardly cursed her lack of experience with men. She wasn't sure how to accept a compliment gracefully. She gave her standard, go-to response, which was a simple, "Thank you," but she wanted to say so much more.

His small gestures had made her feel better about herself than anyone in her life had before, and the desire to tell him burned in her chest. She wanted to share how their limited encounters had been the social highlights of her year. But, of course, she'd never say those things. First, it sounded pathetic even in her own mind. And secondly, she pictured him running from the building at the first sign of some desperate woman who was obviously needy and clingy.

"I'll go put these in a vase of water. Have a seat. I'll be right back." She gestured to an open table.

Aaron took the seat that gave him the best view of her and watched her walk toward the kitchen. He was instantly rewarded when he saw her hug the flowers close to her chest and bury her face in them again.

After arranging the vase on top of the display case, she made her way back toward him with two plates in her hands. He stood and took them from her, placed them on the table, and pulled her chair out for her. Clearly inexperienced with that kind of attention, she hesitated a second before she realized he was being thoughtful and polite. She quickly took her seat, and he moved back to his.

"What have we here?" His voice had an air of excitement and fascination over the scrumptious goody in front of him.

"I remember you mentioned you needed to work out more. So, I brought you some bread pudding with white chocolate sauce to give you a little extra incentive." Christa flirted, much to her surprise, purposely misconstruing his previous words to her.

She had a fleeting thought that this was their "thing," intentionally misinterpreting words and playfully using them against the other at a later time. She quickly pushed that thought aside, thinking that no man as gorgeous as Aaron would be interested in having a real "thing" with her.

Aaron laughed, genuinely laughed, for the first time

in a long time. His deep blue eyes danced with mischief sprinkled in them. "I don't recall saying it *quite* like that." He took a bite of his dessert and groaned with satisfaction as he chewed. Pointing his fork at her, he added, "You are trouble." The sparkle of mischief was back in his eyes, the shade deepening to a rich, dark blue that drew her in until she became a willing victim.

"So what brings you back here today? Severe coffee addiction? Need a sugar rush? Did you get sent home early for falling asleep at work?" Christa teased between bites, trying to steer the conversation away from the thoughts swimming in her head.

Aaron responded with a wide smile and considered turning her words into something dirty and sexual, like he would normally do, but quickly changed his course to try something new. Like honesty.

"I just wanted to see you again. This is my new caffeine spot. The coffee and pastries are the best in the city. But you're the real reason I can't stay away. I'm here twice a day on weekdays and three times on Saturday." He watched her hand freeze in midair, her eyes widen, and her lips part for a second. He had to give her points for recovering quickly as she pushed past the shock and narrowed her eyes at him dubiously.

"Why?"

"Why? Well, because you're beautiful. And sweet. A

great cook—even though you're trying to make me fat. You probably hear this all the time, but you have a *really* nice ass, and I *really* like to stare at it. That blush that takes over your face and neck when I say something remotely dirty is sexy as hell. Like right now, when you're still thinking about how I commented on your ass. But mostly, because I like talking to you and getting to know you."

She narrowed her eyes more, absorbing his words and sizing him up at the same time. "What about your girlfriend?" she asked, not hiding her suspicion of his intentions.

Now it was Aaron's turn to look shocked. And confused.

"Girlfriend? I don't have a girlfriend." His eyes crinkled at the corners, and his brow furrowed at her question.

"Well, no, you have a couple of them, at least," Christa responded. "You brought them in here with you."

"No, no, no—neither of those women is my girlfriend, Christa. I'm an agent, and they're both models. We were on our way to client meetings, and I needed coffee. The first girl didn't meet the client's needs, so I brought the other one by the next day. You know, after you got me hooked on your cooking and your ass. But it's strictly business with the models. You haven't seen me with one in a while, have you?" *As of now, it's strictly business anyway.*

Christa shook her head slowly, pulled the corner of her lower lip into her mouth and bit it while she considered his explanation. Her self-defeating thoughts returned with a vengeance, attempting to deprive her of the tiny bit of happiness blooming inside her.

He was so handsome, and he was interested in her—that just didn't make sense. He was so far out of her league they weren't even in the same zip code. Surely, he'd made some mistake, and he'd come to his senses. Or she'd burn a batch of croissants, and he'd move on to another coffee shop.

Then an unusual thought, for her, took root in her subconscious and urged her to change her mind. *Take a chance. What's the worst that could happen?*

"Well, then I'm glad you came to see me again. And I love the flowers, that was so thoughtful. And...I really like talking to you, too." She finally admitted her feelings aloud, looking shyly at him through her eyelashes. But she was completely unable to hide the huge grin on her face.

CHAPTER THREE

First Date

Aaron stayed at the café with Christa the rest of the afternoon then walked her to her car after closing up shop that evening. Just before she got in, he stopped her with his hand on her arm.

"Christa, before you go, I have something to ask you."

"What is it?" She immediately wanted to facepalm herself. *Couldn't you reply with something a little smoother?*

"I'd like to spend the day with you tomorrow. Is there any chance you can clear your schedule for me?" His confident smile was on full display, but he felt anything but confident as he watched her freeze in place and look everywhere but at him. He'd never worried about being turned down before, but she appeared to search for an excuse to say no.

He wants to spend the whole day with me?

What will I talk about that whole time?

What if I run out of conversation topics?

What if he takes me home early because I've bored him to death?

A lifetime of doubt and insecurity was hard to overcome, especially when someone as overtly handsome and visibly successful expressed interest in her. *Not that anyone like him has ever asked me out before*, she amended internally. His clothes were name-brand. His suits were custom tailored. His car screamed wealth and prestige. Her car screamed to be taken to the repair shop. Embarrassed she'd left him waiting for an answer while she wrestled with her self-confidence, she smiled warmly and replied with the first thought that came to her mind.

"I would love to, Aaron. I'll call Allie and make sure she can cover the shop alone. Saturdays are usually slower since we don't have the nine-to-five crowd first thing in the morning."

"Great. How about I give you a call later tonight just to make sure? That gives me an excuse to talk to you again tonight."

She looked at the ground, hiding her shy smile. "You don't need an excuse to call me, Aaron."

They exchanged numbers then Aaron closed her door and watched her drive off with a smile permanently etched on his face. He'd never been so drawn to anyone so fast and so completely. The foreign nature of those feelings should've been enough to send him fleeing. Instead, he felt it drawing him to her more and more with each passing minute.

Within thirty minutes of when she arrived at home, she'd already called Allie and arranged for coverage, completed her nighttime ritual, and climbed into bed. When her cell phone rang, excitement and anxiety vied for first place in wracking her nerves. She stared at the phone display until after the second ring before she answered it.

"Hello?"

"Hi, Christa. Did you make it home okay?" His voice was low and sexy, the deep timbre of it seeping through the phone and wrapping her in its warmth.

"Yes, I did. I've already called Allie, and she's fine with taking over the shop tomorrow without me."

"That's the best news I've heard all week. I'm so looking forward to forgetting the rest of the world exists and just spending the day with you."

"It sounds like you have an amazing day planned for us." She snuggled deeper under the covers and hugged her pillow close.

"Well, I hope you'll think it's amazing. Are you already in bed?"

"Yeah, why?"

"No reason. I was just thinking about your ass again.

I'm trying to picture what you wear to bed to cover one of your best *assets*." His playful, teasing tone kept the question light and humorous, so she decided to give him a dose of his own medicine.

"You're so funny," she replied nonchalantly, dismissing him with her mocking tone. "I don't wear anything to bed. I've found mixing clothes and sheets is much too confining."

He groaned in physical pain. "You don't play fair."

"You started it." She couldn't help but laugh, feeling slightly more sure of herself than just minutes before. "So, you can dish it out, but you can't take it?"

"Babe, I can definitely do both. I'll be more than happy to demonstrate for you. But before you start fantasizing about having your way with me, you do have to get to know me first. Before you get in my pants, I've set a minimum number of dates you have to meet. That number is only in my mind. You have to earn it."

Christa threw her head back in laughter, loving his sarcastic and frisky sense of humor. "I'll keep that in mind. Let's make a deal. You stop staring at my ass all the time, and I'll stop trying to undress you with my eyes."

"Afraid I can't agree to that. I'd never be able to hold up my end of the deal. I'm not even interested in trying, honestly. So, tomorrow you'll walk in front of me the entire time so I can stare at your ass." He chuckled, and she knew she was in trouble because she thought even his laugh was sexy.

They talked much longer, running the gamut of topics to learn bits and pieces about the other, until staying awake was no longer an option. "As much as I hate to go, I need to get some sleep. Four o'clock came early this morning, and I have a feeling I need to be as rested as possible for everywhere you're taking me tomorrow. Though you haven't told me about a single place yet."

Before letting her hang up, he felt the need to stress the importance of their all-day date. "We have the whole day together, Christa. There are several places I want to take you, just to spend time getting to know you better. But I'd like for my plans to be a surprise. If there's anywhere you want to go, I'll make it happen too."

"That sounds great, Aaron. But I kind of need to know what to wear since I have no idea where we'll be all day."

"Something comfortable—clothes *and* shoes. Dress in layers. Feel free to take off as much as you want. Just don't obstruct my view of that gorgeous derriere. I may need to take pictures of it as you walk."

"Comfy layers and an exposed derriere it is, then," she laughed. "I'll see you tomorrow morning." She rattled off her address, and he promised to pick her up on time.

The next morning couldn't come fast enough for Aaron. He bounded up the steps to Christa's apartment. Part of him hoped she wouldn't be fully ready yet so he'd have a chance to look around her apartment, get an idea of what her life was like and see what was important to her. The other part of him hoped she was waiting for him so they could get away before something unexpected had a chance to ruin his plans for their day. He knocked on her door and completely forgot all about whatever he had been thinking when she opened the door.

"Hi. Oh, wow," he stuttered.

Self-conscious, Christa looked down at her choice of clothing and suddenly felt very insecure. "Is there something wrong with this? I can change." She turned toward the hallway, but Aaron grabbed her hand to stop her.

Her soft skin was like silk in his hand. She stopped in her tracks and looked up at him expectantly and with a hint of shyness.

He physically couldn't make his hand let go of hers. Her hand was small, but he felt the strength in it. It was soft, but he'd witnessed firsthand how hard she worked in her café. But most of all, he knew it just felt right...meant to be...destined.

He smiled sincerely as he shifted his hand to lace their fingers together. "No, you're perfect. That was a good 'wow.' Actually, it was a *great* 'wow' now that I've had a better look. I need to add a few body parts to my list of favorites."

Christa looked down at her clothes again but didn't see anything special. She was wearing a formfitting solid white tank top, faded blue jeans with strategically placed tears, and the high-top Chucks that matched her glittery tan cardigan sweater perfectly. It was very casual and comfortable, but the sweater added a little flair in case they went somewhere nice. Her eyes caught the sight of their fingers laced together, and she felt her stomach do a somersault.

"Well, if you're sure," she replied hesitantly.

"I'm positive. Are you ready to go?" Aaron asked, trying to look around her apartment nonchalantly without appearing overly intrusive.

"One sec—let me grab my phone off the charger," she replied, giving him a minute to glance around the small but neatly decorated living room.

He stopped to look at some pictures on the side table of a much younger Christa. She was riding on the back of a guy a few years her senior; they were both laughing, and neither seemingly knew the photographer had captured the moment. He guessed she was in her teens when it was taken, but it obviously meant something to her since she had it prominently displayed in her apartment.

A twinge of jealousy tried to take up residence in him over the look of pure love on her face as she looked at the other guy. *The guy was a fucking idiot if he couldn't see she adored him*, Aaron thought. He heard her coming out of her bedroom, walking toward him, and he backed away from the picture before he had too much time to contemplate the implications—of either the sudden jealousy or who the other guy could be to her.

Slinging her purse over her shoulder, she stopped in front of him and smiled. "Now I'm ready. You know, you haven't even checked out my ass once since you got here. I'm a little disappointed in you. I expected more."

He took her hand, this time with purpose, and twirled her around to drink in her petite, sexy form. "Perfect. Pure perfection." With her fingers laced in his again, he led her out to his car. Once they were on the road, she noticed he turned away from the Bay Area, heading east out of town.

"Where are we going?" she asked slowly, furrowing her brow and giving him a pointed look.

Aaron chuckled at her stern face. "Somewhere I think you'll like. It's not far, and you're safe with me, I promise."

"I'm sure that's what all the serial killers say," she quickly retorted.

"Hmm. Good point. You're probably right about that," he taunted her.

Aaron burst out laughing when he glanced over and saw her face. Her mouth gaped open, her eyes were narrowed, and she looked like she was about to tear into him. "I'm sorry. You're right—your safety is not a joke."

He fished his wallet out of his back pocket and handed it to her. "Here, take a picture of my license and text it to anyone you want. I promise you're safe with me."

She hesitated just a moment before snatching his billfold from his hand and snapping a picture of his license with her phone. A few clicks later, it was safely on the way to Allie with a note that if she didn't show up for work to tell the cops to find Aaron.

Christa's phone beeped with Allie's reply. *"He can kidnap me any day!"*

Rolling her eyes, Christa handed his wallet back to

him and laughed at Allie's response.

"What's so funny?" he asked, amusement still lacing his voice.

"Oh, just my friend Allie, who is supposed to be my lifeline in case you return without me. She said you can kidnap *her* any day. Big help she is."

By the time they reached the state park, Christa had forgotten any apprehension she had about going off with Aaron. Their conversations flowed much like they had in her café and on the phone the night before, but with a much more personal flair. The occasional brush of his hand against hers sent shivers down her spine, and goose bumps riddled her skin. She couldn't ignore the sparks between them, the intense pull she felt toward him, or the way his smile melted her with how it was so relaxed and inviting.

Christa had taken full advantage of being a passenger by turning sideways in her seat so she could look at him while they talked. She secretly wanted to stare at his handsome profile, but she used conversation as a good excuse. His short hair was messier than usual, but it only added to his rugged good looks. The man simply oozed sex appeal. His blue eyes were fierce and stood out against his tan skin and his eternal five-o'clock shadow.

Every time he looked at her, those eyes pierced her to her very core. If the eyes were the windows to the soul, she couldn't escape the feeling he was gazing directly into hers. She studied all his features, his body language, his overall disposition. He was obviously very successful, cruising fluidly in his Jaguar, but more than that, what made him unique was in his very demeanor. He was confident without being conceited. He was sure of himself without being too cocky.

Okay, he's a little cocky, but in an endearing way.

When he exited the car, Aaron jogged around to open her door then took her hand in his. They walked in comfortable silence until they reached the trailhead. He stopped to look at the signs posted before turning to face her.

"We can go on any trail you want today, but there is one I want to take you on first. It's pretty long, but it's worth it."

"That sounds great. I don't mind a long walk." She squeezed his hand as she replied, amazed at how natural it felt just being with him.

"I was hoping you'd say that."

He led her down a dirt path, covered with natural mulch and lined with huge trees that provided a built-in shelter from the sun high in the sky. He'd been on this trail at least a dozen times and had always enjoyed it. But seeing it through Christa's eyes was amazing. She never let go of his hand as she skirted from one new sight to another, freely sharing her thoughts and excitement with him.

When they reached a clearing in the trees, he lagged a step behind so he could watch her reaction. She'd been busy talking and suddenly stopped in the middle of her sentence and gasped. He kept walking forward a few steps so he could see her face. The trail opened into a lush green field filled with thousands of wildflowers in every color imaginable. The scenery was postcard perfect, but her reaction was his ultimate prize.

He picked one of the yellow wildflowers and slowly reached out to put it in her hair, just behind her ear. "Beautiful," he murmured and brushed his fingertips across her cheek.

She smiled and somehow managed to utter a response. "Thank you."

With his arm wrapped around her waist, he held his phone out in front of them and snapped a picture with the field of wildflowers in the background. She took his phone and studied their picture while he circled around her to gaze at it from over her shoulder. His arm wrapped around her, pulling them closer.

"You captured the beauty of this place perfectly. Maybe you should be the photographer instead of the agent."

"The beauty of this place is in my arms right now."

She playfully poked him in the ribs with her elbow. "Stop teasing me."

"I'm not kidding at all. I love your smile, especially in this picture. It reaches your eyes and warms them even more than usual. You look so relaxed and happy. If I didn't know better, I'd say you enjoy being with me. This is a perfect picture."

He took her hand again and led her down a narrow dirt trail, winding through the wildflowers and over the rolling ridges. Once on the other side, he stopped again to watch her. Her eyes floated across the scenery, taking in the views on the horizon, before stopping on the area he'd waited for her to see.

"How—how did you do this?" she gasped. His smile engulfed his entire face, his ocean-blue eyes sparkling with mischief.

He shrugged his big shoulders. "It's good to have friends."

In a secluded dip between the rolling hills, in the middle of the wildflowers and lush green grass, was an entire picnic feast. The large green blanket was spread out flat with a picnic basket, full place settings complete with wineglasses, and a stainless-steel bucket chilling a bottle of wine.

He held out his arm to Christa to take, and she

absently wrapped her hand around it. She was literally speechless—her standard *"thank you"* was hopelessly insufficient for this kind of gesture. She managed to tear her eyes from the blanket and tilted her face up at him in amazement.

"Why, Aaron? Why would you do something like this for *me*?"

After all his years of indiscriminately fucking willing women, that simple question nearly floored him right where he stood. His movement stopped abruptly, jerking Christa back and causing her to fall into his chest. His arms wrapped around her to steady her and, since she was already so close, he pulled her tightly to him. He looked down into her beautiful, expressive brown eyes and instantly knew he was caught in her spell. One he never wanted to break.

"Christa," he said on a sexy, masculine sigh. His bedroom voice was on full strength without conscious intentions. "This is simply a picnic lunch. I plan to spoil you so much more than this, if you'll let me."

"Let's start with lunch," she responded breathlessly.

They sat on the blanket together, laughing and talking as if they'd known each other their entire lives. She'd never felt as comfortable with anyone so quickly before, except for Jared, but that had been a long time ago. They finished eating, and he stretched out on the blanket, lying on his side with his head propped up in his hand. Christa, sitting with her legs crossed, leaned into his torso and rested her arm on his side.

"I'm stuffed. You made me eat too much," she admonished him playfully.

"That's too bad...since we have some delicious dessert waiting for us," he teased.

Her eyes lit up, and she quickly reached for the picnic basket, ignoring his chuckle. She removed one slice of chocolate cream pie piled high with whipped cream. She cut off a piece and offered it to him. The blue in his eyes darkened, filled with desire and need, as he waited for her to lean into him. The magnetic pull to him caused her breath to freeze in her lungs, but she didn't stop. Leaning closer and closer into him, she finally reached his perfect lips.

His eyes moved up to hers as his mouth opened, ready to take what she was offering him. At the last second before the fork reached him, she flicked her wrist and intentionally smeared the whipped cream on his cheek. It took him an extra second to realize what she'd done. She snickered at first then began laughing uncontrollably. His eyes narrowed, crinkling at the edges and giving him a hard look, but his voice held the key.

"Think you're funny, huh?" he asked playfully.

"Well, it was pretty funny to see your reaction," she amended through her laughter.

"You know, I hear it is bad luck to have whipped cream on your face. The old spirits in these trees, they get offended easily." He spoke slowly, drawing out each detail, keeping her enraptured with him.

"Old tree spirits are offended by whipped cream? Was whipped cream considered witchcraft in the old days?" she whispered to him, her eyes darting all around them, as if she waited for something to jump out at them. He watched her bite her lower lip, trying to keep her laughter contained as she played along with him.

"You'll have to clean it off my face to save us." His voice lowered an octave, instantly pulling her eyes back to his, where she willingly surrendered.

She leisurely raised her hand and reached her fingers out to his cheek, intending to wipe the offensive whipped cream off his handsome face. He grabbed her wrist and brought her hand down to his chest, forcing her to lean over closer to him. He slowly shook his head while keeping his eyes locked on hers.

"Not with your hand. You'll provoke the spirits for sure, then," he whispered seductively.

Feeling more daring than she knew was practical, she kept her eyes locked on his as she pressed her chest against him. Feeling his chest rise with the deep breath he inhaled, she pressed closer until her breath fanned out across his chin, up to his cheek. She first placed a small kiss on the spot marred by the fluffy cream. Licking her lips, she then opened her mouth, and her tongue lightly skimmed the stubble of his beard.

His hand tightened around her wrist, holding her in place close to him. Her next sensation was one of flying through the air at Mach speed and landing on the soft blanket beneath a very hard body. Despite the fact that he towered over her, she noted how they fit perfectly together, their bodies aligned just right with him hovering over her. Aaron dipped his head, his body pressed against hers more, cocooning her in warmth and a deep, carnal craving.

His lips brushed hers gingerly at first. Then just as quickly, the kiss became fierce and commanding. His tongue demanded entrance, easily slipping past her lips to caress hers. His hands rested on either side of her face, cradling her as he tugged it lightly to the side. His kiss deepened as her hands skimmed over his shoulders and up into his hair, pulling his weight down onto her even more.

His knee pushed her leg to the side, and the other leg willingly followed suit. When he was fully seated in between her legs, she felt his erection growing, pushing against the front of his pants, and delightfully rubbing against her core. He moaned into her mouth, sending cold shivers through her and heating her at the same time. Slowing the momentum, he tenderly ended the kiss.

"I've wanted to know how your lips tasted since the first time I saw you," he confessed.

CHAPTER FOUR

The Other Guy

"Don't be a stranger, Sean. I expect to see your fugly mug back in San Francisco soon." Jared shook his friend's hand.

"You can stay and hang out with us for the weekend. You don't have to be at work until Monday morning, Miller." Sean repeated the same argument that had worked too many times before.

Jared pretended to think about his best friend's request for a few seconds before reciting the same sentiments he'd repeated over the past couple of weeks. "I've been here for the last four months since we took the state bar, waiting to see if I passed. Now I have to join the land of the working. Before I can do that, I have to move in to my new apartment. I've put it off until the last minute as it is."

"Don't even pretend your dad didn't pull some strings and help you land that job. You had it in the bag before you even got your exam results back." Sean playfully punched Jared in the shoulder. "Besides, we both knew you'd ace that test. This shit is in your blood."

"Are you saying I couldn't have gotten that job on my own?"

"Absolutely. That's exactly what I'm saying."

"You know, green really isn't your color. No hating on your best friend just because he's got game and you don't."

Sean's laugh echoed across the parking lot. "Whatever, man. Whatever you say. As soon as I get my scores, I expect you to put in a good word for me."

"No need to even ask. You know that."

The diesel engine from the moving truck fired up, drawing their attention as it pulled out of the apartment complex.

"Guess that's my cue. I'm going to hit the road now so I have time to stop by and see an old friend before unpacking my shit."

"This Christa girl must be something if you're ditching me to go see her. She's hot as fuck, isn't she? That's why you've kept her away from me all these years. You know she'd pick me over you."

"You're so full of shit." Jared laughed, dismissed Sean with a wave of his hand, and opened his car door.

"Wait. Are you really not going to tell me about her?"

"No, I'm really not telling you anything about her. Talk to you later. I expect to see you in the next couple of weeks—the minute you get your results."

"Save the corner office for me."

With a wave goodbye to Sean, Jared pulled out onto the highway with nothing but getting to Christa on his mind. His friendship with her developed instantly when they were kids and had somehow endured throughout school. Christa had always been a petite girl. Even when they were in elementary school, she was small for her age. He'd made sure none of the other kids picked on her and had acted as if her protection were his sole responsibility.

Three years her elder, he'd worried about leaving her behind when he graduated high school, even though she'd assured him her spunk and feistiness were sufficient protection. After he graduated high school, Jared left San Francisco and moved to Stanford. Unlike Christa's family, Jared's family was very wealthy and wouldn't miss the money the prestigious college demanded.

He'd been away from home for nearly seven and half years while completing his education, taking the state bar exam, and waiting to receive his scores. The final test before attaining his license to practice law had been grueling, but his focus and determination had paid off when he received notice of a successful score. The drive between Stanford and his new condominium on the outskirts of San Francisco was only an hour at most. With the top down on his Aston Martin DB9 Volante, he enjoyed the rush of the wind in the still-cool morning air in early May. The white noise helped him to think, and he relished the time he spent completely alone.

With all the study groups in law school, time alone was one thing he hadn't had enough of, and his sanity demanded it. But that ride was different because he was looking forward to rekindling his old friendship. Christa was the one person he couldn't wait to see again—the one friend he'd missed the most. If he admitted the truth, he'd been a terrible friend to her, breaking every vow he'd made. His only effort to stay connected to her had been an occasional birthday card and holiday well-wishes sent through his family. But he hadn't personally seen or spoken to her since before he left for college.

Jared's mother and sister remained close to Christa, visiting often, relaying messages from Jared and delivering his gifts. He'd kept tabs on Christa's life through their interactions with her. When he heard she opened her own business, he was extremely proud of her and couldn't wait to tell her himself—in person. The hour drive passed in the blink of an eye, and he'd arrived at his destination.

He walked into The Sweet Spot and looked around her shop. The aroma of freshly brewed coffee and the sweet cinnamon fragrance from the pastries instantly filled his nostrils and prompted him to take a deeper breath. Then he heard Christa's pleas for help before he saw her.

"Allie! Can you come help me before I drop this huge bag of flour and it goes everywhere?" Christa called from the back, the urgency prominent in her tone.

He hastened his steps toward her voice, not seeing anyone else in sight, and found Christa wrestling with an industrial-sized bag of flour nearly her same size. He quickly amended his initial thought to include it wouldn't take much for the bag of flour to match her size, considering how small she was in the first place. His big hand grabbed the top of the bag and easily hoisted it from her grip.

"*Thank you!* I just knew—" She suddenly became mute when the large bag of flour was moved from her view and she realized it wasn't Allie standing in front of her.

He stood still, holding the bag in one hand and an ear-to-ear smile splitting his gorgeous face in two. She was frozen in place, her mouth gaping open, and her hands frozen in midair. At first, she was startled to see the huge, handsome man in her kitchen. But after the initial shock passed, her mind slowly recognized his jaw-droppingly handsome face.

"*Jared!*" she finally shrieked, jumping into his embrace as he dropped the flour bag on the large chef's table in the middle of the kitchen. His arms wrapped around her waist, drew her tightly to him, and lifted her off the ground with no effort at all. Her arms wrapped around his neck and squeezed him tightly.

"What are you doing here?" she finally asked, her delight and love for her friend apparent in her voice. Jared released her back to her original spot and stepped back to get a good look at her.

"I'm finally coming home. The moving company is delivering my furniture to my condo as we speak, but I wanted to stop and see you first. Damn, I've missed you, Christa," he replied with warmth and sincerity infused in his voice and eyes.

She playfully swatted at his arm. "You couldn't have missed me too much. This is the first time you've actually stopped to see me in the entire seven years you've been away."

Jared put on his best, most charming smile. "That's only because I knew I'd never be able to leave you again."

She rolled her eyes, but her face was still alight with her smile. "Jared Miller, you are still such a flirt!"

He was undeniably a flirt, but she never could resist him. He'd been her closest friend and best defender in school where kids' taunts could be downright cruel. Her family life was the polar opposite of

Jared's, but he'd never given her any reason to believe that was what he saw when he looked at her.

"Mom told me you opened this place. I'm proud of you, Christa. Let me buy you lunch," he replied, genuinely happy for her.

"Nope." She almost laughed out loud when his face suddenly fell. His smile was gone, and confusion shone in his eyes.

"No? Why not?"

"Because I'm making your lunch," she laughingly replied. "You're going to eat here, mister!"

"Well, if you *insist*," he teased.

Being back with his friend was the best homecoming present he could've asked for, even without realizing she was exactly what he'd needed before that moment. After they'd sat down with their plates, his tone became serious.

"I've been a selfish asshole and a terrible friend. You shouldn't even be happy to see me right now. There's no excuse for why I've stayed away so long. But I wasn't joking when I said leaving you again would've been too hard."

Internally, he berated himself over his treatment of her. He couldn't deny the fact that he should've sought her out when he came home, but he never could bring himself to do it. It most certainly wasn't because he didn't miss her. He didn't visit her *because* he missed her too much. Parting again, over and over, would have been too much to ask.

Unsure of how to respond at first, she looked down at her plate to collect her thoughts. "Well, I'm glad you stopped by today. It's really good to see you again."

During their extra-long lunch date, one topic easily led into another. Time stood still and flew by simultaneously while they laughed and reconnected. Though the sting was still there, she couldn't deny how good she felt to have him back, until she noticed him checking his watch. Jared stood reluctantly and looked regretfully at the café door.

"I really should get to my condo now," he said hesitantly, not wanting to leave her but knowing he had to go. His resolve waned even more when he saw the crestfallen look on her face at his declaration. "The movers probably just left everything in one room. I'll be lucky to get in the front door."

"Oh, yeah, okay. Well, it was great to see you, Jared," she said warmly. "Don't stay away so long this time. You're back home, so you have no excuse now."

"I'll be around so much, you'll get sick of seeing me."

"Not possible."

She hugged him goodbye and watched him walk

across the street to his convertible. She'd never presume to tell him, but knowing he'd intentionally avoided her all those years had hurt her tremendously. She recalled how his mother was so proud of him and everything he'd accomplished in school. Staying in contact with his mother and his sister provided her with a means for constant updates about Jared. One of them had shared information with Christa after every time Jared came home for their family holidays and birthdays.

One specific visit from Patti stood out in her mind.

"Christa," Patti called out as she entered The Sweet Spot. "I have something for you."

Christa pasted a smile on her face and was careful to keep up appearances. She knew by her singsong tone Patti had a present for her from Jared.

"Hi, Patti. It's good to see you."

Christa would rather he deliver it personally. Using his mother as a courier robbed her of any joy over the thought behind the present. In this case, the thought was not all that counted. Not once did he tell Christa when he'd planned to come home, but Patti always delivered a gift for her from Jared— after he'd left again. The gifts were bittersweet since he'd thought enough of her to send her a small token, but not enough to give her a minute of his time. He didn't think enough of her to pick up the phone and call her or come by to see her. All those times had delivered one crushing blow after the other.

"Jared said to tell you hello, and he's sorry he couldn't come by to see you while he was home. But this is from him. Merry Christmas!"

Inside the expertly wrapped box was a silver frame that held a picture of the two of them from high school. She was riding on his back, leaned over his shoulder, and they were both laughing. Her legs were wrapped around his waist, his hands on her bare thighs while he carried her over the small creek. He'd joked with her over the ankle-deep water, telling her she'd drown if he didn't carry her.

"Tell him I said thank you. If I'd known he'd be here, I would've mailed a present to your house for him."

Patti's smile faltered for only a second before she turned it up again. "I will definitely pass the message on to him."

But suddenly, after seven long years of no-shows, he simply walked back into her life and directly into her business. He offered no real explanation for why he'd stayed away from her, other than the lame excuse of how much he missed her, and she hadn't demanded anything more of him. She scolded herself for simply letting him back into her life with open arms only because she was happy to see him again.

She watched him drive away and felt that old familiar pain in her chest, and she wondered how long it would be before he showed back up again.

Jared reached his new condo and found it exactly as he had suspected. The movers were unable to discern the boxes marked "kitchen" should, in fact, be left in the kitchen. The same could be said for every other room and every box that was carefully labeled. He spent the rest of the day and well into the night moving, organizing, and unpacking the mountain of boxes. When his stomach growled loudly, he realized he'd been so busy that he hadn't eaten since Christa had made lunch for him earlier in the day.

Christa. Just the thought of her evoked a multitude of emotions in him. Seeing her, then leaving her, had been so much harder than he'd ever thought. During their conversation, the first thing he noticed about her was how much she'd changed in the time he'd been away.

It wasn't anything physical because she still looked much like a teenager to him. But her whole presence had changed. The air around her held more confidence; she seemed more secure in herself and her abilities. Her beauty, brains, and poise combined to make her even more attractive than when he'd seen her last.

The musical tone of his cell jarred him from his thoughts. Glancing at the face on the screen, he answered his phone. "Hi, Mom."

"Did you see her today?" Patti immediately questioned.

"I'm fine, Mom. Thanks for asking. No, the movers didn't put anything where it should be, so I've been working on that all damn night. And I just realized I haven't eaten at all since around noon."

"You're a big boy. You'll be fine. Now answer my question." Patti pushed with her determined tone.

"I think I'm close to passing out from lack of sustenance. Can you die from not eating for several hours? I may be dying." Jared continued teasing her.

He knew she wanted nothing more than to marry him off and have grandkids as soon as possible. She hadn't hinted about it at all. She'd downright demanded it of him and even set a timeline before she cut him off from all his favorite foods at family meals. She played dirty, and he loved her for it. She'd been his biggest supporter, and she'd also been the first one to tell him when he was being a royal fuck-up.

"Jared Benjamin Miller!"

Jared had to laugh at that. There he was, twenty-five years old, and his mother calling him by his full given name still made him snap to attention, even over the phone.

"Yes, Mom. I went to see Christa. She even made lunch for me, and we talked for a while," he finally answered her, knowing that small amount of information would never placate her. She was relentless when she wanted something, and what she wanted was for Jared and Christa to hand over their firstborn child to her.

"And? What else?" The frustration in Patti's voice increased with each word, along with the hard edge in it that meant she'd had just about enough of his teasing.

"And, that's all, really. We talked, caught up as much as we could. I told her I had to get to my condo because of the movers, and I left. What did you expect, Mom?" Jared replied, honestly trying to figure out what else she thought he should have done.

"I expected you to spend more time with the one girl who has always loved you but you took for granted. Your boxes could've waited. They'll still be there later. You don't know that Christa will be there for you tomorrow."

The finality of her tone and the very real possibility that Christa could be taken already shook Jared, even if he tried to hide his uneasiness from Patti. Jared ran his hand through his hair, messing it up even more, and then scrubbed that hand over his face. His mother had a good point. Christa may very well be involved with someone.

He didn't see a ring on her finger, but that didn't mean she wasn't in a serious relationship. He didn't ask her and she didn't offer it, but then, he'd given her no reason to even bring it up. He'd approached her as an old friend, the same way he'd always kept it because of their age difference.

"I'll go see her again first thing in the morning, Mom. I promise," he assured her solemnly.

"You didn't even ask to see her again. Did you?"

Jared contemplated for half a second if he should ask who wrote the *Mom's Book of Code Language,* because she'd technically asked a question. But the way she said it left no room for a response. It also held a suspiciously inherent reprimand without the need for saying it aloud. Just as quickly as the thought crossed his mind, he dismissed it, knowing it would only result in a real tongue-lashing.

Patti sighed loudly, signaling her deep displeasure with him and his lack of advancement on her plans for his future. "Son, I don't think you understand how serious this is. Christa was so young when you left for college, but she *always* kept in touch with me and asked about you every time we talked if I didn't bring you up first.

"She was so hurt all the times you came home and didn't bother to go see her. You haven't even tried to fix the pain you've caused that sweet girl. Your actions today just proved to her even more that you don't deserve her. If *you* don't treat her right, *someone else* will. And we both know how you would feel about that."

Patti had never been one to mince words or hold back what she thought, especially from her sons and about how they should treat the women in their lives. She also knew Jared had always carried a flame for Christa, even though he never once allowed himself to act upon it. At first, he'd protected her because she was so much smaller than everyone else. Truthfully, he quickly saw she didn't need his protection—she was fully capable of taking care of herself.

She was quiet and reserved to those who didn't know her. But to those who provoked her anger, she was aggressive and even a little scary at times. Christa had been a pleasant puzzle to Jared. He'd tried to figure her out, tried to box her into one category to define her, but she'd defied his attempts at every turn.

Her family was nonexistent, even though they were somewhat around. She'd grown up with a deadbeat father who only showed up when the gambling money ran out and a drug-addicted mother who was high or drunk more than she was sober. Despite the challenges she faced, Christa rose out of it and made life better for herself, never making excuses or accepting defeat.

Christa spent more time with Jared and his family than she did her own. His family took her in, and she stayed with them for days at a time before going back home. Not once did Christa's mother call to check on her or show the slightest bit of concern about where she'd been. He knew Christa craved the family life his family could offer her—the closeness, the certainty that they would always be there for one another, and the bonds that were unbreakable.

"You're right, Mom. As always. I'll fix it tomorrow. I promise."

"Jared, for your sake, I hope your 'tomorrow' isn't too late. I love you, son."

"Love you, too, Mom."

With that, they hung up, and Jared dropped down on his couch. The gnawing in his stomach had been replaced with a tightening in his chest. Patti certainly had a way with words—and with making him feel about an inch tall. But as a grown man, he knew he couldn't place the blame on his mom. No, that problem fell squarely on his shoulders. He knew he should've asked Christa out when he was with her. He came close once, but, as usual, he counted on her waiting for him. Until tomorrow.

He glanced at his watch and winced at how late it was. He contemplated calling her anyway but then realized aloud, "I didn't even get her fucking phone number!"

Pushing up from the couch and pacing anxiously, he angrily kicked an empty box and sent it flying across the room. Grabbing a beer out of his refrigerator, one of the few things that he did have in his nearly bare kitchen, he took a long swig out of the longneck bottle, walked out onto his balcony, and propped his forearms on the rail.

It'll be a long fucking night, he thought wearily.

CHAPTER FIVE

A Day Late

Jared arrived at The Sweet Spot just after the lunchtime crunch. He'd spent a sleepless night, looking at the clock every hour, tossing and turning. He finally got up and made a bigger dent in unpacking his boxes and getting his condo halfway arranged. He thought about what he'd say to her, revising and rehearsing his speech over and over, until he finally felt somewhat confident he'd nailed it. He'd walk in, tell her how he felt, and see where it went from there.

"Christa, I've waited a long time to say this to you," he began. *No, that's not right.*

"There's something I need to say. I moved back here to be with you." *No, that's not it, dammit!*

"In all the years I've been gone, you are the one person I've missed the most. I'm here now, and I want to give us a chance to be more than friends. I hope you want that, too."

Yes, that's it.

Reciting those words in his mind over and over, he walked down the street toward The Sweet Spot just after the lunch crowd had dispersed. He'd planned it that way, hoping to find Christa available to talk to him. He didn't want to wait another day to tell her how he felt. He'd waited long enough, stayed away from her for too long as it was, and he felt like shit for hurting her over and over.

He walked into the café and looked around, not seeing Christa anywhere. The girl behind the counter was a little taller than Christa and had long brown hair with curled ringlets throughout. She offered him a full-on flirty smile as soon as she saw him.

Her name tag read "Allie," and he remembered Christa had called that name out when she was wrestling with the life-size bag of flour. He approached the counter with a smile.

"Hi, Allie," he said, making a point to look at her name tag. "How are you today?"

"I'm great. How are you?" she asked, meeting his gaze directly then raking her eyes over him without hiding her salacious intent.

"I'm good, thanks. I'm actually looking for Christa. Is she around?" he asked, leaning his hip onto the counter, crossing one foot over the other and his arms across his chest. He gave her his best smile, still openly flirting with her in hopes of getting some information out of her.

"No, she's not. She won't be in at all today. She took the day off. You want some coffee or anything else?" She tilted her upper body toward him, leaned on the counter, and lifted her eyebrows.

Quite the flirt, he thought. *But she's also sizing me up. She's obviously protective of Christa.*

"Sure, a cup of coffee would be great. Black." He tried to hide his disappointment. He'd built the scene up in his mind all damn night and morning, only to find she wasn't even there.

Allie handed him a steaming mug of coffee. "You sure I can't get you anything else?"

"Very tempting, but I'll have to take a rain check. My name is Jared, by the way. I'm an old friend of Christa's. Do you know how I can get in touch with her? I really need to speak to her."

Allie tapped her finger against her lips and narrowed her eyes at the stranger inquiring about her best friend. She didn't know him, and she had no way of knowing if he was a friend, as he'd claimed. His name wasn't familiar, and she'd never seen him around. He wasn't someone a woman with a pulse would've forgotten. He was a gorgeous man—tall, muscular build, blondish-brown hair, and soulful brown eyes. But since Christa's safety was at stake, Allie decided to play it safe.

"Sorry, I can't give her number out. But if you want

to leave yours, I'll make sure she gets it."

"Fair enough," he responded, his best smile still intact. He accepted the paper and pen Allie offered and wrote his name and number down. He handed it back to Allie and intentionally grazed his fingers across hers. "Don't go selling it on eBay," he joked.

"Wouldn't *dream* of it," Allie retorted in a playful, sarcastic tone.

He took his coffee and sat at a table close to the door. He couldn't help but hope Christa would decide to come by and check on her business, even though it was her day off. He picked up a newspaper left on a nearby table and tried to catch up on the news. Every time the door opened, his eyes lifted to see if it was her. After more than half an hour, his coffee had long gone cold, and he had no excuse for waiting around any longer.

His phone rang just as he reached his car. *Mom.* She seemed to have a sixth sense about whatever he was doing, and it became stronger the closer he was to home. The option to ignore the call crossed his mind, but he realized she was the one person who had Christa's number and would give it to him. He took the call reluctantly, knowing what was coming.

"Hey, Mom," he answered casually.

"Don't '*hey, Mom*' me, young man. You know why I'm calling," she chided.

"I'm leaving her shop as we speak, but she's off today. I was hoping you'd send me her number so I can call her." He used his best *I'm-your-favorite-son* voice to get his way.

"Don't think I don't know what you're doing when you talk to me like that. The only person you're fooling is yourself, young man," she laughingly replied. "But I will let you get away with it this one last time. I'll text it to you right now."

"Thanks, Mom. You're the best. Love you."

"Love you, too, son."

A minute later, his cell buzzed with Christa's cell phone number and a message from his mom telling him not to screw it up. After saving it to his contacts, he immediately called her. His call went straight to voice mail, indicating her phone was either off or she was out of range of the cell towers. With his frustration at epic levels, Jared climbed back into his Volante and sped away toward his condo.

CHAPTER SIX

Evening the Odds

Allie was cleaning up in the kitchen when she heard the bell jingle over the front door of the café. Since she'd locked it at closing, she knew it must be her friend. "Christa, is that you?"

"Yes, Allie, it's just me," she yelled back.

Allie grabbed a towel to dry her hands and continued talking, loudly, to Christa as she walked down the hall to the front of the café. "There was some *hot* guy here to see you earlier. I mean, he was *fucking hot*, Christa. He asked for your cell, but I didn't give it to him. If you're not going to tap that, let me know. I'll jump on him like he's my own personal pogo stick."

When Allie reached the end of the hallway, she saw a noticeably shocked, deeply red-faced Christa. Then her eyes lifted slightly to see a different extremely hot man standing behind Christa. She instantly recognized his expression—the gritted teeth, the muscles ticking in his jaw, and the way his chest rose and fell with each deep breath. He attempted to project a calm appearance, but Allie knew intuitively he felt anything but calm at that moment.

Unable to stifle her laugh, Allie chuckled lightly. "Oops, didn't know we had company. Sorry about that."

Christa tried to avoid talking about the obvious pink elephant sitting squarely in the middle of the small room. "I don't know of anyone who'd be looking for me. Did he say what he wanted?"

"He just said he's a friend of yours, and he acted like he really needed to talk to you. He left his name and number over there by the cash register," Allie answered while still watching Aaron with amused curiosity.

His reaction to another man showing interest in Christa intrigued Allie. He seemed genuinely threatened. Not in a crazy, jealous way, but in an insecure, endearing way. As if he was afraid of losing Christa to another man. She watched his eyes dart nervously over toward the cash register, where the competition's number waited for Christa to retrieve it.

As Christa picked up the paper, Allie watched Aaron take a deep breath and place his hands on his hips. Wondering how long he could hold his breath before he passed out, Allie broke the silence. "Well, do you know him?" Aaron's eyes snapped to Allie's, and she smiled when he finally released his breath.

"Oh, yeah, it's just Jared," Christa said casually.

"Yeah. That's what he said his name was—I couldn't remember," Allie lied. She knew exactly what his name was, but she was enjoying this little show way too much to end it sooner. "So, how do you know him?"

"From school. We were friends forever before he went off to college."

Christa laid the paper back down on the counter then walked back to Aaron's side. Allie watched them both with her keen eyes, noting their closeness and their obvious comfort level with each other. Aaron snaked his arm around Christa and pulled her close to his side while Christa wrapped her arms around his waist, snuggling in close to him.

"Oh, that's sweet," Allie said aloud. When Aaron and Christa looked at her questioningly, she quickly added, "That you're still friends after all this time. You two must be pretty close."

And Allie watched as Aaron tensed again. *Interesting.*

"I guess we were back then, but he's been away for more than seven years. He just moved back here yesterday," Christa explained.

And Aaron relaxed again. *Yeah, the boy has it bad,* Allie laughed inside.

"Well, I'm heading home now. Are you two just hanging out here or what?" Allie asked.

"I just wanted to check on you before Aaron takes me home," Christa said with a nonchalant shrug, but Allie knew how to read between her lines. "Thanks for covering the shop again by yourself. We had a great day."

"I'm fine. Everything here is done, so you two kids go on home."

Christa knew Allie was onto her ploy to hide behind her friend and avoid what would come next.

Even in the cool San Francisco night air, Christa's palms were sweating profusely as they approached her door. She pretended to adjust her sweater and wiped her palms dry. Then she dug into her extra-large purse, pretending to look for her keys, then checked her pants pockets, again wiping her palms. The nagging worry that Aaron would think she was some mutant with nasty, sweaty palms only made it worse. Truth be told, Christa knew exactly why she was so nervous and so...soggy.

She wanted to invite Aaron in because she wasn't ready to end their time together. However, it had been a long time since she'd invited a man inside, and the last time didn't go very well. When she wouldn't have sex with him, the guy had stomped off, throwing less than flattering epithets over his shoulder as he stormed out. It wasn't like she'd led him on—she'd been very upfront about it, but that didn't change the outcome.

Christa already felt like she was getting way too attached to Aaron. Being with him was effortless—everything about his personality was laid-back, affable, and genuinely inviting. Their day together had been amazing. After the impromptu lunch make-out session, complete with whipped cream and chocolate cream pie, they spent the rest of the day exploring the park hand in hand. There was one specific moment that stole Christa's breath, and very likely her heart, and she'd been reliving it over and over, making herself crazy.

At one point on the trail, they stopped to take in the panoramic views of the Sacramento River, and Aaron unexpectedly lifted Christa's hands to his lips. His blue eyes turned a darker shade and never left hers as he slowly placed featherlight kisses on each knuckle, one hand at a time. Wordlessly, he pulled her closer to him until her breasts were pressed firmly against his torso, and he bent so her hands could reach around his neck. Slightly stooping, he wrapped his arms under her ass and lifted her off the ground, slowly sliding her body against his until they were finally eye to eye.

Her capacity for rational thought was nonexistent. His expressive blue eyes spoke volumes to her without saying a word. They told her how much he wanted her. They conveyed his innermost thoughts without restraint. The instant connection she felt to him gave her an unfamiliar full-body tingle and immense pull deep in her core. Christa was certain she'd been struck by lightning of the best kind.

She didn't know how long he held her like that, flat against his body. His strong, muscular arms were flexed from holding her full weight, without the slightest hint of straining. Unable to resist his silent requests any longer, Christa pulled his face to hers and, at first, lightly kissed his lips. A dam suddenly released inside her, and she took what she wanted without asking. Her fingers fisted his hair, and she crushed herself to him even tighter. She licked his bottom lip and felt his groan rumble through his broad chest.

That was all she needed to hear to give her more courage than she knew she possessed. Her tongue darted into his mouth, caressing and sucking on his tongue. When she lightly pulled his bottom lip into her mouth, running her tongue over it seductively, she felt the moment when he lost his composure. Walking off the path, Aaron put her back on a massive tree and used his knee as a perch for her, freeing his hands to glide over her body.

He broke the kiss to inhale deeply and cupped her face in his. With a deep, sexy rasp, he broke the silence. "Damn, Christa, how are you doing this to me?"

"Doing what?" she whispered back.

His eyes pleaded with her, but she didn't know what he was asking of her. She stroked his face with her fingers, reveling in his stubble and how good it had felt rubbing against her skin. She urged him with her eyes to tell her what he meant.

"How can you walk right through every wall I've ever built like they were never even there?"

That moment had instantly become Christa's all-time favorite memory. Aaron proved his sincerity in his every thoughtful deed throughout the whole day. He'd planned every detail of their excursion and left nothing out. True to his word, he was spoiling her, and she loved every minute of it. No one had ever gone to such great lengths just for her, to impress her, and to make her day so special.

That was exactly why she was so nervous to approach her apartment door with him in tow. That would be the defining moment—when he realized all his efforts would not culminate in a night full of every sort of debauchery known to man...and woman. She couldn't deny she also wanted that—the connection, the intimacy, the promise of more nights together.

But she wasn't ready.

Will he storm out on me? Will he leave me brokenhearted?

These were the real questions at the root of her nervousness. She was afraid to find out the answer—no matter what the answer actually turned out to be. On one hand, if he stayed and they continued seeing each other, it meant she had to let him into her carefully constructed world. She'd have to trust him and put herself in a precarious position where she could possibly get her heart broken. On the other hand, if he stormed out, she had no doubt she'd be heartbroken anyway.

There's really no way to win, Christa thought as she nervously pulled her keys out, having run out of time and excuses to avoid opening her door.

She looked up at Aaron shyly, meeting his intense gaze through her eyelashes. She again called upon her courage and asked the dreaded question.

"Would you like to come in for a drink?"

Aaron immediately recognized the trepidation in her face and her voice. His protective instincts were already in overdrive for this petite, beautiful lady who had stolen his ability to think rationally. He wanted to alleviate her anxiety, not add to it. It occurred to him that this was the first date he'd been on where he didn't expect a roll between the sheets at the end of it. He didn't want the night to end, but mainly because he truly enjoyed her company. Determined to put her fears at ease, he responded thoughtfully.

"I would love to, Christa. But I should warn you..." He paused to emphasize his point with a deep breath. "You're not having your wicked way with me tonight. I'd like to enjoy your company without the pressure of you undressing me with your eyes. If you think you can manage that, I'll come in for a little while." He kept a straight face and waited for her to process what he'd said.

The moment of levity worked like a charm. Christa burst out laughing and placed one hand on his chest. Aaron's gorgeous smile splayed across his face. She knew he understood completely and was giving her the out she needed without putting her on the spot. And she felt her heart melt for him even more.

"I will try, Aaron. I'm not making any promises, though," she laughingly replied before opening her door. "To even the odds, that means you can't stare at my nice ass anymore tonight."

"I never made that promise, and you didn't make that stipulation with your invitation. So, I reject your evening of the odds."

Much more relaxed now after he'd expertly diffused the tension, she was able to enjoy spending more alone time with him.

"Can I get you something to drink? Beer? Coke?" she asked as they walked in.

"No, I'm good, thanks," he replied as he took a seat in the middle of the love seat.

She looked around her small apartment living room for a moment, considering where she should sit. He was smack in the middle of the love seat, so it would be awkward to try to sit beside him. But then she would also feel awkward sitting on the couch away from him.

Why does dating have to be so hard? she wondered.

Finally deciding on the couch, she took a step past Aaron, and he grabbed her hand and pulled her into his lap. "I have your seat right here," he teased with a sexy smile. "I can't stare at it, but I can feel your sexy ass on me."

Taking her seat, Christa found she fit perfectly in his lap. She nestled into the crook of his arm and laid her head on his shoulder. Aaron's arms closed around her, holding her in his safe embrace. He lowered his mouth to her ear and whispered, "Mmm…I could get used to this."

"To what?" she whispered back.

"You in my arms," he replied, his warm breath feathering across her cheek just before his lips made contact with her skin.

As she raised her head, her lips met his and she became lost in him. Her hands found his hair, and her fingers twisted the silky smoothness around her fingers. Pulling him closer, unable to resist and feeling her body on fire, Christa drew herself up until she was fully facing and straddling him. He splayed his hands out across her back, holding her so close to him that she felt the taut buds of her nipples scraping across his shirt through her clothing. The warmth of his hands on her skin, underneath her shirt, scalded her in the most erotic way.

Aaron's hands followed the line of her bra, lightly grazing her skin and causing her nerve endings to fire uncontrollably. His thumbs found her hard nipples and brushed across them, causing her to moan audibly into his mouth. He increased his pressure with the second pass, and she was certain she'd go up in flames at any moment. Since she had completely given up her rational sense, it took her a few seconds to realize she was actively grinding against his growing erection.

Aaron slowed their fevered kiss, moved his hands to her face and held her there, forehead to forehead, while he took a minute to get himself back under control.

"That was so fucking hot," he finally said. "That was the best damn kiss ever."

Coming down off her sensual high, Christa suddenly felt very embarrassed at how she'd let her feelings escalate so quickly. "Aaron, I-I don't normally—" She started to explain herself, but he put one finger across her lips to stop her.

"I know you don't, Christa. I can read people well enough to know one-night stands aren't your style. And neither is fucking on the first date. But I am glad I affect you as much as you do me," he finished with a sexy, half grin.

"I can't deny that," she confessed.

"It's getting late. I'd better be going now," Aaron said but made no attempt to get up. Christa reluctantly moved from his lap to give him room to stand.

"I had so much fun today, Aaron. Thank you for everything—the park, the picnic, all of it. You really shouldn't have done so much."

Aaron placed his hand on her cheek, and she leaned into it instinctively. "I told you, I've only just begun to spoil you. It was all my pleasure, trust me, but I'm thrilled you enjoyed it."

They walked together toward the door, and Aaron stopped just over the threshold.

"Can I see you again tomorrow?"

"Yes, definitely." She couldn't contain her biggest and brightest smile.

Aaron leaned in and kissed her again. "Be sure you lock up. Sweet dreams, beautiful. Good night."

"Good night," she said wistfully.

Aaron walked off, and Christa closed and locked her door behind him. She leaned against the door, reliving the events of their day together with a smile, when a sudden knock startled her.

She slowly opened the door and peeked out to see Aaron standing there. He spoke before she could say anything.

"It's tomorrow. I couldn't wait any longer," he explained with a shoulder shrug and a smile. He wrapped his muscular arms around her in a sensual embrace and gave her another panty-melting kiss. When he put her down, she looked up at him starry-eyed and giddy as he gently stroked her cheek with his hand.

"Get some sleep, beautiful. I'll be back in a few hours to pick you up." He moved away from the door. "Oh, and next time someone knocks on your door in the middle of the night, ask who's there before you open it. I'll get to spank that sexy ass if you do that again."

Christa laughed. "Okay, okay. I don't normally get any visitors in the middle of the night. It's your fault—you distracted me!"

Aaron's smile beamed back at her before he turned and walked away. Sighing happily, Christa locked up and got ready for bed. She was beyond keyed up from the whole whirlwind named Aaron, she thought she'd never fall asleep. Dreams of him soon overtook her and, before she knew it, the irritating noise from her alarm clock woke her just as she was getting to a good part.

Annoyance quickly turned to excitement when she realized she didn't need the dream since he would soon be there in person.

CHAPTER SEVEN

Meet the Millers

Jared had run out of unpacking tasks to take his mind off Christa. Waiting for her to call him was excruciating, though. He'd checked his phone at least fifty times the previous night, hoping she'd stopped by her café and got his message before she went home. He'd stayed busy all night, making sure all of his belongings were perfectly arranged, only because it helped take his mind off her for a few minutes at a time.

Then he found he had a full day ahead of him with absolutely nothing to do but think about her. When he'd been patient long enough, he dialed her number and waited. She picked up on the third ring.

"Hello?" Her voice was tentative and cautious.

"Hey, Christa. This is Jared."

"Oh, Jared! I don't have your number in my phone, so I didn't know it was you. What's up?"

He thought she sounded genuinely glad to hear from

him. But then, he was talking to Christa—she was always glad to hear from him.

"I just thought maybe we could spend the day together. It's been a long time. I've missed you," he persuaded.

"I'd love to see you, but I already have plans for today. Can I call you later? Or maybe you can come by the café tomorrow, and we can have coffee together? It'll be on the house."

Jared recognized that tone of voice. It was cheerful and sincere, but also distracted. Whatever plans she had for the day were obviously all she could think about.

"Yeah, sure. That sounds great." He tried to keep the disappointment out of his voice. "I start my new job tomorrow, but I'll try to come by after work. If not tomorrow, then definitely one day this week," he promised.

"That'd be great, Jared. It's good to have you home. I'll see you later, okay?"

After they hung up, Jared had a sneaking suspicion her time was being taken up by another man. Not that another guy had never stopped him before, so he reasoned he wouldn't let it stop him this time. He'd waited years to move their relationship to the next level. If another man thought he could take Jared's place in Christa's life, that man would be sorely disappointed.

Undaunted, Jared decided to visit his parents while he had free time. They had always been supportive of him, and he recognized he was fortunate to have them. When he walked into their house, he instantly smelled Sunday dinner on the stove and heard the chatter and laughter of his family in the kitchen. The years he'd been away suddenly melted away to nothing, and he was immediately glad to be back home.

He walked into the kitchen unannounced, lowered his voice a couple of octaves and let the deep bass sound fill the room. "What's going on in here?"

Everyone jumped, and faces snapped to look in his direction. After the initial shock, his siblings and parents all called out to him at once.

"Jared!"

"We didn't expect you today, son!"

"Come sit down and eat!"

He took his seat and filled his plate, joining in on the friendly ribbing of his siblings. He spent the rest of the afternoon catching up with his older twin brothers, Jessie and Josh, and his younger sister, Jennifer. Being back in the fold felt so right.

"So, Jared, when are you going to man up and ask Christa out? I saw her the other day. Man, she looks good. If you're not interested, just let me know, I'll take her off your hands," Jessie teased.

"Yeah, right, Jessie. She's too smart to fall for the likes of you." Jared laughed while tossing a bottle cap at Jessie's head.

"Man, who are you kidding? I am the stud muffin around here. She'd pick me in a heartbeat!" Josh chimed in.

Jared rolled his eyes. "You two are identical twins, Josh. And she wouldn't pick either of you over me."

"Willing to put your money where your mouth is, brah?" Jessie challenged.

Jared laughed good-naturedly, knowing his brothers were only razzing him and seeing how far they could push him before he went off on them. They'd used the same routine on him all his life.

"No chance, *boys*. Mom's on my side this time."

Jessie's and Josh's faces both fell at the same time. Everyone in the family knew that anytime *Mom* took sides, the game was over. There was no point in arguing any further.

"That's right, boys," Patti chimed in. "Jared is finally going to put things right with Christa. And it is well past time, if you ask me."

"Well, that may be a little hard to do *now*," Jennifer

piped in. All heads jerked to her. Patti looked shocked, and Jared looked a little panicked.

"Why is that, Jen?" Patti asked.

"I went into her café yesterday, and Allie told me that Christa was on a date—an *all-day date*. She's seeing some guy that came into her café, and she apparently really likes him," Jen explained.

Patti and Jared continued to stare at Jen like she was an alien who'd just crash-landed in their living room.

"What? Why are you both staring at me like that?" Jen demanded. Being the baby of the family, she'd always endured the brunt of the bullying from her older brothers. Especially when it came to dating, guys calling her, going to her high school proms, or anything else that was even remotely interesting and involved the opposite sex.

"Who is he?" Jared asked.

"I don't know—some guy who came into her café is all I know. Allie said they really hit it off, and she's never seen Christa this interested in a guy before," Jen answered. "Maybe you should ask Allie out instead."

Jared pretended he didn't hear that last part. He wasn't interested in Allie—he wanted Christa. He looked at his mom and could instantly read her thoughts because they mirrored his own. *I waited too long... I'm too late.*

"You know Allie very well?" Jared asked, suddenly realizing Jen had called her by name.

"Yes, I have a couple of classes with her at UCSF," Jen responded absently. Then, as if it suddenly hit her, she added, "Oh, no, you don't! I'm not getting involved in whatever scheme you are planning for Christa. She's my friend, and so is Allie."

Jared grabbed his chest and put on his best "hurt" face before he said, "I can't believe you'd think I would plan and scheme against Christa!"

"Yeah, whatever, big brother. I grew up with the three of you," she said as she gestured at her three brothers. "I know damn well what you're all capable of doing!" Jen responded with a laugh.

For all the torture her older brothers had put her through in her life, she knew they loved her and would do anything for her. And she loved them back with all her heart.

The three men eyed her suspiciously for a moment, then slowly closed in on Jen. "That sounds like an insult to me. What do you think, Josh?" Jessie spoke with a crazy half grin and a completely wicked look in his eyes while he approached from her right.

"Oh, most definitely, Jessie. That was *definitely* an insult about growing up with the awesome Miller brothers," Josh agreed, moving toward her left.

"You'd think she'd know better after being under our guidance for the last twenty-one years," Jared chimed in, walking directly toward her. Her gaze darted nervously between her three brothers. They were all crazy-eyed, and she watched them with a guarded stance.

They always found the most humiliating way of making her succumb to their requests. When she was eight, her parents had instructed the older boys to babysit her while they went out. Her brothers decided she was possessed and needed to be baptized to exorcise the demons. They proceeded to try to baptize her head in the toilet while holding her upside down by her ankles and trying to stuff her head into the toilet bowl water. When she got free, she chased the three of them around the yard with a baseball bat for an hour.

Being grown now didn't change the relationship between them very much. They would still try to baptize her in the commode water, and she would still beat the shit out of them with a baseball bat for even attempting.

But there was also a lot of love in their family, and they could always count on each other. If Jared pushed this, Jen knew she would be pitted between her brother and her friends. There was no easy way out.

"I have my Louisville Slugger, and I know how to use it." Jen warned them with her sternest expression, but she still looked around for a way out.

"Boys, leave her alone," the older, gruff male voice called out. Even grown, Ethan's voice stilled the brothers' movements. "Jared, you're a man now, son. No games. Get the woman on your own and quit trying to use your little sister to get dates for you."

Jen breathed a sigh of relief and smiled at her daddy. He winked at her and smiled when the boys weren't looking. "Don't let them push you around, baby girl," he said with a kiss on her cheek.

Being the baby and the only girl, she'd always been treated a little differently. But she was also "Daddy's girl," and the boys had always been jealous of his protection of her.

"Thanks, Daddy." She laughed and kissed his cheek. "I didn't know how I was going to get out of that."

Ethan walked off, and Jared approached Jen nonchalantly. "Don't think you're off the hook, little sister," he muttered under his breath as he lifted his glass to his lips.

Jen smiled at Jared and whispered back, "I *am* off the hook, big brother. You're on your own."

"You still have a thing for Rory, don't you?" Jared asked calmly, knowing damn well she did and that

Rory was her one and only weakness. Rory also happened to be one of Jared's best friends.

"I don't know what you're talking about," she stated defiantly.

"Oh, I think you do, little sis. In fact, I know you do. What if I had a talk with him? Let him know that you've carried a secret flame for him for the last several years? How would that be?" he asked coolly.

"You wouldn't," she said, but her voice lacked conviction. In fact, she knew he would. She mused to herself, *"Why did I have to have brothers?"*

Jared didn't respond verbally. He simply tilted his head and gave her a devilish grin that told her she should know better.

Resigned to the fact that she had no other choice, she conceded. "I won't help you hurt her, Jared. If Christa is happy with someone else, she deserves to be happy with no interference from us."

Jared flinched at that statement. He wanted Christa to be happy. Of course he did—she deserved so much more than she'd been given. But he also wanted her to be happy with *him*. Though he'd never told her, he just always assumed she'd be there waiting for him when he returned home. He hadn't considered any other scenario when it came to Christa. Now he was being forced to envision her with another man. That scenario just didn't sit well with him.

"I just need a chance with her, Jen. I should've done so many things differently with her, but at the time, I thought I was doing her a favor. I didn't want to ask her to wait for me. To just…take a few visits now and then when I came home on breaks. I don't want to be too late."

Jared's explanation somewhat made sense to her, even though she, along with the rest of her family, had stressed how wrong he was on a regular basis. But his voice was filled with disappointment that spilled over into his expression. Right or wrong, he was her brother, and she loved him.

Jen sighed deeply as she thought about what he'd just shared with her and what it would require of her. "I will do what I can to help you, Jared. But don't ask me to betray my friend. That's not fair for you to expect me to do that."

Jared nodded in agreement and pulled Jen to him for a hug. "I was just kidding about telling Rory. I wouldn't do that to you."

"Yes, you would," she replied into his chest, and she couldn't hold in the laugh when she felt his chuckle rumble through his chest.

He kissed her on top of her head and let her go. "I start my new job tomorrow, and I already know I'll be swamped. Can you see what you can find out for me?"

"Yeah, okay. I'll try to get the scoop," Jen replied. "I need to get going. I have a full day tomorrow myself. It's good to have you back home, Jared."

"Christa, I need caffeine! Stat!" Jen called as she walked into The Sweet Spot. Christa was behind the counter and quickly looked up when she heard someone yelling like a lunatic. Seeing her long-time friend coming through the door warmed her heart, and the crazy-woman thought instantly made sense.

"Jen! It's been too long! Where have you been, girl?" Christa called back to her while she started making Jen's favorite drink—a white chocolate mocha with an extra shot of espresso.

"At work. They're trying to kill me." Jen laughed, acknowledging her penchant for theatrics.

"Jen, you work in the pediatric department of the hospital. I seriously doubt the little kids are trying to kill you," Christa snickered.

"Never underestimate them, Christa. They're devious and cunning. And...*cute*," Jen argued, making Christa laugh loudly.

Christa took a seat with Jen as she set her coffee in front of her. "Mmm, that is so good."

"So, what brings you in today? I haven't seen you in a long time. Visits from two Millers in the same week…maybe I should go buy lottery tickets." Christa smiled warmly, genuinely glad to see Jen, and Jen felt her stomach roil in response.

"I actually came the other day, but you were off on some hot date. Who's the lucky guy?" Jen asked, leaning in and whispering secretively.

"Actually, he's someone I met here in my shop. He came in every day over the past month for coffee and to have breakfast with me. We really hit it off," Christa explained, her shyness bleeding through her tone and revealing she was clearly holding back. The intrigue only made Jen more curious about Christa's new mystery man.

"And? Come on—you know how my brothers tortured me all my life. I know torture tactics!"

"Okay, we spent the whole day together Saturday. He left a little after midnight and then came back yesterday morning to pick me up. We spent the whole day together again, and he left late last night." Christa was now beaming. Her smile and excitement were contagious.

Jen was genuinely happy for her friend and a little sad for her brother. Her brother who had waited too long to make a move and took for granted that Christa would just wait around for him for however long he decided to take.

"So, tell me about him. What's his name? What does he do? What does he look like? Is he good in bed?"

Christa choked on her coffee at the last question. "Um, well, I don't know about the last question, Jen. But his name is Aaron Rivers. He's an agent—he pairs up models and ad companies, completes the sale, signs the contracts, and whatever else agents do. He's *so* handsome, Jen. He is just...drop-dead gorgeous. He has black hair, and he's tall and muscular. He has one of those sexy, eternal five-o'clock shadows and the most beautiful blue eyes I've ever seen. I still can't believe he's interested in me, of all people."

"Why wouldn't he be? You're gorgeous, Christa. He's probably saying he can't believe you're interested in him."

Christa smiled down into her coffee mug. "Jen, I'm really falling for him. I know it's way too soon to even think about that. I mean, it's only been a few weeks since I first met him, but I just can't help it."

"That's great, really, it is. But maybe you should take it a little slower? A little safer?" Jen suggested.

"You know, I thought about that myself. That was my first inclination. But I decided I've played it safe my whole life. I've had a few boyfriends but nothing too serious—nothing long term. I've done what was expected of me and worked hard for everything I've been blessed with. I really want to let go of the reins I've held on to so tightly and just *have fun* now." Christa began getting more animated, livelier, the more they talked. "I want to live a little, take a few chances, and see where it goes. If I get hurt, I get hurt. What's the worst that can happen? We eventually split up? Maybe. But at least I took the chance to *live* while I'm young."

"I've never seen you like this, Christa. He's really good for you," Jen said thoughtfully. She watched Christa's face, as she was far off somewhere, reliving a past moment. "You're in love with him, aren't you?"

Christa jerked up. Her spine suddenly made of unbending steel, her face serious, and her voice hushed. "Why do you say that? It's too soon to be in love."

"No, Christa," Jen said, shaking her head slightly. "It's never too early to be in love. You know when it's real. It's your mind that tries to fight it, tries to hide the feelings behind logic and reason. It's your mind that tries to tell you you're wrong. But the heart—the heart knows what it wants."

Christa stared at Jen, dumbfounded, for several seconds. "Oh. My. God. Jen." She leaned back in her chair, dropped her head and stared at her hands for a moment. She had to gather her thoughts. *Could Jen be right? Isn't it too soon?*

"You're right, Jen," Christa said, feeling better having said it aloud instead of turning it over and over in her mind. Saying the words made it more real—but less of the untamable monster she'd created in her mind. "I think you're right. I think I'm already in love with him. At least, with how he makes me feel. How he treats me. The way he finds time to spend with me, call me, or text me." Her smile crept across her face, raising her cheeks and lighting her eyes as she looked at her friend.

Jen decided to test the waters. "You know, I always thought you and Jared would end up together," she said wistfully. "Then you and I would be sisters."

Christa laughed at the thought. "Yeah, right, Jen! Jared and I were only ever just friends. Anyway, he never saw me as anything but a little kid. Then he went off to college, and I barely heard from him the whole seven plus years he was away. It's good to have him home, though. I *have* missed him."

"Maybe *you* should ask *him* out," Jen pressed.

Jen laughed at the look of sheer terror on Christa's face. "Um, I don't think so, Jen," Christa laughed nervously. "Besides, I'm not really one to date around. I like spending time with Aaron," she finished with a shrug.

"Sounds like he's the one, Christa," Jen replied with sincerity. She could see it in Christa's face when she talked about Aaron. She was completely taken with him. Jen had picked up Jared's protective nature over Christa after he left for college. She wanted to test Aaron and see if he was as enamored of Christa. "So, when do I get to meet him?"

Christa glanced down at her watch. "If you can hang around, you'll get to meet him in just a few minutes. He'll be here any time now." Christa beamed.

The bell over the door drew her eyes up, and she saw the most gorgeous man standing in the doorway, looking for her. When his beautiful blue eyes found hers, she felt that same tingle in her stomach and tightening in her chest. He was really there for her.

He strolled to her table and drew her up from her seat, into his arms. They wrapped around her, pulling her firmly against him as he lifted her feet off the floor and claimed the kiss he'd been waiting all day to enjoy.

"Hello, beautiful. How was your day?" he murmured to her, keeping his lips against her cheek as he spoke.

"Mmm...so much better now," she purred back, melting into his arms and into the warmth of his body against hers.

Aaron's eyes met Jen's, and he saw a mixture of emotions in them. She looked amused at their public display of affection, but there was something else there he couldn't quite place. He gently put Christa's feet back on the ground and looked at her face as he stroked her cheek with his hand.

Christa took his hand in hers and turned to Jen. "Aaron, I want you to meet a good friend of mine. This is Jen Miller. Jen, this is Aaron Rivers."

Aaron and Jen shook hands, and each said hello before Christa continued. "Jen and I were just talking about you."

Aaron gave her an amused look and a sexy smirk. "Is that right? So that's why my ears were burning."

"Yep, you caught me." Christa laughed and wrapped her arm around Aaron's waist.

"I hope I have." Aaron's sexy voice probed as he lowered his head to kiss her again. "So, what were you two saying about me?"

"Hold that thought," Christa interrupted, "Do you want a coffee? Jen, refill?"

"Sure," they both answered in unison.

Jen took the opportunity to question Aaron as soon as Christa left the table.

"She's great, isn't she?" Jen began.

"She's the best person I know," Aaron answered truthfully.

"Are you two serious?" Jen wasn't one to mince words, and she didn't have the luxury of time to pry information out of him.

Aaron smiled knowingly as he leaned back in his chair to look Jen fully in the eye as he spoke. "I appreciate you looking out for her. But believe me, I'm very serious about her. I just hope she feels the same about me."

CHAPTER EIGHT

Breaking Hearts

"You know, I think I know who you are." Jen narrowed her eyes, recognition dawning on her. "I've seen you on TV and in magazines with models." Her tone was just a notch away from accusatory, but her eyes sized him up thoroughly.

Aaron shifted uncomfortably in his seat. "Yes, I'm an agent for Rivers Forte, so I'm frequently seen with the models."

"No, that's not it. These pictures were of you escorting them to red carpet events. You were in a tuxedo and everything. They were your *dates*," she emphasized.

"Yes, in the past, I have dated models. But that was a while back," Aaron explained.

"Don't hurt her, Aaron," Jen stated firmly. "She's too good of a person to be strung along."

"I agree. And I won't hurt her. Ever," Aaron replied resolutely.

Jen leaned in and lowered her voice menacingly. "That's good. Because if you do, I will hunt you down, cut off your balls, and stuff and mount them for my new dining room centerpiece."

Christa arrived with the coffees just in time for them to avoid a further exchange of words, but the air was obviously thick with tension between Aaron and Jen.

"What's going on here, guys?" Christa asked, breaking the silence and getting straight to the point.

Aaron took her hand in his. "Jen was just putting me in my place. Letting me know what I have to look forward to if I hurt you."

"I can always count on the Millers to take care of me," Christa replied jokingly. "Now that that's out of the way, can we all be friends?"

"Sure. I think we're all clear," Jen answered with a smile that Aaron returned.

Once they'd finished their coffees and the ladies agreed on a girls' night out in the near future, Jen said her goodbyes and left the café. As soon as she got in her car, she called Jared.

"Hey, sis. What's up?" Jared was distracted, and Jen heard the distinct sound of papers shuffling and falling in the background. "Shit!"

"Sounds like you're having a good first day on the job," she deadpanned.

"Yeah, just great. Shit, is that really the time?"

"Afraid so, big brother. I'm on my way home. I've been at The Sweet Spot with Christa—"

Jared interrupted her before she could finish. "And? Did you find out anything?" She suddenly had his full attention.

"I did, Jared. She's seeing this guy, Aaron, and he came in while I was there. They are crazy about each other. I saw them together. I think...I think you need to stay out of it, Jared. She's *happy*," Jen emphasized.

"Well..." He paused. "There's no reason we can't still be friends. Right?" Jared asked.

"Jared." The warning in her tone was unmistakable.

"We've always been friends, Jen. We're still friends now," Jared rationalized.

He knew it was a stretch, but he wasn't giving up on Christa completely. Staying in her life meant being there when the chips fell, helping pick them back up, and being the one she could depend on. He'd let her down too much while he was away at school, and he had too much to make up for to turn away now.

Another week passed by before Jared made his way back to The Sweet Spot and back to Christa. His new job was the definition of the tenth level of hell, and demanding didn't begin to describe his caseload. He'd expected somewhat of a shitty caseload when he first started—that was just how it worked out for the new guy on the block. Starting out already late on several cases had severely hampered his plans to spend more time with Christa. That day, he left work on time and drove straight to see her.

Walking into the café in the late evening, Jared knew it wasn't going to be the reunion he planned to have. His feet stopped in midstride when he saw her sitting in another man's lap, leaning in close to him and sharing an intimate joke. Christa looked up when she heard the bell.

"Jared!" she exclaimed, but Jared noticed she didn't move from the man's embrace. "Come on in. I want you to meet someone."

She sounded so happy and sincere, Jared didn't have the heart to tell her he had no interest in meeting the man who was trying to take her away from him. Except, she wasn't his. He'd left her behind more than seven years ago, and he had no claim to her then or now. His head knew that. His heart and his ego argued the point, though.

Jared crossed the café to join Aaron and Christa. As

he watched them together, he felt like a third wheel, completely unwanted and out of place in their intimate setting.

"Jared, this is Aaron Rivers. Aaron, this is Jared Miller, Jen's brother. Jared and his family were like my own family growing up. He's practically my brother." Christa finished the introductions with a beaming smile that tore Jared's heart out.

A brother.

Aaron and Jared shook hands, each man silently sizing the other up, identifying the potential threat the other posed. Jared saw a flash of recognition in Aaron's eyes, like he'd seen Jared before, but he quickly dismissed it. Knowing they'd never crossed paths, Jared thought no more of it and moved on to bigger issues. Like how to get Aaron out of Christa's life.

"Good to meet you, man," Aaron said with a smile, shaking Jared's hand but still holding Christa with the other arm.

"Likewise," Jared responded.

"Can I get you anything, Jared? Coffee? Sandwich?" Christa asked, ever the hospitable host.

"I don't want to interrupt you two. I just wanted to stop by and see you. It's been a long time." Jared spoke directly to Christa, never moving his eyes to include Aaron in the conversation.

"It's no problem. It'll only take me a minute. Have a seat here with Aaron, and I'll be right back." Christa rose from Aaron's lap and extended her hand to the other seat at the table.

She left the two men alone while she played hostess. Aaron and Jared sat in uncomfortable silence for a few moments before Aaron spoke.

"So, I met your sister, Jen. She's very protective of Christa."

"Yes, we all are, actually," Jared replied, his threat lying just under the surface of his words. "My parents love Christa—my mom, especially. They've been close for a long time."

"Yeah, Christa told me you two were friends, but you've been away at college for, what was it, a little over seven years, right? She said she didn't see you much during that time." Aaron indirectly challenged him in return.

The tightening of Jared's jaw muscle was obvious, and Aaron knew he'd hit a nerve. Aaron kept his face neutral so as not to give away his satisfaction at putting Jared in his place.

Christa arrived with Jared's dinner just in time to avoid a confrontation. Jared had to force it down, though, as he watched Christa take her seat back in

Aaron's lap. Her arm was around his neck, and both of Aaron's arms were wrapped around her waist, claiming her as his own. Jared noted that Christa looked genuinely happy, just like Jen had described. He wasn't happy about it, but he decided, for Christa's sake, he wouldn't cause any trouble between them.

When he finished eating and talking with Christa and Aaron, Jared got up to leave, and Christa walked him to the door. Aaron kept his seat but also kept a watchful eye on them—mainly on Jared. He hugged Christa and thanked her for the dinner.

"Don't be a stranger, Jared. It's good to have you home," she said sincerely.

"You seem happier, Christa," Jared replied, inclining his head toward Aaron. "Does he have anything to do with that?"

"He does, Jared. He's been really good to me. We haven't been seeing each other long, but it just feels...*right*," she explained. The words crushed him inside, but outwardly, he somehow maintained his smile, for her sake.

"He'd better be good to you. Or he'll have to deal with me," Jared warned.

Christa laughed and swatted his arm. "You'll have to get in line behind Jen. She's already warned him enough for both of you."

Jared kissed her cheek goodbye, waved to Aaron, and left the café. He sat in his car for several minutes before driving away, thinking about what could have been, what should have been had he not been so self-absorbed all those years. Had he not just assumed she would wait for him to come home.

After Jared left, Christa returned to her seat with Aaron. "So, what'd you think?"

Aaron had anticipated this very question. "He seems like a good guy. He looks familiar. Is that him in the picture in your apartment?"

He'd already known the answer before he asked, but he wanted to open the dialogue to get her talking. He wanted to find out as much as he could about her previous relationship with Jared. The man was protective of her. Hell, the whole family was protective of her. But there was a different look in Jared's eyes when he looked at Christa. And Jared couldn't hide how he felt or what he thought when Christa sat in Aaron's lap. The man was jealous with a capital green.

"Yes, that's him." There was no hint of hesitation in her voice. "We were so young then—or I was anyway. Jared's a few years older than I am. Anyway, I had gone to his family's BBQ one weekend, and all the kids had a three-legged race. I was paired with Jared, so you can imagine how that worked out with his long legs and my short ones. We were getting beaten, very badly, so I hopped on his back just before we crossed the stream and he ran the rest of the way to the finish line. His mom was laughing so hard she could barely take that picture."

Christa's laughter increased the more she talked about that weekend. Aaron immediately noticed she wasn't reminiscing about Jared as much as she was the whole family get-together. The partial confirmation that there was nothing more than friendship there made Aaron feel a little more relaxed. That, and she made no secret about their relationship in front of Jared. When she'd sat back down in his lap in front of Jared, Aaron had felt invincible. And his little sweetheart had no idea she was breaking hearts.

Aaron stayed after all the customers left and helped Christa clean up the kitchen, get breakfast items set up for the morning rush, and walked her to her car after they locked up. He kept his hand on her lower back, enjoying the contact and intimacy it implied. Just as they reached her car door, he moved his hand to her arm, lightly gripping her elbow and turning her to face him. Aaron gently stroked her cheek, leaned in, and placed a dry, chaste kiss on her lips.

Once wasn't enough, so he closed the gap again, taking her mouth with his, using his tongue to gain entry. He lifted her up and sat her on the hood of the car. She wrapped her legs around his waist, holding tight and pulling himself to her core. The kiss became urgent, fueled by desire, and the fire only grew hotter. His hands covered her face, cradling it as he devoured her, tasting her with a fevered frenzy. His hips surged forward, the evidence of his arousal pushing into her through their clothing.

Christa's breathing hitched, and she moaned softly into his mouth. Aaron's hands rapidly moved across her body, leaving a trail of fire in their path. Christa pulled him closer to her, pressed her chest firmly against his, and her tender nipples rubbed against the hardness of his muscled chest. His thumb found her already erect nipple and lightly rubbed it in circles. The sensation shot straight through her body to her core, igniting her nerve endings and sending a delicious shudder through her.

As much as Aaron wanted to continue this very public display of inappropriate affection, he didn't want to get Christa arrested for indecent exposure. And while a big part of him, mostly the part below his belt, wanted to continue this erotic dance in the privacy of her apartment, or even her car, the other part of him wanted something more. He'd always had one-night stands, or sometimes, a couple of nights, but never more. No real connections, no real feelings, and no real future were ever possible.

With Christa, he already wanted more of everything—more time with her, more getting to know the real person, more intimacy, and more connection. He showed more restraint and self-composure than he knew was humanly possible when he slowed the kiss until he could pull away from her. Her eyes were wide, her pupils dilated, and her breaths were heavy and fast. He found little consolation in knowing she didn't want their impromptu display of public affection to end any more than he did. It only made him want to take her even more.

Aaron put his hands back on her face and kissed her lips softly. He kept his kisses controlled, smooth and sensual. Her natural taste was so intoxicating he couldn't get enough. With a deep sigh, he put his forehead to hers and moved his hands to interlace their fingers together.

"You should get going. It's late. Can I follow you home—just to make sure you make it safely? I don't like you walking in alone at night." Aaron's voice was low and possessive.

Christa's heart melted at his words. She couldn't believe she had found someone who cared enough to go out of their way to make sure she got home safely.

"You don't have to, Aaron. You must be tired." She offered him a way out of his offer.

"Christa, I can't rest without knowing you're all right. I won't try anything, I promise. I just need to know you're safe." His tone pleaded and commanded at the same time.

"Okay." Christa gently stroked his stubble. At that very moment, she could honestly say she was falling hopelessly head over heels in love with Aaron.

Aaron followed her into her apartment, checked to make sure everything was secure, and kissed her good night at the door. Christa closed and locked it behind him and then floated on cloud nine to get ready for bed. Everything in her life was finally looking up—her new business was picking up, she had big plans to expand her catering, and her love life was definitely getting better and better.

June

Over the following month, Jared buried himself in his work and stayed away from Christa and her café. And her new boyfriend. The thoughts of her with another man were killing him, but he wouldn't be the one to cause her any more pain than she'd already suffered at the hands of her family. His long days spent working the extra heavy caseload the senior associates had piled on him were starting to pay off. He had managed to settle several cases out of court, creating lucrative deals for both the firm and the clients. He'd also spent most of his evening work hours with another junior associate, Faith Wells. She wasn't Christa, but she was nice and she helped fill the lonely hours.

It was when he was home alone after work when the thoughts invaded his mind relentlessly. He tortured himself thinking about the sounds Christa must make, how good it must feel to hold her, and what it would feel like to wake up with her in his arms. Not to mention the dreams he had almost nightly. The ones where she writhed underneath him, calling his name as he buried himself deep inside her. He woke every morning with the thought he was too damn old to be having wet dreams. He was right. He just woke with an unresolved erection that couldn't be fully satisfied without her.

Jared had never had a problem in the *getting a date* department, and Faith made it obvious she was interested in him. He decided maybe it was time for him to spend some time outside of work with her and see how it progressed. He hadn't heard from Christa in the past month, so he reasoned he wasn't as important to her as he thought he was.

This must be exactly how she felt all those years I treated her the same way, he thought solemnly.

The next evening after they finished with more of the case files, Jared asked Faith to go to a local jazz bar to have a drink with him. She readily agreed, and they left in separate cars, agreeing to meet at the club.

The dimly lit room matched Jared's feelings. Even though his brain told him to move on without Christa, his heart hadn't quite followed suit yet. Jared and Faith found a small table away from the crowds and quickly ordered their drinks.

"So, I thought you'd never ask me out. What took you so long?" she asked brazenly while smiling seductively. He cringed inwardly, instantly comparing her to Christa and noting that Christa would've never been so bold.

"Just been busy, I guess," he replied with a shrug of his shoulder, not wanting to tell her what he honestly thought.

After a few drinks loosened him up, he felt a little better without Christa on his mind every second. Faith laughed and flirted with him, touching his arm and moving her chair closer to his in her obvious attempts to draw him into her.

After a couple more shots, he was past the point of caring that she wasn't really Christa or that he wasn't really that attracted to her. She was a warm, willing body, and he had already decided he would use her body in any way she wanted.

A cab ride and a stumble through the door later, he

grasped her hair in his hand and covered her mouth with his. His tongue slid in with no resistance; she matched him stroke for stroke. Her hands found his belt, and within seconds, his dress pants were on the floor, and she was stroking his growing erection through his briefs. Faith pulled away from Jared and dropped to her knees, freeing his cock as she knelt. Without warning, she'd taken him into her mouth, working him with a hurried frenzy. Jared closed his eyes and held her head in his hands.

When she slowed, he gripped tighter, jerking his hips quickly in and out of her mouth while moaning loudly. Faith relaxed the muscles in the back of her throat, allowing him deeper penetration. Jared groaned one last time as he lost the battle with control. She took all of him and stood with a knowing smirk on her face. Jared quickly tugged her pants down to her ankles, bent her over the back of the couch, and fucked her from behind after quickly sheathing himself with a condom. No foreplay, no words of affection—just the fast, hard pounding she so obviously wanted.

Faith cried out when he thrust inside her the first time. "Isn't this what you wanted? Didn't you want me to fuck you?"

"Yes," she hissed back.

"That's what you're getting." Jared continued to surge into her, over and over, until she was screaming, her fingers gripping the cushions while her pussy gripped his cock. He growled loudly as he came. "Fuck, Christa!"

Jared immediately stepped away, looking for the bathroom to clean up, when Faith stood from her bended position.

"My name isn't Christa." Her voice dripped with venom and disgust, aimed at him.

"What the hell are you talking about?" Jared asked with a furrowed brow and confusion etched on his handsome features.

"Just now, when you were fucking me, you called me Christa. My name is Faith."

Jared gave a half shrug. "I know your name. I don't know what you're talking about. You must have misunderstood me." *I just wanted you to be Christa.*

She gave him a hard look, as if she were trying to decide if he was lying or not. He didn't really care, but he knew it would make their working relationship more awkward, so he hoped she believed she'd just misunderstood what he'd said.

"All right, if you say so. Do you want to take a shower with me?"

"Sure." *No. What the hell have I done?*

Showered and dressed, Jared used the excuse of not

wanting to leave his expensive car parked anywhere overnight to get out of Faith's apartment. On the cab ride back to his car, he envisioned his new working relationship with Faith. She wasn't the one he wanted, but the only one he wanted was in the arms of someone else. If he shunned Faith now, how would that affect his career? If he didn't, how would that affect his career?

For his sanity's sake, he decided to tell her they needed to keep their arrangement under wraps to maintain a professional relationship at work and not to let their late-night activities interfere with their ambitions. Faith was career-driven, too, so he didn't think she would take offense at his request. Then, when it all naturally died out between them, they could remain professional coworkers. His last thoughts of her were along the lines of "the best-laid plans." Distractedly, he paid the cab driver, got in his car, and drove home.

He took the long way home—the path that took him directly in front of The Sweet Spot. He had avoided this route for the past month simply because he didn't want to see Aaron's car parked out front. Slowing as he passed the café, he was treated to a special view through the large picture window in front. Christa had her back to the window, standing on her tiptoes, her arms around Aaron's neck as he bent down toward her, and their mouths were locked in a passionate kiss.

Jared hit the steering wheel with his fist as he yelled, "Fuck!" Glancing at the clock, he assumed Christa was just getting everything ready to start her day. He knew she had to start early to have her pastry case filled before all her customers started coming in. But since Aaron was so obviously there with her at five o'clock in the morning, Jared assumed they had spent the night together.

A thump on the steering wheel in cadence with each curse didn't make him feel any better. "Fuck! Fuck! Fuck!"

There was no chance of getting any sleep with those mental images repeatedly playing in his dreams.

CHAPTER NINE

Breakfast Buffet

June

"I can't believe you're here to help me this early in the morning," Christa cooed sweetly as she wrapped her arms around Aaron's neck.

"I've missed you." He slanted his mouth over hers. "I don't get to see you enough."

"I know, I've missed you, too. Work just gets in the way of life, doesn't it?" she responded with a laugh. "But it was just a few hours ago when I last saw you..." Her voice trailed off.

"A few hours too long, Christa," he replied, his eyes full of love and desire. This time, his kiss was more urgent, more possessive, and more aggressive. She responded in earnest, pulling him closer to her as he did the same. The sound of a car gunning its engine caught his attention, and he slowly broke their kiss.

"Maybe we should take this to the kitchen. Anyone can see us in here through this window," he suggested.

"Maybe you're right," she purred. She turned to walk toward the kitchen, grabbing Aaron's tie in her hand and pulling him behind her.

"Damn, woman, you are so hot." He growled in her ear when he caught up with her. "Now turn around and let me watch that hot ass of yours sashay in front of me."

"You only want me because of my ass, don't you?"

"Not only." He paused. "Your croissants are out of this world."

She threw her head back in laughter, feeling pure happiness with how natural their relationship felt. She felt protected and desired when he wrapped his arms around her from behind and walked the rest of the way with his body connected to hers.

She giggled as she leaned back into him. She snaked her hand to stroke the back of his neck, playing with the soft tendrils of his hair, and driving him crazy with her touch. By the time they reached the privacy of the kitchen, Aaron's fingers found refuge under her shirt, rubbing circles on her stomach. They traveled up her torso, raising her shirt as he continued his exploration of her skin.

He bowed his head and placed wet, openmouthed kisses on her neck. His tongue flicked across her sensitive skin, licked from her ear to the base of her neck, then back again. Christa's head tilted to the side, giving his tongue full access to the sensitive skin below her ear as his hands found her breasts. He deftly unhooked her front-clasped bra, then palmed and gently kneaded her breasts. Her moans of pleasure increased with his pressure until his fingers found her sensitive nipples. He grasped each nipple between his thumb and index finger and lightly squeezed then rolled them.

His growl in her ear nearly brought her to her knees. "Christa, you feel so damn good. Fuck, I want to taste you right here on this table. Let me have you for breakfast."

She turned to face him, and their mouths immediately clashed in a frenzied rush. Their tongues danced, their caresses adding more and more heat to their desire. Christa lightly sucked on Aaron's tongue, pulling it into her mouth and gently caressing it before releasing and repeating the actions on his lower lip. She always loved his lips— so perfectly kissable. Aaron's hands moved down to her waist, then to her ass.

She was suddenly lifted to sit on the chef's table, and he placed himself directly between her legs. He placed kisses along the slope of her neck again, then reached her breasts where his mouth continued to deliver the most exquisite torture she'd ever experienced. His mouth worked wonders on one breast while his hand tended to the other. Then he switched sides to ensure she was thoroughly and completely loved.

When he raised his head, his hooded eyes conveyed his thoughts wordlessly. He helped her remove her shirt and bra, freeing her completely to him. Ever thoughtful of what she needed, he spread the shirt out on the table beneath her to shield her back from the cool surface before he helped her lie back.

"Don't worry, baby. I'm still taking it slow with us. One step at a time. Just let me love you this way, okay?" His voice was so kind, so caring, it completely melted her heart.

Apprehension radiated from her petite frame. Her muscles tensed under his touch, uncertainty taking hold. On one hand, she was ready for the next step, to let him take everything. But something held her back. Fear of the unknown, perhaps. Lack of experience, definitely.

"Christa, if you want me to stop, I will. I'll never pressure you, baby." He soothed her, but his voice held a trace of concern in it. Worry that he'd already pushed her further than she was ready to go.

"No, Aaron, I don't want you to stop," she assured him, and she meant it. "Don't stop."

He kissed her softly as his hands worked first to remove her skirt. Hooking his thumbs in the sides of her panties, he slowly dragged them down her legs, allowing his hands to rub against the entire length of her as they went. Her heavy breathing was evident in the rise and fall of her beautiful, perky breasts. Once he'd removed her panties, he started at her dainty feet, giving every inch of her body his undivided attention.

He lifted her leg, licked the back of her knees, and ran his tongue upward, across her hamstrings to the perfect globes of her ass. Her sharp intake of breath was his only verbal cue that she was excited.

"Feel free to make as much noise as you want to, baby. Hearing your moans of pleasure only turns me on and makes me want to pleasure you more."

Her responding whimper sounded like a challenge, one he gladly accepted.

"What kind of sound do you make when you come? Is it a scream? A moan? Tell me. I want to know." His lips continued exploring her skin.

"I don't know...I haven't—" Words escaped her along with her ability to breathe with his next move.

He picked up her opposite leg, his tongue making quick work of it. This time, she allowed the moan to escape her lips. It was so pure, so honest, and so full of passion, it caused his erection to bulge painfully behind his zipper. Knowing he was probably the first person to make her cry out like that made his chest swell with pride. He vowed he would also be the last person who would elicit those sounds from her.

He hooked his arms under her legs and pulled her until her ass reached the edge of the table. "You can scream my name anytime you need to, baby," he challenged. Flattening his tongue, he found her wet core with his mouth, and he licked her from bottom to top. Finding her clit, he circled his tongue around it several times before he lightly sucked on it. Her moans and squeals were just starting. He wouldn't stop until he heard his name fall from her lips.

After his warm, wet tongue flicked her clit repeatedly, heating it in the process, he pulled back and blew lightly on it. She moaned louder, but it still wasn't what he wanted to hear. He plunged his tongue deep inside her, rolled it around, and lapped up her desire. Increasing pressure and intensity, he went from her wet channel to her sensitive folds to her clit, over and over again. She was writhing underneath him, moaning loudly and grasping at his hair.

Aaron eased his hands under her ass, lifted it off the table while leaving her resting on her shoulders, and commenced to his intensely intimate sexual assault on her senses. The scruff of his beard scraped the sensitive skin of her thighs, increasing the sensations flooding her. He moved one hand, still holding her petite frame with the other, and added his fingers to the barrage.

One finger dipped inside her, collecting her juices then spreading the wetness on her folds. Lubricating her to avoid hurting her, he pushed his finger into her, slightly crooking it and scraping against her inner walls as he slowly withdrew it. His movements were slow at first, giving her body time to accept his invasion.

His goal was in sight when she moaned next. "More, Aaron. *Please.*"

"Whatever you want, love," he answered.

Then he applied more pressure with his tongue, devouring her clit and licking, sucking, and delving deep inside her. His fingers joined the assault, first one plunging hard and deep, and then adding a second. He felt her muscles clamping down on his fingers and knew she was close. His thumb found her clit, and he pressed down lightly in small circles, adding to the overall pleasure and breaking down her resistance.

Her cries of pleasure increased until, unable to hold it in any longer, she screamed his name while she soaked his hand with the rewards of all his work. His warm tongue lapped her up, consuming all she offered him, until she was spent and limp in his hands.

"Oh my God, Aaron. That was amazing," she panted breathlessly.

"You are amazing, Christa." He placed soft kisses on her body, everywhere, as he lowered her body back to the table.

He leaned over her, covering her beautiful naked body with his. Christa's legs circled around his waist, pulling him in closer to her as she wrapped her arms around his neck. His kisses were addictive, each one making her want more. But she felt selfish for taking all the pleasure and not giving him any in return. Aaron had been so patient with her over the last month. Their heavy make-out sessions had resulted in a couple of cold showers for them both—separately—but he'd been a perfect gentleman about it. He never pushed her for more than she was ready to give. He never even asked why she was so reluctant to take their relationship to the next level. He acted as if he had his own reasons for holding back.

Their intimacy that morning took them to a whole new level, and Christa's body was on fire. Nothing could quench this insatiable thirst but Aaron himself. When Aaron rose off her, she watched him as his eyes raked over her naked body. Aaron helped her to sit up and wrapped her shirt around her shoulders. He held the front of her shirt together as their eyes met.

"I want to give you something I've never given anyone before. If you'll have it," he murmured softly.

"What is it?" she whispered back, mesmerized by the adoration in his eyes.

"My heart," he said as he placed her hands on his chest. "It beats only for you now. If you take it, don't ever give it back to me. It'll be yours forever. I will be yours, forever."

Tears filled her eyes—tears of happiness, tears of requited love, and tears of relief. Having real love reciprocated without strings, without conditions, and without unreasonable expectations was foreign to Christa. But the way Aaron freely offered his love, in such a romantic manner, was by far the best moment of her life so far.

"I love you. I think I loved you from the moment I first met you, Christa. I can't help it. The more I'm with you, the more I need you."

"I love you, too, Aaron. I could never give your heart back." She pulled his hands to her chest. "Feel it beating? That's *your* heart—and I will take care of it like it's my own."

He stared at her—amazed, grateful, and even more in love than he was just a moment ago. This demure, beautiful, inexperienced creature had accomplished what the most skilled, acrobatically inclined supermodels couldn't come close to doing. She had tamed him, domesticated him, and even made him want it.

He held her face in his hands and softly, slowly, and repeatedly kissed her lips, her eyes, and her nose. "You never cease to amaze me," he said as he rested his forehead against hers. His hands moved down to her shirt and pushed it back off her shoulders. Her eyes widened, partly in fear and partly in anticipation, and Aaron smirked at her. He reached behind her and picked up her bra. With the utmost skill and care, he slowly redressed her until he fastened the last button on her shirt.

She sat still the whole time in astonishment at the care he was taking in making sure she was fully clothed. Somehow, the entire process of dressing her was just as erotic and sensual as undressing her had been. All the additional attention he'd given her made her feel extra special. He was never too busy for her, never had an excuse for not showing up when she needed him. He even came to the café, out of the blue, at five o'clock in the morning just to help her get ready for the morning crowd.

"You are the best man I've ever met, Aaron," she said sincerely. His hands froze in midair, the stunned look on his face conveying his inner thoughts without saying a word. He looked as if he was waiting for her to laugh after making that statement, as if he was waiting for the other shoe to drop.

"What is it?" she prodded.

He shook his head from side to side while

maintaining eye contact with her. "No one has ever accused me of being a good man before, Christa."

She scrunched her brow up in confusion. "What do you mean?"

Aaron huffed out a deep sigh before answering. "Christa, I've never been in any real relationship before. I won't lie. I won't sugarcoat it. I want you to know me—the real me—and that was part of me."

He looked away from her, suddenly ashamed of the life he'd wanted before he met her. "I was never with one woman for more than one or two nights. But it's not like that with us. With you, I want it *all*. And if I have to wait a year to prove it to you, then I will wait. Without question or complaint."

"Did you...date...the models you work with?" she asked tentatively.

"Yes, if by date, you actually mean have a one-night stand with them," Aaron answered truthfully. Then held his breath, praying she didn't kick him out.

"But you're done with that?" She tried to hide the quiver in her bottom lip. She was trying so hard not to cry, not to be upset with him, and it was killing him.

"I was actually done with that just before I met you that first morning. You gave me extra incentive, though."

"How so?"

"I wanted to be the kind of man you would want to be with," he stated plainly. When she didn't speak for a minute, Aaron continued. "Are we okay, baby?"

"We're okay. I told you I can't give your heart back. It already beats inside me."

Aaron wrapped his arms around her and squeezed her tight to him. He hoped he wasn't crushing the breath out of her, but he couldn't loosen his grip just then. He felt like he had to make sure their connection was set in stone before she figured out that he wasn't worthy of her love. Before she came to her senses and ran for the damn hills, he had to make sure she was as in love with him as he was with her.

"I guess we should get busy. You'll have customers soon," he said softly into her hair. She nodded but made no attempt to leave his arms.

"What about you?" she asked so softly he almost didn't hear her.

"Me? I'm here to help you. I'm not leaving. It's Saturday, and I'm off today."

"No, not that," she said shyly. "All you did for me...earlier... I didn't do anything for you."

Aaron pulled away from her just enough to have room to tilt her head up. She closed her eyes. Smiling, he said, "Sweetheart, what I did for you was because I *wanted* to, not because I expected anything in return."

She finally opened her eyes and saw his gorgeous smile. "What if I wanted to do something for you, too?"

"I will take you up on that—later. We have work to do now, missy, and you've been slacking long enough this morning," he joked and swatted her ass playfully. "Now, what do you need me to do?"

Christa stood on her tiptoes and placed a soft kiss on his cheek. "All right, let's get busy, then." After getting him set on his tasks, she started making all the pastries for the morning crowd. She noticed that every time she took a fresh batch of chocolate croissants out of the oven, she was short at least one.

"Aaron, if you eat one more chocolate croissant, you are going to be sick."

"I can't help it!" he responded with a mouthful of pastry. "You make them taste too good."

"And stay out of the espresso! You're already not going to sleep for a week."

"You make it taste too good, too," he called back to her.

With everything finally ready, Allie came rushing in at the last minute to jump behind the register. When Aaron came around the corner with an apron that read The Sweet Spot on it, Allie raised one eyebrow at him.

"Oh, I didn't know we hired a new employee. Christa, did you *thoroughly* check him out first?"

"It's on my to-do list," Christa retorted, accustomed to Allie's brand of teasing. Aaron gave her a shit-eating grin and waggled his eyebrows.

At the end of the day, Aaron had worked hard and loved every minute of it. He'd worked side by side with Christa and Allie, loving the fast-paced but laid-back atmosphere Christa had created. She and Allie had a natural camaraderie that the customers loved even though their personalities were night and day apart.

"Christa, you and Aaron can take off. I'll close up alone," Allie offered.

"I don't feel comfortable leaving you here alone." Aaron's voice was filled with concern.

"I'm a big girl, Aaron. I can tie my shoes and everything," Allie boasted.

"Let's go, Aaron. You'll never win when she's like this." Christa pointed at Allie, who was standing with her arms crossed, her brow furrowed, and an evil grin on her face. She was openly daring Aaron to argue with her, but he wasn't biting.

"Okay, okay. But for the record, I don't like it."

"Duly noted. Now get out," Allie ordered.

Once they stepped outside, Aaron wrapped his arms around Christa and walked as if he was glued to her. His deep voice in her ear sent chills down her spine. "Now, about that offer…"

CHAPTER TEN

Baby

June

Monday morning when Aaron walked into his office building, he was still feeling the exhilaration of the weekend with Christa. His happiness was short-lived once he reached his office, however. His smile disappeared from his face when he saw his brother waiting for him.

"Where the hell have you been hiding? I've hardly seen you over the last month," Lance barked.

"I've been here every day, Lance. My office is three doors down from yours. I'm not that hard to find," Aaron replied scathingly.

"I have a new client for you—Kylie Rae Romano. She's personally overseeing her new clothing line, and she has very specific requirements for the next face of her company. Plus, she's also planning a huge runway show and needs a whole host of models who can pull off her unique designs. I need you to go to San Diego and work with them directly for the next two weeks. I've already told her you'll do it. You leave next Monday morning." Lance had made his decision without bothering to ask Aaron for his input. Yet again.

"You'll need to pick out the best models you can find. Wine them. Dine them. Do your normal thing," Lance said, adding his own flair of sarcasm and disgust. "Just don't screw it up."

Aaron's blood ran cold in his veins. Lance was ordering *him*, the *co-owner* of their business, to handpick and personally oversee a project that any of their lower-level partners could handle without his oversight. He was beyond frustrated and disgusted with his brother's continuously ridiculous demands. Their relationship had been strained at best, but Aaron's unhappiness was steadily increasing—with his job and his brother.

"You told her *what*?" Aaron's fingers curled into fists, and he placed them on his hips. "Since when do you assign my fucking work for me? I own this damn company, too, Lance. And I will decide if it's an account I need to handle personally or not. You don't get to fucking decide that for me."

"It's already decided, and you are committed to it. Kylie specifically requested you, and you are going. This deal cannot fall through," Lance snarled. "Look, it's two weeks in San Diego with a shitload of beautiful models. All the eager beavers you can stand, jumping in your bed every night to willingly fuck your brains out. Then you can send them on their way the next morning, no strings attached. That's right up your alley. What the hell are you complaining about?"

"I'm not interested in any *eager beavers*, Lance."

"What?" Lance asked disbelievingly as he dropped into the nearby chair. Aaron frowned because that meant Lance intended to stay longer than Aaron wanted him to stay. "Since when?"

"I met someone. I've been seeing her for more than a month now, not that you'd notice or even bother to ask. I'm not interested in fucking any of the models or anyone else, Lance. And I don't want to be away from her for two weeks." His hands clenched the back of the chair in front of him, and he readied himself for all-out war with his brother.

They had never gotten along under normal circumstances, but their relationship made sense where business was concerned. Their parents had encouraged their joint venture and, even though Aaron inwardly cringed at the thought, he gave in to make them proud. When his good looks and natural charm won over even the most beautiful models and clients, he realized his gifts were more than lucrative. Lance's chosen profession was a huge plus for all their contract and representation agreements.

When they started their business with less than

nothing to their names, Aaron was glad to have a partner who was responsible and dependable. The more successful they became, the more demanding Lance became. He was convinced Aaron would tarnish their good reputation with his manwhoring ways and drag their business down. That was the topic of the majority of their arguments.

Now Lance was actually pushing him to do just the opposite. He was seriously encouraging Aaron to fraternize with the models in San Diego. *Isn't this ironic? He changes his mind when I have absolutely no interest in it*, Aaron thought to himself.

"This client is important, Aaron. This could set us for life." Lance spoke slowly as if Aaron didn't understand plain English and without trying to disguise his annoyance.

"We're already set for life, Lance. What more could you possibly want?" Aaron snapped.

"There's always more, Aaron. Don't be naïve." Lance stood and walked to Aaron's door. "A week from today, you'd better be on that flight to San Diego. Barbara has your travel itinerary."

After he had the last word, Lance left Aaron standing in the middle of his office fuming mad and disgusted with himself as much as he was with Lance. Aaron briefly considered the consequences of quitting his own company. *How would I even do that? Turn in a two-week notice to myself?* Aaron thought dismally.

He felt like a caged animal, trapped against his will and against his better judgment. One thought got him through the day without just quitting his job, his company, and his brother—*Christa*.

The smell of coffee and sweets assailed his senses as soon as he walked into the café, but it was the sight of Christa that stirred his hunger. She was helping an elderly lady to a nearby table, trying to balance coffee and a brownie in one hand while the little old lady walked slowly, leaning on Christa for help and talking nonstop.

Aaron rushed to her side to take the lady's order before Christa dropped it. Just as the plate started to tip, Aaron grabbed it and smiled at a stunned Christa when she looked up at him. Aaron placed the items on the table and pulled the chair out for the customer to sit.

"My hero," Christa said, wrapping her arms around his waist and pulling herself close into him. "You got here just in the nick of time."

He smiled against the top of her head. "Your hero? Now that's a title I could definitely get used to hearing."

"Mrs. Cushing, this is Aaron. Aaron, this is Delilah Cushing. She owns most of this block, and she's my landlord. She's also the sweetest lady I've ever met," Christa said while moving to Delilah and putting her arm around her shoulders. Delilah's face lit up, and her wrinkled hands moved to wrap around Christa's arm affectionately.

"Don't believe her for a second, young man. I'm old, crafty, and I'm not one to be trifled with. She just met me on a good day," Delilah countered impishly, but her love for Christa was obvious to Aaron.

Christa kissed Delilah on the cheek and told her she'd check on her later. Delilah watched Aaron as he followed Christa behind the counter. Her keen eyes had seen plenty over the years, and when she looked at Aaron, she saw a young man head over heels in love. Delilah wasn't kidding when she said she wasn't one to be trifled with—and she would defend those she loved with all her considerable might.

Christa had earned her favor when, without knowing who the older woman was, she had helped Delilah when no one else even noticed her. From that moment, Delilah considered Christa as her own granddaughter and secretly helped her. She knew Christa was too proud to accept any handouts, so her craftiness came in handy on more than one occasion.

She smiled to herself when she thought about how this fully furnished café suddenly became available at an unheard-of low cost for the prime real estate. The area it was in justified at least three times the amount Christa was currently paying for it, but Delilah wanted to repay a kindness with a kindness.

She had convinced Christa by renting the space she was doing Delilah a favor, helping an old lady out with overhead expenses. Delilah didn't need the money, though Christa had no idea who she was. Delilah took the monthly payment Christa always made on time and put it in a special savings account. Someone needed to look out for Christa, and Delilah reasoned she should be the one to do it.

She watched Aaron with her adopted granddaughter, pleased to consider that maybe Christa had found someone else to care for her and love her. He worked tirelessly by her side, helping to fill orders, learning to run the register, and restocking the pastry case. He never complained and rarely took his eyes off Christa. When Delilah stood to leave, Aaron offered his arm to help her to the door.

"May I have this walk?" Aaron joked as he extended his arm to her.

"Why, yes, young man, you may!" Delilah answered jovially.

"Is someone picking you up, or do you need a ride somewhere?"

"My driver is waiting outside, but thank you for asking," Delilah said while holding his arm. "You're a good boy. I know you'll be good to my girl over there."

"Yes, ma'am, you don't have to worry about that," Aaron replied with a smile.

"Oh my feet! It's been a long day!" Christa complained as they entered her apartment.

"I will gladly massage them for you, babe," Aaron offered.

"I just may take you up on that." She stood on her tiptoes to kiss him.

He bent so she could reach him better, then wrapped his arms around her and picked her up. He kicked the door shut with his foot, carried her to the couch, and laid her down while never removing his mouth from hers. His hands roamed over her body, over her clothes, taking time to memorize her every curve and plane. He broke off their kiss, sat back on his heels, and gently stroked her cheek with his hand.

He picked up her legs and sat on the couch, placing her feet on his lap. He removed her shoes and began massaging one foot, taking his time to help her relax. After a couple of minutes, she closed her eyes and moaned in appreciation. He massaged up her calf, the back of her knee, and finally her thigh.

Instinctively, she spread her legs wider as his hand slid upward. He started over with the other foot, rubbing, massaging, and working his way up her leg. Her sighs and murmurs were intoxicating. Aaron wanted to keep going just to continue hearing her sweet sounds.

"Christa," he said softly as his hands continued to work their magic.

"Hmm," she muttered.

"I have to go out of town next Monday on business. I'll be gone for two weeks." He didn't want to ruin their time together, but he couldn't wait until the last minute to spring it on her.

Her eyes flew open, and he saw the flash of worry in them. "Two weeks? Why so long?"

"It's not my choice, believe me. And if I could take you with me, I would. I didn't think you could leave the café that long, though." He stopped to look at her, raising his eyebrows in question. She shook her head side to side to indicate no.

"This client has several business lines, and they are coordinating an entire reengineering of their company. So, over these two weeks, I'll meet with the department executives to learn their marketing plans and set up reviews of the models who meet their specific needs. It really is a big deal for my company—both the money and our reputation in the industry," Aaron explained.

Christa was silent a little too long for Aaron's comfort.

"Talk to me, babe," he urged.

She blew out her breath in frustration. "It's me, Aaron—it's just my...insecurity." She waited another minute longer before shrugging her shoulders. "I guess I'm just afraid you'll find someone better than me."

Aaron shook his head. "There is no one better than you, sweetheart."

She gave him a small smile. "Will you be back on the weekends?"

"I will do my best to be," Aaron promised.

"Well, we have a week before you go, right?"

"Right," Aaron said with a smile.

"Then let's make the most of it," Christa cooed.

Aaron's eyes widened for a split second before narrowing suspiciously at her statement. *Of course* he wanted to make the most of it, but he wasn't convinced that she was ready for that part of their relationship yet.

"What do you propose?" he asked seductively, giving

her all the control and letting her take whatever she wanted.

Christa's tongue darted out nervously to wet her lips as she slowly licked them before she pulled her bottom lip in between her teeth. She was completely unaware that her unassuming actions were heating Aaron beyond measure. When she looked up into his eyes, she gasped at the unbidden longing she saw in them.

A sudden boldness took root as Christa sat up, leaned toward him, and crawled into his lap, straddling him so that they were face-to-face. He watched her with a curious and amused expression, still giving her full control to do as she pleased. She held his face in her dainty hands, leaned in, and softly brushed her lips against his. He eagerly reciprocated the kiss, spurring her on as she moved her body closer to his.

She lightly sucked his bottom lip into her mouth, skimming it with her tongue before releasing it and slowly pushing her tongue into his mouth. His hands moved to her hair as their kiss deepened, their tongues performing an erotic and sensual dance, moving and gliding across the other.

She moved to his jawline, placing kisses while her hands stroked his chest through his shirt. She moved back, giving herself room to reach more of him as her fingers unbuttoned his shirt one at a time. His growl vibrated through her core when her hands found his bare skin underneath.

When she pulled back and looked directly into his eyes, a moment of confusion flashed across his face as she moved off his lap and onto the floor in front of him. It was quickly replaced by reverence and need when her fingers moved to unbutton his pants.

Wordlessly, she motioned for him to stand, and he complied with only a moment of hesitation. As his pants fell to the floor, she stroked the length of his already hard shaft through his boxer briefs. She slowly, tortuously, and purposely peeled them off him, freeing his erection in the best possible position directly in front of her.

She lifted her eyes, watching Aaron through her lashes, as she ran her tongue around his girth before lapping up the clear bead balanced on the tip. The primal groans emanating from Aaron conveyed all she needed to know and gave her all the confidence she needed to continue.

His head fell back as his fingers wound through her hair. She took him into her mouth with her warmth and wetness instantly enveloping him. Her tongue felt like the finest silk, swirling and circling his girth, before flattening and taking him deeper.

His fingers held fast to her head, gripping and fisting her hair as she worked him faster and faster with her mouth and her hand. Relaxing the muscles in the very back of her throat, she held him deep in her mouth as she moaned and allowed the sensations to vibrate through him.

"Fuck, baby, you're killing me. Damn, you feel so good," he huffed out, quickly losing his self-control. "If you don't stop, I'm going to—"

She could tell he was close, feeling every muscle in his beautiful body tense and hearing the edge of his voice, she worked him harder. Aaron lowered his face, looking down at her as she looked up at him with her determined expression, and he was completely undone. His knees nearly buckled under him as he watched her take his very last drop. The act itself was so intimate and personal that he instantly felt even more protective and possessive of her.

He gently stroked her hair as she pulled back from him. She could almost see his love for her cascading from his eyes, pouring into hers as their gazes locked. He moved his hands under her arms to help her stand before he lifted her, her legs wrapped around his waist, and he thoroughly and completely kissed her. All his emotions were just under the surface, bubbling and boiling, ready to break through.

There was no doubt he loved her, no doubt how important she was to him. There was absolutely no doubt about her place in his life. His own insecurities warred in his mind, begging to be let out and made known. More than anything, he wanted to make her understand that she belonged to him. Not in a Neanderthal-caveman type of belonging...but in a much deeper, more profound respect.

To emphasize his sincerity, he spoke softly as he held her tight against him. He didn't want to break the spell between them, but there was a lingering doubt that nagged him with relentless thoughts. A question that he needed answered to make sure they were on the same wavelength.

"I want to be everything you need. The only one you crave. My name—the one you scream. My touch—the one that burns you, melts you, and excites you. Only mine. I may be selfish, but I won't share you. Tell me you're mine—*only mine*."

His eyes bored into hers with a fierceness that made her heart palpitate. She marveled at how his strong arms so easily held her petite frame suspended off the ground. But it was the possessiveness, coupled with an intense, deeply rooted need in his voice that had her unraveling at the seams.

"I am yours, Aaron. Only yours. There's no one else I want, and I would never do that to you," Christa answered earnestly, searching his eyes for answers to her unspoken question. When he didn't respond, she continued, "Baby, tell me what's wrong."

His eyes softened, and his lips twitched upward in

one corner, making her lean in and kiss the corner of his mouth.

"What was that little smile for?"

"You've never called me 'baby' before."

"You don't like it?" she asked, the concern obvious in her voice.

He kissed her softly, leaning his forehead to hers. "I love it."

She captured his mouth with hers, and their kiss quickly turned urgent once again. She felt his erection growing again, hardening between her legs as he held her body tight against his. He stepped out of his pants that lay puddled on the floor as her hand snaked down between them to grasp him. He carried her down the hall to her bedroom, their bodies locked together and their tongues tied in mutual ecstasy.

CHAPTER ELEVEN

Making Plans

June

All the years Christa waited, all the other men she'd turned down, and all the questions and ridicule she'd received suddenly made complete sense. Being head over heels in love with Aaron gave her more confidence than she realized she had. She'd dated and had her fair share of close encounters, but she'd never felt taking the next step was right. The guy wasn't the right man. The intense feelings weren't there, or the timing was off. She wasn't specifically waiting for her wedding night, but more for the *right* man to come along. No one had fit the complete bill before Aaron came into her life.

That night, as he carried her to the bedroom, she was ready—her feelings for him were deep and passionate. He'd spent time with her, put as much effort into their relationship as she had, if not more. With every beat of her heart, she wanted to consummate the relationship by giving him the part of herself that she'd never shared with anyone before. The only reason she was nervous about telling him was because she didn't know how he'd react to the news of her being a twenty-two-year-old virgin. Building up the courage to confess was wrecking her nerves.

"Aaron," she said breathlessly. The need for him was evident in her voice. She wanted him to hear it, feel it, and take her to places she'd only read about.

"Shhh, baby, it's okay. I've got you." He reassured her by placing kisses on her face and neck as he made his way to her bed.

They climbed onto the bed, and he quickly covered her body with his. He snatched his shirt up and off with one hand and cast it aside, but his eyes never left hers. He peeled her clothes off one piece at a time, purposely taking his time and showering her body with as much love and attention as possible. By the time he reached her bare skin, she thought she would die of intense desire and unmistakable sexual frustration. Aaron sensed her intense yearning for him, the wordless way she tried to rush him, her desire for him to make her his.

"Relax," he whispered, his lips a breath away from her skin. "We're in no hurry."

"Aaron, I don't want to wait any longer," Christa pleaded.

He let out a long, frustrated sigh. "I want you so bad

I can't see straight. I'd love to bury myself deep inside you, make you come so hard, and scream my name until the neighbors call the cops."

He waited a second before continuing. "But I've never had a relationship that was special before. Every time I've been with someone, it's simply been fucking. Never making love. Nothing I'd remember by the next morning. I want our first time, and every time, to be special. I don't want to rush into it just because we're both so worked up we can't stand it."

Her silent response was dubious at best. The thought that kept running through her mind was one of self-doubt.

"What man would turn down sex from a willing participant?"

"One who isn't really interested in me, that's who."

"Hey. Stop that."

"Stop what?" She raised her eyes to meet his and tilted her head to the side as she spoke.

"Doubting how I feel about you. Questioning my motives. Thinking I wouldn't kill for one minute of your wet pussy wrapped around my cock." A lazy, sexy grin spread across his face. "Believing I don't want to see that beautiful pink tinge of embarrassment when I talk dirty to you all fucking night long. *When* I ruin you for every other man and make you beg to rest after I wring every single orgasm you have from your body, it won't be a spur-of-the-moment encounter."

Her chest heaved with heavy breaths. Her eyes widened, and her fingers gripped his shoulders tightly. "No one has ever said those things to me before."

"I'm only getting started, babe. A sneak peek at my opening act. My words alone can make you come. But where's the fun in that? Every part of you will burn for my touch. You won't beg for it—you'll *demand* it."

"Oh my God." Her breathy reply was a mixture of a plea and a prayer.

"But not tonight. Tonight, you'll come several times—in my mouth. When I leave here, I'll take your scent home with me. Your taste will be all over my tongue. Now, lie back. And you might want to hold on to something."

Before her mind could formulate a coherent response, his warm tongue laved her clit, circling slowly before his lips closed around her. Her eyes closed, her head dropped to the pillow, and her hips lifted toward him involuntarily. When his fingers plunged into her wetness, she gripped his hair with her hands, her body automatically curling upward from the intense pull low in her belly.

"Aaron," she cried out as she toppled over the edge.

"You taste so fucking good." His lips hovered over her as he spoke, his murmurs sending ripples through her already overly sensitive core. His stubble rubbed against the delicate skin of her inner thigh, bringing an erotic mixture of pleasure and pain. She writhed underneath him when he alternated between lightly blowing on her clit and covering it with the warmth of his mouth. "I could stay right here all night, drowning in every drop of you."

"Don't think I would refuse that offer."

"Am I a bad influence on you?" One corner of his mouth lifted, mischief played in his eyes, and unmistakable pride shone on his face. "Nice. Now, if I can just get that sweet mouth to talk dirty to me."

With a nervous laugh, she squeezed her eyes shut and shook her head. "I don't know what to say."

"We'll start with something easy, then. Tell me what you want me to do to you. Whatever you want, just say it, and it's yours."

She opened her eyes and chanced locking gazes with him. "I loved what you were just doing."

He shook his head from side to side slowly, intentionally, maintaining eye contact with a devilish grin plastered on his gorgeous face. "Nice try, baby. But that's cheating. I want to hear your words."

"Aaron."

Her gentle chide couldn't save her. "Don't be embarrassed when you're with me. About anything. Everything about you turns me on. So will anything you say and however you say it. Now, let me hear the words from those beautiful, plump lips of yours."

"I want to feel your mouth on me again. Your lips and your tongue—I want you to taste me with them. Then use your fingers..."

"What do you want my fingers to do?" He kept his voice barely above a whisper then held his breath while waiting for her reply. *Will she let me in? Will she trust me?*

"I want you to..." She paused, speaking painfully slowly. "...finger me while you taste me." Her tense muscles relaxed, and she exhaled a deep breath. "Use your fingers to fuck me while you lick my pussy."

"Fucking hell, that was the hottest thing I've ever heard. Your wish is my command, whatever you want."

He lowered his head and resumed what he'd started with renewed fervor. Every time she began to return to earth from her carnal high, he catapulted her to the stars again. When she had a chance to catch her breath, he stole it again. With every caress, she somehow worked her way deeper into his heart. With every pleasure-filled moan, he fell further under her spell. With every cry of his name that dropped from her beautiful lips, he came to understand why he'd never been in love before.

The connection he felt to Christa was unlike any relationship he'd had in his life. She accepted him—his true self. Not the arrogant agent most knew him to be. Not as his family saw him, the royal fuck-up whose only talent was his good looks. Not the highly-paid gigolo his brother tried to use him as to obtain the next lucrative contract. She saw past the flash and hype. There was no pretense when he was with her, no need to put on a good show to keep up appearances.

He was just a man, falling desperately in love with a woman who'd known very little about his life, or his reputation, before she changed him for the better. Before she became his inspiration to treasure their time together.

"Aaron, I can't believe I'm about to say this...but you have to stop."

A roguish smirk lifted the corners of his lips. One eyebrow arched upward slowly. A shining beacon of pride lit his eyes. "Why's that?"

"My body is spent. I can't take any more. You've

zapped all my energy and left me as useless as a rag doll."

"Since your words do wonders for my ego, I'll give you a break for now."

"So chivalrous."

"That's exactly right. You're very lucky to have snagged such a catch." He slid over her body, caging her underneath him before dipping his mouth to capture a thorough kiss.

"I'd say I'm very lucky. There must have been hundreds of women who've tried to snag you before we met."

A shadow of regret floated across his features, and he settled on the bed beside her. "Christa, you deserve to know about my past. I haven't always been the most stand-up kind of guy."

"You mean, you're not a twenty-seven-year-old virgin?" she whispered loudly, her eyes open wide, her jaw slack. "I'm afraid I'll have to ask you to leave. I can't have someone of questionable morals in my home. While I'm naked. And completely spent from the multiple orgasms he just gave me."

He dropped his forehead to her shoulder, his body shaking with laughter. "Okay, okay. You made your point. Everyone has a past. Maybe I should be more specific then, my beautiful little smartass."

"I'm afraid of what other shocker you plan to hit me with tonight."

"Do you want to know anything about my past? I'll tell you anything you want to know. Any questions you have at all."

"There's only one answer that matters to me."

"Then it matters to me. What's your question?"

"Is there anyone from your past who could affect our future?"

"No. There isn't anyone in the world who could do that. Not in my world anyway. What about yours?"

"Not a single person."

His fingers floated over her bare chest, drawing invisible lines between her breasts. His gaze followed his hand, his focus slightly too intent on avoiding looking at her when he asked his next question. "Even Jared?"

The pointed pause following his question made his stomach knot, and dread filled his chest. With no other choice, he finally looked up and met her confused expression. "Why would you say that? I told you he's just a friend and has been for years."

He laid his head on her chest and tightened his arms around her. "You did, and I believe you. But I also saw the picture of you two when you were younger, and I recognized the same expression on his face when he came into your shop. Maybe you don't even realize it, but he's holding on to a pretty bright flame for you. My impression is you held a torch for him, too—at least, at one time anyway."

"Yes and no. Seven years ago, when I was *fifteen*, I had a huge teenage crush on him. But he's been a friend for much longer than that—his whole family has been. He went off to college, not far from here at all, and not once stopped to see me when he came home. Holidays. Birthdays. Nothing. He didn't even come home for summers because he rented an apartment near campus.

"That really hurt me, Aaron. Not because I was in love with him, but because he was *supposed* to be my friend. If he were really a friend, would he have hidden his trips home from me? Would he visit his family and not even stop by here to say hello to me for a few minutes? I felt so unimportant...so *disposable*... He's trying to make up for that now, and that's fine. I'll be his friend again. But I just don't see how our friendship can ever be what it was before. He hurt me too much for that.

"So, if you're questioning whether I'll run to Jared should he suddenly declare his undying love for me, my answer is no. Even if you and I weren't together, I'd say no. But, in all honesty, you've just given me a lot more incentive to reject him, if he ever did proposition me."

"Oh, so you only love me for my orgasm-inducing tongue?"

The words were spoken in jest, a playful lover's banter, but they hung heavy in the air between them. He could see the wheels spinning in her head, questioning his meaning, looking for clues of underlying significance.

"If it's the last thing I do, I'll erase every doubt from your eyes. Christa, you have completely captivated me with your natural beauty, your delightful personality, and your tender heart. I am undeniably totally and completely in love with you."

"I love you, too, Aaron. So much it scares me."

"Never be afraid of me. You have my love—just don't ever give it back to me." His lips brushed softly across hers, his murmurs of love lingering between them. His pensive expression betrayed his thoughts as he rested his head in his palm.

"What's wrong?"

"Next Monday is my two-week trip to San Diego. I know you can't take off the entire two weeks to go with me on such short notice. But can you take off Friday and Saturday to go away somewhere else with me?"

"I'm sure I can work it out with Allie. Where are we going?"

"If I tell you, will it spoil the surprise of it all?"

"Nothing can spoil it as long as I'm with you."

"All right, I'll tell you. I want to take you to Vegas for the weekend. My friend Logan and his wife Mindy can go with us. We'll have a great time before I leave you for the longest two weeks of my life. Are you in?"

"That sounds so exciting. Of course I'm in! I've never been to Vegas—I can't wait to go with you!"

He slanted his mouth over hers, his tongue delving in and gliding across hers. The passion between them was hot enough to ignite the room with uncontrollable flames. But he held back, though his body cursed and revolted against him for it. "We'll have our own suite. Just you and me. Can I apologize now if I never let you see the bright lights of the Strip while we're there? As much as I don't want our relationship to be based solely on sex, I don't think I can stay there with you all weekend and abstain."

"What if I told you I don't want you to abstain? Or that I don't care anything about seeing the bright lights if it means I have you to myself all weekend?"

"Friday night. *You. Are. Mine.*" He spoke the words as an oath, a promise of pleasure and ecstasy to come.

"Baby, I'm yours tonight. You just haven't taken advantage of me yet."

"If I can last three more nights past tonight, I have wonderful plans for us. Can you stop being such a cunning temptress until then?" A smile teased on his lips, but his resolve was waning swiftly.

"For you, until Friday. After that, I can't make any promises."

July

The week dragged by, day after day stuck in the office with his brother breathing down his neck. Thursday afternoon, Aaron walked into Lance's office to face the music.

"Hey, Lance." Aaron knocked lightly on the open door before walking in. "Just letting you know I'm leaving now, and I'm taking off tomorrow."

"Big plans for the weekend?"

"Yeah, Christa and I are going away together for the weekend."

Lance narrowed his eyes and leaned back in his

executive leather chair. "You're spending the weekend with just one woman? Who are you, and what have you done with my brother?"

Aaron shrugged. "She's different from the others. I look forward to spending time with her, seeing her. You'll like her too when you meet her."

"I get to meet her? When?"

"Soon. When I'm sure you can't run her off with your winning personality and overall friendly disposition."

"You said she owns her own business. How much money does she have? How successful is she?"

"You have to be the rudest person I've ever known. You don't ask someone how much money they have."

"Fucking hell, Aaron. You haven't even talked to her about anything important, have you? As usual, you're just drifting through life, expecting everyone else to take care of the details while you close the deal. I don't even know why I'm surprised anymore." Lance stood and paced across his office, agitation driving his steps. "Has it ever occurred to you that she could be playing you, getting close to you because she knows exactly who you are?"

"Who am I? I'm just an agent and co-owner of a business. I'm no one famous. No one special." Aaron fired back against his brother's accusations.

"You're a highly successful agent who has helped build a nearly billion-dollar business from the ground up. You rub elbows with some of the most well-known and instantly recognizable people in the entertainment and sports industries. Your net worth alone would bring out the claws. But add in the overall business and future endeavors we have on the books, and any woman alive would do anything to trap you."

"She's not like that, Lance. You haven't met her. You haven't spent any time with her. You're in no position to judge her. Or me, for that matter. This conversation is over. I'm off tomorrow, out of town for the weekend, and I'll see you Monday."

"Don't forget the mistake you made before and what it cost, Aaron. Mom, Dad, and I can't always be there to save you from yourself."

"Fuck off, Lance."

CHAPTER TWELVE

Memory Lapse

July, Present Day

Aaron sat in his extravagant high-rise condo overlooking the Bay, staring out the floor-to-ceiling windows at the horizon without seeing anything past his own failures. The vaulted ceilings and spacious floor plans at one time were a sign of his accomplishments. A testament to his talents. But as he stared out into the night, all he saw was his reflection staring back at him. Mocking him. Telling him he was a failure, like his brother had insinuated during their last heated argument.

He hadn't left his condo in the past four days, from the moment he arrived home with Christa's wedding rings clutched tightly in his fist. They still sat on the coffee table in front of him. Taunting him like every other thought and memory that riddled his mind. He refused to answer his phone. Lance had come by, but Aaron refused to open the door. When yet another knock drew his attention, he was tempted to ignore it again. After a quick glance through the peephole, he recognized the courier uniform and opened the door.

"Mr. Rivers?"

"That's me."

"Just need your signature for the package right here." The courier gave Aaron the small stylus to sign his name on the handheld device.

"Who is it from?"

"Affairs of the Heart Wedding Chapel of Las Vegas."

Aaron's brow furrowed as he took the package and absently thanked the delivery man. He moved back to his chair, tore the strip off the top of the package, and dumped the contents out on the coffee table. His heart thundered in his chest as he stared, captivated by the images spread out in front of him.

The image of Christa in a simple but elegant wedding dress, her face beaming with happiness, stared back at him. But what held his attention was the instantly recognizable expression of love on his own face. He stood beside her, in a white tuxedo with tails, with his arms wrapped around her waist. While she looked at the camera and smiled, his eyes were on her.

In the next photo, she stood in front of him with his arms wrapped around her from behind. He was leaned over, his chin resting on her shoulder and their faces cheek-to-cheek. The radiant smiles on their faces were impossible to miss—they were blissfully happy.

He surrendered to an overwhelming urge to speak to someone who could shed light on the time leading up to his departure from San Francisco. With his cell phone in hand, he quickly found the pilot's number and hit *Call* before he lost his nerve.

"Mr. Rivers. What can I do for you?"

"Todd, this will sound strange, but I need to ask you a few questions about our last trip."

"Your Vegas wedding trip. Sure. What's on your mind?"

"This is confidential, but I'm having some…health problems…neurological, to be exact. Can you walk me through everything you remember from the time I arranged the flight until we landed back home? I'm trying to pinpoint what could've been the catalyst."

"Sure. I hope you're okay. Let's see. You called me Tuesday evening and scheduled the private jet for first thing Friday morning. You were very specific about the time to leave because you'd already secured dinner and show reservations. We left on time, the car service was waiting at the private strip to take you to your suite. I didn't see you again until you and your party boarded the plane Sunday evening and we flew home."

"Did I seem odd or different to you? In any way? The smallest change may help me identify important details."

"The only difference, honestly, is you finally looked and acted *happy*, Aaron. I've never seen you so thrilled before. You were going on and on about a new business venture you and your new wife were going to start together."

"Did I tell you how I planned to propose to her? Or anything about the ceremony?"

"You told me all about it," Todd confirmed. "Tuesday night when you scheduled the flight. You'd already arranged for Bellasara's to open after hours for just you two because you wanted it to be fairy-tale special for Christa. With how you two tried to refuse to use separate seat belts for takeoff on the return trip, I didn't even question if everything went as you'd planned. It was obviously even better."

"Thanks, Todd. I appreciate your time."

"No problem. So, I'll see you tomorrow, right?"

"Tomorrow? For—what?"

"Lance called earlier and said you have to be in San Diego for a meeting first thing Monday morning. Sounds like it was very fortunate the meeting was pushed back a week, especially since you haven't been well over the past few days. But it evidently puts the kibosh on your upcoming two-week honeymoon trip, though. I guess that's why Lance originally wanted you to head down Friday morning instead, so you'll have some relaxation time first. Will Christa be joining you?"

"Uh, no, not this time," Aaron hedged. *What two-week honeymoon trip?*

"That's too bad. I'm sorry to hear that."

"Yeah, so am I. Let me talk to Lance about a possible change of plans, and I'll get back with you later."

"Sounds good. Just let me know when you're sure of the arrangements, and I'll file the flight plan." Aaron finished his conversation with Todd, every nerve in his body firing instantaneously with anxious energy.

Aaron rifled through the other contents of the package and found a video, no doubt documentation of their nuptials. Unable to resist, he put the movie in and watched with rapt attention. He was there of his own volition. The camera zoomed in on him as he recited his vows. He repeated the words exactly as the official instructed, then added his own twist.

"With this ring, I'm not only giving you all my love, but every part of me. Mind. Body. Heart. Making you fall in love with me all over again every single day will become my life's ambition. If the day ever comes when you give these rings back to me, I'll

know you're throwing my love away, tossing us aside. I'd never be able to love anyone again after that. Hold on to us no matter what the future throws at us. Our love, our marriage, and our life together are all that matter. Never give up on me, Christa, and I'll make you the happiest woman who ever lived."

"The words Christa said to me in Lance's office." He felt an invisible sledgehammer slam into his chest.

Watching himself on the video of his Vegas wedding but having no recollection of a single moment troubled him beyond belief. Not remembering a single word, not knowing how he'd managed to function throughout the entire ceremony bothered him on a deep-seated level. But having no recollection of their wedding night nearly broke him.

When the camera panned out, his gaze left Christa's face long enough to realize his best friend Logan was standing beside him during the ceremony.

He fired off a text to Logan next.

Aaron: **Need you to come to my place. Urgent. Hurry your ass up.**

Logan: **Get your panties out of a wad. On my way.**

Twenty minutes later, Logan walked in and went straight to the kitchen, grabbed a beer from the fridge, and made himself at home.

"So. How's the happy couple? How long do you think the honeymoon phase will last?"

"I don't remember any of what happened last week. How we got there. How we got married. How she moved in with me."

"Yeah, right." Logan guffawed at Aaron and took a long draw from the longneck bottle.

"I'm serious." Aaron looked up at Logan, concern etched on his features. "What happened? I don't remember any of it."

"What was the last thing you remember?" Logan moved to sit on the couch across from Aaron when he realized his friend wasn't kidding.

"I woke early Monday morning and felt like I had the worst hangover headache I've ever had. When I sat up, I realized Christa was in bed with me, which was unusual. Then I got up and saw her clothes in my closet. Her empty suitcases sat at the foot of my bed. There was a wedding band on my finger, and even in the fading moonlight, I could see the ring on her finger.

"I called Lance, freaked out because I had no idea what was going on. He said he'd warned me about her. That she knew who I was. She knew about my money, my company, and she'd found a way to get around signing a prenup. He was convinced she'd drugged me and reminded me of what an idiot I was for falling for her innocent act."

"What did you do, Aaron?" Logan's tone held both concern and a hint of warning. "I know your brother and how ruthless he is. What did the two of you do to Christa?"

"Lance drew up the divorce settlement papers to buy her off while I played it cool. Told her we had to go by the office first thing, but I didn't tell her why. We presented her with an offer to take money and just walk away. Not push for a bigger settlement."

Logan dragged his hands over his face and blew out a disgusted huff. "You blindsided her and turned Lance loose on her? Have you lost your fucking mind?"

"I feel like I have. What happened? Did anything odd happen to me? Why can't I remember anything?"

"Give me a second to catch up here, man. Christa didn't drug you. She didn't force you into marriage. She didn't trick you into it. *You* were the one who wanted to get married. *You* kept pushing it—she tried to get you to wait, to include your brother, not to make rash moves that would further strain your relationship. She married you because she loved you."

Logan pushed up off the couch and began pacing

across the room. "You were pissed off about the two weeks in San Diego deal. You told us on the plane how you didn't want to be an agent anymore. You wanted to sell your part of the company and start something new. Man, Aaron, I've never seen you as happy as you were with Christa last weekend."

"Think, Logan. Did anything at all happen? *Anything?*"

"No. Noth—wait. Yes. We were wearing the slick-bottom tuxedo shoes and messing around. While we waited for the girls to come out, we ran and slid up and down the hall. Your feet went completely out from under you one time, and you fell, hit your head on the concrete floor. It took you a few seconds to get up, but you were laughing and rubbing the back of your head. You said you were fine."

"Maybe I wasn't. I need to get in to see my doctor right away."

"What did Christa say about the divorce settlement?"

"She gave the wedding rings back to me and refused to take anything from me."

"Christa gave you the wedding rings back? I don't believe it."

"She said I told her if she ever gave them back, it meant she was giving back my love. Then she said she wasn't giving them back, but I was taking them away from her. I watched it on the DVD before you got here. I don't remember a word of it, Logan."

"You were adamant about that when you took her to Bellasara's, Aaron. Those rings were the bonds between you two, and once the bond was broken, it couldn't be remade. You said there would be hard days ahead, but she had to hold on to the promise you made her that night."

"Logan, you have no idea how bad this fucking sucks. Not to remember any of it. To know I've fucked things up so badly I may not be able to fix it. Ever. First I have to figure out what's wrong with me. Why I can't remember any of it. If hitting my head had anything to do with it."

"Yeah, you do. Then you'd better figure out a way to get your wife back."

Aaron sat in the waiting room of his doctor's office, filling out forms and impatiently anticipating speaking with the doctor. His leg jumped with nervous energy, and his eyes darted around the room, searching for something to hold his attention.

When he heard voices outside the door, his senses went on high alert. The doorknob turned, and the doctor stopped midway through the door to speak to someone in the hall. Aaron briefly considered jerking the doctor into the room and slamming the door shut.

He needed answers. Immediately.

"So, what's going on with you today?" The doctor was cordial and professional, so Aaron tempered the aggravation consuming him while he explained his issue, what had happened over the weekend, and how he needed to know what he could be facing.

"Do you remember anything about hitting your head? Did you lose consciousness at all?"

"I really don't know about losing consciousness because I don't remember any of it."

"Okay. We need to get some pictures of your head first. We can rule out a few conditions first and let it point us in the right direction."

An hour later, Aaron was lying on the CT table while the machine circled around his head. Although he was concerned about his health, the dread settling in his gut over Christa felt like a lead weight.

Have I just made the worst mistake of my life?

When the scan finished, the technician told him to wait in the room until the doctor reviewed the results. A few minutes later, the technician brought the phone to him.

"Aaron, don't be overly alarmed. You're not dying. But I need you to come back to my office and let's talk about the results and next steps."

"Okay. I'm on my way."

When he walked back into the medical building, the nurse escorted him directly back to the doctor's private office.

"Have a seat. Dr. Batton will be with you in a few minutes."

No sooner had the nurse left than Dr. Batton walked in. "Aaron, I just spoke with the radiologist about your scans. I'm piecing together what you've told me with what he saw on the CT, but it seems you had a slight concussion after hitting your head. I believe you had a post-traumatic seizure at some point over the weekend that impaired your memory. The amount of alcohol you consumed on top of that most likely dulled any effects you would've felt."

"Will my memory ever come back?"

"Since the concussion was minor, I'd like to think your memory will return fully. Most symptoms and injuries to the brain are unfortunately a 'wait and see' type of diagnosis. You'll need to take it easy over the next couple of weeks. Avoid too much stress, too much stimulation. Give your body time to fully heal, and your memories could return. It may be a little at a time, it may be all at once. Or it may be not at all."

No stress. No stimulation. For two weeks? Yeah. That'll happen.

Aaron slid behind the wheel of his Jaguar and used the solitude of his car to collect his thoughts. "I'm stressed just thinking about going back to the office, over every single thing that's happened with Christa. I don't fucking want to go to San Diego."

Resigned to the unavoidable waiting argument with Lance, he drove to their office building on autopilot, barely remembering the trip once he'd arrived. The last time he'd been there was with Christa, dropping the surprise divorce bomb on her. So many aspects of that trip were the same. Ty was at his guard station. Employees hustled around him with determined strides, the next big meeting waiting in the wings.

Yet nothing felt the same.

CHAPTER THIRTEEN

No Stress, No Excitement

"You are going, and that's the end of the conversation," Lance bellowed, his voice carrying through the closed door and across the rows of cubicles. Heads turned and eyes widened, but no one appeared overly surprised at his outburst.

"I just left the doctor's office. He gave strict instructions—no stress, no excitement. Rest for two weeks."

Lance stopped and, for once in as long as Aaron could remember, real concern for his little brother covered his expression. "What else did he say? That little whore drugged you, didn't she?"

"No, Lance, she didn't, and don't talk about her like that. I fell and hit my head with no help from her. Logan was with me when I did it. The doctor thinks I had a post-traumatic seizure from the concussion late Sunday night, and that impaired my memory. Lay off her already. She didn't do anything wrong—I did."

"You sure as hell did. Now all of this is documented in your medical history. It could cast doubt over whether you knowingly entered the marriage." The anger and disappointment in his eyes were back, wordlessly berating Aaron's stupidity.

"Are you kidding me right now? My memory from the past week or so is gone, but you're only worried about what she could use against me in court?"

"No, that's not what I meant."

"It's exactly what you meant. This conversation is over. I'm done. I'm not going to San Diego. I'm not meeting with the new client. I'm not wasting my time finding the perfect models. If it's so important to you, then go do it yourself." He strode toward the door, and Lance stopped him just before his hand touched the knob.

"Aaron, I'm sorry. Of course I'm worried about you. Your health, the business you've helped build, and your future. You're my younger brother. I'm just trying to look out for you."

"I don't need another father. You're my *brother* and business partner. Act like it."

"You're right. I'm sorry, okay? I haven't even had a chance to tell you I'm going on this trip with you. You've been stressed, and I thought you could use some R&R at the beach. A warm, sunny location. We can be two brothers simply having a little fun instead of working nonstop for a change.”

“What’s the catch?”

“No catch. I’ll handle all the contract negotiations, and you handle finding the perfect faces and bodies for the campaigns.”

“This isn’t like you at all. You’re not a nice person. You’re never supportive. Why now?”

“Because I’ve been a dick, and I realize it.”

“Huh. You talked to Mom. Told her everything. She crawled up your ass, so you’re acting like the good son again.”

“No. I just calmed down and acknowledged your well-being is more important than anything else. This trip is a chance for us to be brothers.”

“I’m not staying two weeks, Lance. I’ll find the talent, and then I’m leaving.”

Lance nodded without giving a verbal agreement, but that was fine with Aaron. When Aaron was nowhere to be found, Lance would realize he’d meant exactly what he said. Aaron’s sense of obligation to his brother and their company wouldn’t allow him to leave Lance in the lurch at the last minute. But he vowed that trip would be the last time he put the company ahead of his own needs.

“As good as you are at your job, it’ll probably be no

more than a long weekend away." Lance slapped him on the back and smiled encouragingly.

"Who are you, and what have you done with my brother?"

Lance chuckled and dropped his eyes to the floor. "If you have to ask that, I guess I've been a real dick to you."

"You know you have. Ever since—"

"Don't. Don't even bring it up. It's in the past, so we *both* need to leave it there. I'll say it again—I'm sorry. We good?"

"We're good."

"I'm sending Barbara by your place this evening to pack your clothes for the trip so you can rest. We'll head out early in the morning and have all day Friday, Saturday, and Sunday just to hang out together."

The weekend went surprisingly smoothly, despite the inherent sibling rivalry that had plagued the two men throughout their lives. Lance couldn't completely shed his fatherly big-brother tendencies. With the tentative diagnosis of a concussion and possible seizure, Lance wouldn't budge on his alcohol ban out of an abundance of caution. After a weekend of decompressing, destressing, and not discussing work at all, Aaron was rejuvenated.

And he'd finally decided what he'd do once he returned home. What he needed to do. What he *wanted* to do.

Monday morning, Lance and Aaron entered the executive office building of Kylie Rae Romano Enterprises, a high-end clothing designer taking the industry by storm. Lance had sent a junior agent down the previous week to take headshots of the models without makeup, bundle them with the composite cards, and separate them into groups. Aaron's job was to take the client's vision and identify which models would best fit the specifications.

If he brought the best models to the table, they'd win the entire contract.

If he completely missed the mark, they'd be dismissed without a second chance.

Lance was counting on him to work his magic and exceed their expectations, to show them what they didn't even realize they needed or wanted.

The competitive nature of the business was fierce and unrelenting. Someone new and upcoming always waited in the wings to take the top-billed spot away. Reaching the top didn't seem as hard as staying on top.

None of this is stress-free, Aaron thought.

"Good morning." Lance turned up his charm factor when he approached the receptionist. *Always get the assistant on your side first*, he'd repeated ad nauseam. *They run the show behind the scenes.* "Are you Miss Ramano's assistant or one of the models?"

"I'm her assistant, Brandy. Definitely not a model." Her face brightened from the offhanded compliment.

"Then it's obvious Miss Ramano surrounds herself with beauty at every corner. I'm Lance, and this is my brother, Aaron. We're with Rivers Forte. Can you point us to the...um—" He stopped to verify the name on his itinerary for the fifth time that morning, convinced it must be wrong. "The Spunky Misunderstood Genius room?"

Brandy giggled at his discomfort and confusion. "Sure. And yes, that's the correct name of the room. Kylie likes to change things up."

After signing them in through security and getting badges to the secure building, she escorted them to the conference room. Stacks upon stacks of model profiles sat on the oversized conference table, heckling Aaron and his plan for an early escape.

"You had quite a turnout for this call." Aaron walked to the table and began identifying which sorting system the junior agent had used.

"It was incredible. Last week was crazy around here.

We had to extend the dates because models were outside waiting in line before we opened and were still here waiting when we closed. Kylie didn't feel right turning anyone away when they were here during the hours we advertised." Brandy moved to the table beside Aaron. "I've never seen so many beautiful women in one place before. You have your work cut out for you."

"Beautiful women are his specialty." Lance jumped into the conversation before Aaron could reply. Aaron turned his head and glared at Lance over his shoulder. No words were needed to convey his ire. "Thank you so much for your help, Brandy. Can I get your extension in case we need to get in touch with you?"

She and Lance stepped away from the table while she gave him internal dialing instructions, and Aaron inhaled deeply as his eyes drifted over the hundreds of folders awaiting his perusal. He shrugged out of his suit jacket, loosened his tie, and sat in front of the first pile. The faster he got to it, the faster he'd finish the job. He put every other worry out of his mind and set his laser-focus on the hundreds of pictures.

Some were discarded with a quick glance, some were put in a "second look" pile, while others were a definite pick. He labored until his neck and shoulders became stiff from looking down at the pictures for an extended time. He stood, rolling his head and shoulders to help limber up his neck. A quick glance at an image sticking out of the folder knocked him off-kilter. The white dress the model wore clung to her curves. The silky material flowed like water naturally over her chest.

An image of Christa walking down the aisle toward him came out of nowhere. Her wedding gown was more of a dress she'd wear to a black-tie affair, but it cascaded over her so beautifully, he hadn't been able to tear his eyes from her. His hands had longed to touch her. He'd consciously forbade his feet to move, not to rush to her, when every other part of him hungered for her.

"Fuck," he muttered under his breath, gripping the table and dropping his head forward.

"Are you okay?" Lance's tone held honest concern. He moved quickly to Aaron's side and gave him a hard once-over. "You need to take a break. You've been at this for hours now. Let me show you where the break room is. Drink some water or something."

Aaron took a long drink from the cold water, staring out the window, but the scenic view couldn't hold his attention. A memory had flashed into his mind, and he saw it as clearly as if he were there again.

"Forget her." Lance spoke softly, interrupting his thoughts. "Even if it was your idea, it was a bad idea all the way around, Aaron. You've only known her, what, a couple of months? Have you even met her family? Do you know anything about her past? How can you even really know her in a few short weeks?

"Maybe you got caught up in the moment, made a rash decision. But she's coming back in to sign the papers. After the mandatory six-month waiting period, all this mess will be behind us."

"Six months?" Aaron jerked his gaze up to meet Lance's, certain he'd misheard him.

"Yes, the waiting period is California law. No divorces are granted within six months of filing."

"You've barely left your apartment for the past week. Come to Mom and Dad's with me tonight. The whole family will be there, Mom's cooking, then we'll watch a movie or something. You know Jessie and Josh will have you rolling in no time." Jen tried patiently to coax Christa out of her bed. Allie had called Jen, concerned when Christa didn't show up for work again.

"Jen, normally, I love your family. But the last thing I want is to be around a bunch of people. That's why I haven't been to the café—I can't even think about pretending to like anyone right now. Especially happy people."

"And maybe part of you wants to wait here to see if he comes back for you?"

Tears slid down her cheeks as Jen's question hit its mark. "Maybe. But maybe I just want to lie here and die, alone and peacefully."

"You know I can't allow that. Don't make me call in backup to get you out of the bed. Jared can be here in an instant if I need him."

Christa groaned and threw her forearm over her eyes. "You know, I don't even care if he sees me looking like an old hag. I'd tell him the same thing. I just want to be left alone."

"I can understand that, but your solitude is reaching unhealthy levels. How long has it been since you showered? Because you stink. Bad."

Despite her best efforts to refrain, Christa started to laugh along with Jen. "I hate you."

"You love me, and you know it. Now get up, shower, and let's go to my parents' house for an evening of good, old-fashioned Miller torture tactics."

"Fine. I'll go with you for a little while. But I'm only agreeing because I know you'll bring them all over here if I don't."

"That was going to be a surprise."

"You're the worst friend ever." Christa tried to hide a

small smile as she swung her legs over the side of the bed.

"And shave your legs. You just shredded your one-thousand-thread-count sheets with those barbs." Jen heard Christa laugh out loud after she closed the bathroom door.

Christa smelled the aroma of the food cooking the moment she stepped inside Patti and Ethan's house. She'd barely eaten in days and had passed the point of hunger pangs, and instead, fought the waves of nausea that made her stomach roil.

Ethan approached her first and hugged her, the same as always. "How's my favorite daughter?"

"Thanks a lot, Dad," Jen feigned offense.

"Uh-oh. I forgot you were here." Ethan grabbed Jen and pulled her into his empty arm. "How's my other favorite daughter?"

"Sure, now you remember me. Is dinner ready yet, Mom?" Jen smiled at her dad as she called out to Patti.

"Almost. You girls come set the table. The boys are on the deck making homemade ice cream."

Jen and Christa joined Patti in the kitchen. "It takes all three of them to make ice cream?"

"We heard that." Jared stood at the sliding glass

door, the wicked smile across his handsome face silently threatening his little sister. Then his smile faded when Christa stepped out from behind her, moving around the table with the plates and forks. "You're lucky you brought company, or you'd have to pay for that disparaging remark right now."

"Hi, Jared." Christa gave him a small smile. But it lacked the warmth he'd always seen in her.

Jen had already filled Jared in on what had happened, at least from how Allie explained the events unfolded. But he wanted to get Christa alone to get the full story firsthand, to help her through it, to comfort her as best he could.

"Hi, sweetheart. Don't I get a hug?"

"Of course." She stepped into his arms and nearly broke down sobbing in front of everyone from just the warmth of his embrace.

Conversation over dinner was purposely kept lighthearted and self-deprecating by Jared, Jessie, and Josh. When they'd finished eating, Ethan dipped the ice cream out for everyone and delivered it to them in the media room. When they'd settled in, Christa found she felt a little better from the comfort of company, until Aaron's picture filled the screen from the local news station.

But he wasn't alone. A beautiful model was draped around him in an intimate embrace.

"You may recognize Aaron Rivers of Rivers Forte, San Francisco's leading talent agency. Aaron has just secured the largest account in California, for a fashion line that's quickly becoming a household name. You are looking at the new face of Kylie Rae Ramano. Her name is Daria Volodina, and she has just become the most envied woman in the world.

"Not only has she just signed a seven-figure deal with Kylie Rae Ramano fashions, but it appears she's snagged one of San Francisco's most eligible bachelors...and its most notorious playboy. Neither has confirmed a relationship, but if Aaron's past relationships are any indication, Daria will be on his arm for many red-carpet events."

"Excuse me." Christa quickly stood and rushed out of the room.

When Jared heard the front door slam, he jumped up to run after her.

"No, Jared. Not now," Jen warned. "She's in no shape to hear your declarations of love."

"I'm not just going to let her run off, hurt, alone, and with no one to talk to about all of this. Maybe I can help her."

CHAPTER FOURTEEN

File The Papers

Jared and Christa sat in the swing under the gazebo in the family's backyard. His arm was wrapped around her shoulder while her head was nestled into the crook of his shoulder. His fingers stroked her arm lovingly, lending his strength and shelter from the turbulent storm raging in her emotions.

"Let me get this straight." The muscles in Jared's jaw ticked from gritting his teeth so hard, but he kept the anger out of his voice when he spoke to her. She had more than enough pressure on her already. "They offered you ten million dollars, and you turned it down?"

"Yes. I don't want their money. I don't want anything from them at all."

"I'm sure the prenuptial agreement protected him anyway, especially in the first few years."

"We didn't have a prenup."

Jared stopped all movement—the swing, his fingers,

his breathing. "You didn't sign a prenup before you married *Aaron Rivers*?"

"Nope."

"Christa, you could get a lot more than ten million dollars, then. We could take half of everything from him, especially with how he's treated you. Pretending not to remember the wedding when he carted you off to Vegas. I'll represent you—and I won't even charge you. Every dime will be yours." Just the thought of taking Aaron Rivers down for what he and his brother did to Christa was payment enough for Jared. And he'd have a front row seat to watch Aaron crash and burn.

"No."

"Christa, did you have any idea who this guy was before you ran off and married him? Didn't you know what his business was? How much he's worth?"

She sighed heavily, embarrassed to admit the truth. "No, Jared. I had no idea who he was, what he owned, or how much money he had. Evidently, I'm much less experienced than even I realized. I fell for everything—no questions, no proof, nothing. Everything he told me, I just believed it all was the truth. I've been to his condo. It's nice, but it's nowhere near as extravagant as your parents' home or their vacation houses.

"Why would he want to marry me only to humiliate me like this? I'm nobody. I have nothing. I don't understand this at all."

"And you still don't want to take him for half of everything he owns?"

"No. I really wish I could just make it all go away."

Jared was silent for a moment, the wheels in his head turning at lightning speed. "If that's what you want, we can file for an annulment before you sign their divorce papers. We can show fraud. It won't hurt him financially, but the repercussion ripples could impact his business when it's made public. They'll question his integrity as a businessman."

"I'm not trying to hurt him or his business. Just erase the fact that it ever happened and give my last name back to me."

"Consider it done, sweetheart. I'll take care of this mess, and I'll take care of you."

"So you'll draw up the papers for annulment for me?"

"Of course. I'll do it first thing in the morning and bring them by your place when I get off work."

"Thank you. I appreciate your help, and you're saving me from going back to their office."

"You won't ever go back there without me. That

Lance guy sounds shady as fuck."

"He is an asshole. Jared, I'm ready to go back to my apartment now. I'm just not good company today. Jen refused to let me drive, so can you give me a ride?"

"Of course. I'm ready when you are."

After she thanked his parents and said goodbye to everyone, Jared dropped her off at her place with the promise she'd call him if she needed him for anything. She forced a smile as she closed the car door, then turned and trudged into the privacy of her apartment.

She dropped her keys on the side table and stopped dead in her tracks. The picture in the silver frame of her riding on Jared's back had been replaced with the one from her date with Aaron in the park. He stood behind her with one arm wrapped around her waist, the field of wildflowers in bloom behind them, and expressions of sincere happiness on their faces.

"Was it all a lie?" She picked up the frame, held it to her chest, and walked to her bedroom. With her back against the door, she sank to the floor, hung her head, and cried.

When she awoke the next morning, she stood under the scalding water until she was ready to face the day. Her tears had dried despite the broken heart she still carried. Somehow, knowing an annulment rather than a divorce was in her future lightened her mood. She viewed it as she was expunging her record, wiping the slate clean and starting anew rather than leaving a permanent black spot as evidence of what might have been.

She arrived at The Sweet Spot earlier than usual that morning. Since Allie had managed the business alone unexpectedly for an entire week, Christa vowed to make it up to her by taking over as much of the workload as possible. Determined to put all her focus and energy into her business rather than her failed marriage, she worked nonstop during the dark morning hours. Breads, pastries, sandwiches, coffee—everything was ready and waiting by the time Allie arrived.

"Wow. Did you stay here all night working or what?"

"Might as well have. I came in extra early and was on a mission."

"Mission accomplished." Allie tilted her head to the side, examining Christa with her keen insight. "You'd feel better if you snuck into his apartment and replaced his shampoo with Nair hair-remover lotion. Put Icy Hot in the crotch of all his underwear. Squirt toothpaste in the holes of his electrical outlets. Or, we could print flyers and put them up all over the city."

"Flyers?"

"Yes, a flyer. We'll start a contest for the best Chewbacca roar with a grand prize of $1,000. We'll list his home phone number and instructions to leave a voice mail and contact information. It'll be great."

"You truly scare me sometimes."

Allie shrugged. "It's who I am."

"As much as I'd love to pull all those pranks on him and his brother Lance, I don't have time to focus on them anymore. I've wallowed in my self-pity for the last week, and I'm nowhere near getting over it, but I didn't come this far to roll over and die. I have a business to run and expand. Before I met Aaron, I had goals I wanted to attain. Goals centered around me—no one else. That's what I have to focus on now."

"There's my spunky little munchkin. I knew she'd reappear before too long."

"You called Jen and told on me. You were worried." Christa cut her eyes at Allie and arched one eyebrow, daring her to try to lie her way out of it.

"That's right, I did. And I'd do it again, so don't test me," Allie winked. "The truth is, I *have* been worried about you. All of this hit you harder than anything I've ever seen. You wouldn't talk about it. I was desperate."

Christa nodded slowly, her gaze fixed on the floor. "I haven't been able to talk about all of it with anyone. Somehow, I managed to repeat what happened in Lance's office to Jared. He said he'll help me file for an annulment instead of a divorce, though he tried to talk me out of it since Aaron and I didn't have a prenuptial agreement.

"The truth is, if I can't have Aaron, I don't want anything from him. I have this stupid fantasy where the annulment erases my memory so I won't have to think about it ever again. As much as I know that'll never happen, I know I'd never move on if I accepted any kind of settlement from him. It would almost be like I was still connected to him, and I can't have that."

"I can sort of understand that. But I'd still rather have an ass-ton of money while I sulk on a yacht, floating in the Caribbean, as sexy, oiled and naked cabana boys serve me frozen drinks with little umbrellas."

"We all have life ambitions, don't we?"

At the end of the day, Christa was exhausted and

headed straight to her tub to soak until the water turned cold. She pulled her hair up into a messy bun on top of her head, leaned back, and let the hot water drown her worries. She tried to, anyway. Random memories and feelings kept popping back into her mind uninvited, until she wanted to literally drown them—by finding the bottom of a bottle of rum.

By the time she wrapped her thick robe around her and tied a towel around her hair, she'd forgotten Jared had said he'd stop by. Until the knock on her door and a quick glance at the clock reminded her.

"Hey," she said sheepishly. "I didn't have time to put on something other than my robe. Today was so crazy busy, I actually forgot about the papers for a while. Come on in, but don't look at me."

Jared chuckled and shook his head then softly kissed her cheek. "You're beautiful, as always. I'm sorry I'm here so late. As the low man on the totem pole, I don't really get a say in what time I leave the office. It depends on what case we're working and what information we need."

"You know you're welcome here at any time. Plus, you're doing me a humongous favor, and I appreciate it more than you know."

"Helping you is my pleasure. No need to thank me." He motioned to her small kitchen table. "Let's have a seat and go over the documents before you sign. I need to make sure you understand everything in them, and what you're giving up, before I file these."

"I know what I'm giving up, Jared. You don't have to reiterate that point. I don't want anything of his. I don't want a divorce. I don't want alimony that'll tie me to him for the rest of my life. This just has to be over and wiped away so I can start fresh." By the time she finished her speech, her voice had increased two octaves. She'd grown weary of explaining herself and what she wanted, or didn't want, regardless of how helpful her friends tried to be.

"Fair enough. I won't bring it up again. Let's go over the legal terms so you understand what they mean, because there will be questions once it hits the media. He's very well known in certain circles—and becoming even more so with this new deal. The paparazzi will want answers."

"Shit. Tell me all about it, then."

They sat, and he spread the papers across the table. "There are *very* few instances where an annulment will be granted. One of those is unsound mind. You said he claims he doesn't remember anything about the ceremony, the weekend in Vegas, or when you moved in to his condo. We can argue he has a preexisting medical condition that impairs his cognitive abilities, one he didn't alert you of, and convince the judge to grant the annulment.

"When the media learns of the reason for the annulment, his business ventures will be called into question. He's half owner of a very lucrative talent agency. He manages billion-dollar contracts. There's no way to go through with this plan without some damage to his reputation."

"This is the only way to get an annulment?"

"It's the only condition you could possibly meet. The judge can still rule against it. The upside of an annulment is we don't have to wait the six-month period a divorce requires. He'll have thirty days to answer the summons. You'll have to testify before the judge and explain why you should be awarded an annulment instead of a divorce. If there's an opening, we can get on the judge's calendar on day thirty-one."

"I understand." Her confirmation wasn't a commitment.

He pushed the pen over to her and pointed out where her signatures were required. She picked up the pen and clicked the end several times while she stared at the signature lines.

"Christa?"

"I'm having a really hard time making myself sign these papers, Jared. I'm not in the right frame of mind to think this through."

"Tell you what. Go ahead and sign them, I'll take them with me, but I won't file them until you give me the go-ahead. That way, when you're ready to make a move, you won't have to wait any longer than it takes to serve him. If you decide not to go through with it, I can shred them and no harm done."

"Okay." That time, her reply was emphatic and resolute. With one last click of the pen, she signed her marriage away.

She lay in bed that night, flipping through the channels, when a familiar face caught her attention. Aaron's face filled her screen—tanned, smiling, and happy. On his arm was yet another model undressing him with her eyes. Her perfectly manicured hand slid up his lapel and stopped on his chest. He wrapped his hand around her long, slender fingers and moved her hand, not letting go as their arms simultaneously dropped to his side.

The agony of watching that scene play out in front of millions of viewers was too much, all while the news anchor speculated on his relationship with yet another model. With hot, angry tears rolling over her cheeks, she picked up her phone and fired off a text to Jared.

File the fucking papers. Tomorrow.

CHAPTER FIFTEEN

Prepare for the Shift

"I've had enough of this. I'm leaving." Aaron zipped his suitcase and turned to face Lance. "My part of this job is finished. The models have been chosen, and the contract is signed."

"We haven't even been here a full two weeks yet. You can stay and enjoy summer in San Diego for a while longer."

"No, I can't. On one hand, I'm glad I came with you because it gave me time to clear my head. I've had to face some hard facts about myself—and it's time I change what I don't like."

"Interesting. Let's hear it." Lance inhaled deeply, drawing up to his full height while puffing his chest out. "I'm all ears."

"And yet I don't have time to have this conversation with you because I'm flying back to San Francisco as soon as possible. Then I'm getting my wife back. Which I'll follow up by selling my half of the business. If you're interested in buying me out, I'll be glad to talk to you sometime in the next few weeks."

"What do you mean 'getting your wife back,' exactly?"

"It doesn't matter how much wealth I've acquired or how successful I've been. I lost all self-respect and my self-esteem after what happened my sophomore year in college. Ever since then, you've told me every move to make, when to make it, how to act, and what to think. It really didn't hit me how much I've depended on you until we were here, just relaxing, and you were still doing it. And I allowed you to.

"But the gut-punch I didn't see coming was how you completely sabotaged my relationship with Christa— and enjoyed every minute of it. Oh, the head injury was all on me. The memory problem wasn't your fault. But when I called you that Monday morning, freaked out because my memory was gone, you purposely used what happened back in college against me. You made me question everything about my judgment.

"The real reason you were worried had nothing to do with her drugging me and tricking me into marriage. You were worried about yourself. What would happen if I'd screwed up and picked the wrong girl? What would happen if she realized how much money we have and decided she wanted half of it? How badly would it hurt you and the precious agency? I don't have time to argue, and I wouldn't even if I had all the time in the world."

"All I've done is try to look out for you. Your best interests. You fucking know that, and I shouldn't even have to say it."

"She is my best interest. Because *I love her*. It was my idea to get married, not hers. I know that without a doubt now. You know, I remember everything about her up until the week of the Vegas trip. I know for a fact she is the best person I've ever known, and I've hurt her in ways I'll never be able to take back. Christa deserves better than how you and I have treated her. My job now is to make sure she gets exactly what she deserves—and more. Anything and everything she wants."

With that, Aaron strode out of the hotel and hopped in a taxi to the airport. He saw everything so clearly after shaking the blinders off. Family had a unique ability of making or breaking someone, and his family had been overbearing since the incident years earlier. The wake-up call came when he realized he'd not only allowed it, he'd depended on their intervention and direction. When the time came for him to make decisions for his own life, his own happiness, he took a long, hard look in the mirror, and he didn't like the reflection.

Taking control of his destiny felt damn good—liberating. Mistakes from the past could no longer haunt him, but making another monumental mistake would rob him of the happiness he'd found.

"One way or another, I'll win her back. I'll show her how much I miss her. How much I love her," he muttered to himself. "And remind her why we're perfect together." *And hopefully, regain my full memory.*

Hours later, he opened the door of his condo, tossed his suitcase inside, and headed straight for his car. He hadn't seen his wife in weeks, and it was past time to rectify that. He didn't take time to rehearse any lines or try to figure out how to break the ice. He couldn't blame her for the thick layer surrounding her heart since he'd been the one who put it there.

Once in the garage, he jogged to his car but stopped abruptly when someone called his name.

"Aaron? Aaron Rivers, is that you?"

Aaron turned to find a man in a suit and tie approaching with a friendly smile covering his face. "Yes. Do I know you?"

The man's smile broadened into a toothy grin. "Aaron Rivers, consider yourself served." He slapped the envelope on Aaron's chest and quickly released it, forcing Aaron to grab it before it fell.

"Hey! Wait a minute. What the hell is this?"

"You should really ask your attorney about that. My job is only to provide proof you received the papers.

Have a nice day."

Aaron tore the envelope open and dumped the papers out. There, in black and white, lay his shredded heart.

Request for nullity of marriage.

He snatched the papers off the ground and jumped into his car, his heart racing faster than his vehicle ever thought about going. With tires squealing and horns blowing as he weaved through traffic, he arrived at The Sweet Spot in record time. His feet carried him into the café, while his eyes searched out his love.

She rounded the corner into the main area from the hallway just as he reached the display case. His heart slammed against his chest, but he couldn't breathe. His eyes searched her for an answer, but he couldn't voice the question. Unspoken words had done so much damage to them both already. *Divorce. Annulment.*

The time for them to talk had arrived—as husband and wife.

"Christa." The inflection in his voice when he spoke her name sounded like a plea and a prayer. Hope and desperation. Pleasure and pain.

"You shouldn't be here, Aaron. We have verification the process server has already been to see you. The final papers are being filed as we speak. Don't make me add a restraining order to the list." She stood her ground, her shoulders back and her head held high. Had he not been looking for a sign, he would've missed the fraction of a second she lost her bravado and showed her brokenness.

"We need to talk, baby. There are so many things I have to tell you, so you'll understand what happened. Please just hear me out. Then if you still want me to leave, I'll go."

"Fine. You have five minutes, so you'd better talk fast." She turned to the counter and told Allie she wouldn't be away long.

They slid into his car for privacy, and she looked at her watch. "Tick-tock."

Speaking quickly, he explained his head injury and subsequent seizure that robbed him of his memory. He urged her to call Logan and verify their conversation, how his best friend could vouch for what happened that night.

She couldn't hide her concern for his health. Even as hurt as she'd been, she still cared. "How much of your memory have you lost?"

"Everything in the week leading up to the wedding is gone, except one flash I remembered. You, in your wedding dress, walking down the aisle to me. And me, having to forcefully keep myself in place and not run to you. You're so beautiful, but the way you looked that night was simply amazing." He reached over and covered her hand with his, sealing the moment between them with his touch.

But his feeling of triumph was short-lived when she snatched her hand away from his. "You remember everything up until the week before the wedding?"

"Yes." His confirmation was tentative. Unsure.

"You're telling me you remember everything about us except *that* week?" Her voice rose with each word, along with her anger. "Only that one week is missing, yet you still sprang divorce papers on me without talking to me first? You humiliated me in front of your brother and everyone in that office building. You tore my heart out, stomped on it, and killed every hope I ever had for a lifelong love.

"Waking up with no memory of the past few days would freak me out, so I'll give you that. But if I'd remembered you, and who you were to me *before* that week, do you know who I would've turned to first? *You*. But that's not at all what you did."

"Christa, baby, I'm so sorry."

"Don't call me 'baby.' The papers have been filed. I've requested a court date as close to the thirty-first day as they can squeeze us in. This conversation is over. *We* are over."

She slammed the door shut behind her, leaving a stunned and speechless Aaron sitting alone in his car. Watching her walk away, unable to stop her.

In that moment, he vowed he wouldn't give her up without a fight.

And here, buttercups, is where the fun begins. Which man will get the girl? That's still to be seen. Which one deserves her is the real question.

Delilah

I slid into the passenger seat of Aaron's car and flashed a big, toothy grin at his shocked expression.

"Hello, Aaron. Seems you've made quite a mess of your marriage already. I must say, I thought you'd make it longer than a few days before the groveling and begging for forgiveness would be necessary."

"Mrs. Cushing?" His brows furrowed, and his head shook from side to side slowly in his confusion after my interruption.

"Call me Delilah."

"Did Christa tell you about us? What did she say? Do you think she'll forgive me?"

Poor boy was grasping at any straw he could find.

"Pay attention, Aaron. That girl in there is like a granddaughter to me, and I protect her fiercely. Make no mistake about it, I will crush anyone who hurts her. You and your brother came very close to being a bug under my boot for two reasons. First and foremost, you hurt Christa. That alone was enough for me to unleash my wrath on you. Secondly, you made me doubt myself. I've always had an uncanny ability to read people instantly, and for a while there, I thought I'd lost my touch.

"When I first met you, I sensed you were a good-hearted man. One who would honest to God take care of my girl, but more importantly, shower her with the type of love she's never had. You've been given a rare second chance with me, Aaron. Don't screw it up."

"I'm sorry, Delilah. I'm still trying to catch up with you. Where'd you come from? Are you alone? Is someone helping you?" He turned to look out the back window of the car.

"Stop looking for my babysitter and wheelchair. The only reason Christa had to help me that day was because I was still recovering from a minor surgical procedure. I'm perfectly capable of taking care of myself. Now, what do you intend to do to win her back?"

"That's exactly what I was just thinking about—I don't know yet. I tried to apologize to her a couple of minutes ago. But all I managed to do is make her even madder, and for reasons I didn't even think about before I showed up here. Wait—how'd you know I was even here?"

"My name is Delilah Cushing Hayse. Ring a bell?"

"Oh. Shit."

"So, you do know my name."

"Definitely. You started out as a real estate tycoon, but there's not much you're not involved in and influence today. You've moved more into the financial arena now. Whatever you buy or sell impacts the stock market. Major investors follow your lead."

"That's right. That also means I have friends in all kinds of places—high, low, and everywhere in between. Friends who have information I need, favors to repay, and a willingness to help an old lady out whenever she needs it. Good thing I called off that help when I saw you pull up here with your heart on your sleeve. Here's what you're going to do to win her back: *whatever it takes to make her happy.* Figure it out. I'll be watching."

With that advice, I exited his car and left him to wonder who my sources were. To be honest, Christa had been under my protection since the day I met her. She reminded me so much of myself when I was her age. Her timing couldn't have been better since I was in the office closing another real estate deal when she contacted a corporate Realtor on my staff about the vacant bakery building.

With the phone call on speaker, I knew how unfair life had been to her the second I heard her voice. I'm not usually overly sentimental, but something in her tone resonated with me. Determination. Grit. The drive to rise above her circumstances and be what no one believed she could be. That was when I decided to handle the terms myself and instructed my Realtor to let her have it at a ridiculously low price for such a prime location. Per normal protocol, we conducted a thorough background check on her— much more in-depth than the standard. Every aspect of her life was investigated, giving me a full picture of her current and past circumstances.

That was when she became my personal responsibility, though I've never told her. That was when I decided anyone who hurt her would deal with me.

.

CHAPTER SIXTEEN

Just Friends

Christa

"Jared, Aaron just came to see me." I blurted out the news the second he answered the phone, barely giving him enough time to say hello.

"What did he say? Don't leave anything out."

I repeated the entire conversation, including Aaron's claims to have hit his head and suffered a seizure that robbed him of any memory of our wedding night.

"At first, I was genuinely concerned about him. I thought he had total amnesia, and I couldn't imagine how terrible that would be. Then he so nonchalantly said only the week before our wedding was missing.

"But then what he didn't say hit me. *What about the rest of the time we were together?* Those memories were still intact. Yet he had no problem throwing me to the wolves—or wolf, in this case.

"The more I thought about what he said, the harder it was for me to believe a single word of it. I've been vacillating between hurt, anger, and disbelief. Then he urged me to call Logan to verify his story, as if Logan wouldn't lie for his best friend."

"Did he say what his doctor's name is?" Jared asked, bringing me back to our conversation.

"Yes, he said he went to Dr. Batton."

"It'd be almost impossible to subpoena his medical records and get them back in time at this point, especially since he'd have to agree to release them without a court order. But we can use this information to help your annulment request. He hit his head before the wedding, and he doesn't remember any of the events surrounding it now. He wasn't of sound mind during the ceremony and proposed a settlement to get you to agree to a divorce."

"Thank you, Jared. I'm sure you're busy with other work and don't need my drama right now. But I really do appreciate your help."

"You're not bothering me, Christa. In fact, I'd love to see you tonight. How about I pick you up around eight and take you out to eat?"

"That's so sweet of you. I'd really love to, but I

wouldn't be very good company after today. We've been so slammed in the shop. I haven't been off my feet all day, and they're killing me. I've already planned a hot date tonight—with a good book and an entire bottle of wine."

"You'll hurt my feelings if you don't have dinner with me. I'll have to sit there all alone."

I conceded with a soft sigh. "Fine. Only because you'll guilt-trip me forever, otherwise."

"Great. I'll pick you up at your place. See you tonight."

"Where are we going?"

"Somewhere nice. It'll be a surprise. You deserve to be spoiled."

"Dressy. Got it. See you later, Jared."

With my phone back in my pocket, I turned to start another carafe of coffee and found Allie staring me down. The expression on her face said she was less than pleased with me. "What?"

"You're going on a date with Jared tonight?" She put her fists on her hips and pinned me with her irritated gaze, daring me to deny my plans for the evening.

"It's not a date. I'm only having dinner with a friend, and he's helping me with this mess with Aaron."

"Going to dinner somewhere with a dress code isn't just a friendly outing, Christa. And that man doesn't look at you as just a friend. Don't be naïve." She grabbed the towel from under the counter and began cleaning. Angrily.

"Wow. Where is this coming from, Allie?" I stepped in front of her to make her stop and talk to me.

"Christa," she started, already exasperated with me, and threw the towel down. "You know I love you. You're my best friend, and I want nothing but the best for you. I'm warning you now, nothing good will come from this."

"Allie, I love you too. I've told you we're only friends. But I seem to remember you offering to make Jared your own personal pogo stick. So, why the sudden change?"

"He's handsome." She shrugged. "I'm not looking for a forever kind of love. A night or two with him would be enough for me. He's no different—I know guys like him.

"What Aaron did to you was really shitty, and part of me would like to feed him a sandwich using his balls as the sliced lunch meat. But he showed up here for you, didn't he? He came crawling back, asking for forgiveness, trying to explain what happened. Your *husband* asked for your forgiveness, Christa."

She stomped off to the back of the shop, leaving me

to digest her words alone. Hearing Allie call him my husband felt like a knife stabbing me directly in the center of my heart. I looked down at my left hand and could still feel the weight of my wedding rings even though they were long gone. My tether to Aaron was still very real, whether I was wearing the rings or not. Pride wouldn't let me show him how much he hurt me...or how very much I still loved him.

Then I remembered the betrayal. The sting of his disloyalty. The utter disregard for my feelings when I cried and begged him in Lance's office. The way he didn't defend me against his brother's accusations. And just like that, I was right back in the raging storm of anger and depression.

I marched to the back, where Allie was hiding after making her cutting remarks, ready to throw a few barbs of my own. "I know you think you're helping, in your own twisted way. But if you recall, my *husband* admitted he remembered everything except the week leading up to our trip to Vegas. That means he remembered me. He knew who I was. He knew how he felt about me and how I felt about him. But none of that mattered when I begged him—in front of his asshole brother—to just talk to me. Like an adult. Like a *human being*. I asked him if he wanted a divorce, if he truly didn't want to be married to me. He didn't. So, excuse me for trying to protect myself from that kind of hurt again. Apparently, Jared is the only one on my side, helping protect me."

"If you think Jared is only trying to protect you from Aaron, you'll end up making another colossal mistake because you're fucking blind. Aaron fucked up, no doubt. But he loves you, and he's trying to make amends. I'm not saying to run and move in with him. But you can give him a chance."

"Give him a chance, huh? A chance to hurt me again? A chance to humiliate me? A chance to toss me aside like I mean nothing to him—just like my parents did? Hell no."

"Then you'll miss a chance to be truly loved for who you are. He's not your mom or your dad. He's a man who had a medical condition and freaked the fuck out. I don't know how I'd react if I woke up married one day and my spouse had already moved in, but I had no clue how any of it happened. I'd probably beat the shit out of him with a baseball bat, no matter how long I'd been with him. Or maybe I'd play it off like I knew exactly what was going on because I'd finally convinced someone to marry my crazy ass. The point is, neither of us knows how we'd react because we've never been put to the test before."

Allie and I finished the day speaking only when we were forced to and only about work. She wasn't mad at me—she was disappointed in me, and that was almost worse. She waited for me to call Jared and break our friendly dinner reservation, but I didn't.

It was not a date.

As I locked up for the night, my phone pinged with a text.

Jared: *I'm looking forward to our date tonight.*

The inadvertent cringe that message caused was impossible to ignore. I never wanted to date again. Not Jared, not any man. Because my heart and soul still belonged to Aaron.

Damn you, Aaron.

Me: *I'm sorry—can't make it tonight. I'm too tired, and I'm definitely not ready to date.*

He answered immediately. *Date was the wrong word. Just dinner with a friend.*

When I didn't reply for a minute, he sent another text.

Christa, let me be there for you. I haven't been for so long.

Me: *All right. Dinner with a friend it is.*

When I reached my apartment, all I really wanted to do was sink down into my tub and stay home for the night. But I showered and dressed instead. No doubt Jared would take me to one of the best restaurants in the city. The ones where it takes months to get a table unless the right names are dropped and connections contacted. Jared's family had those contacts, so I had no doubt he'd called in a favor.

When he showed up at my door promptly at eight, wearing a fresh suit and tie with hair perfectly styled, I knew he went home after work to change. He cared about his appearance, I got that, but I couldn't help comparing him to Aaron. Jared took time to primp and groom himself to the exact right degree. Aaron was sexy and striking without even trying.

"You are absolutely stunning. I love you in heels and a sexy dress." His eyes raked over me from top to bottom, then back up again.

Though he meant it as a compliment, his actions only made me feel uncomfortable.

"Thank you. You look very handsome yourself." I grabbed my clutch and locked my apartment door on our way out. "Where are you taking me?"

He rattled off the name of the newest, most exclusive restaurant in the San Francisco area, as I expected. The memory of the impromptu picnic with Aaron in the wildflower clearing popped into my mind. How relaxed I felt with him on our first date. How I never wanted it to end. How I'd give anything to be back there again in his arms right now. It was all I could do to keep from running back into my apartment and barricading myself inside.

But I didn't. Because I had to move on no matter how much it hurt.

The drive to the restaurant was quick, or maybe it

just seemed it was because I was lost in my head. I blamed it on the long day I'd had and apologized for my silence. Inwardly, I was thankful Aaron allowed it. I meant *Jared*. Jared allowed it.

The chic restaurant was a refurbished two-story warehouse, with floor-to-ceiling windows covering the front. We climbed the few steps to the front door, and a doorman was there to greet us. Once we were seated, I took a minute to absorb the posh and pomp surrounding me, and I felt completely out of place. An older couple stopped briefly to say hello to Jared, filling the dead air in our nonexistent conversation. When we were close friends before he left, I couldn't remember a single time we ran out of conversation topics.

"I'm sorry I didn't introduce you to them. I couldn't remember his wife's name, and all I could think about was making a fool of myself if I called her by the wrong one."

That visual made me laugh, and it felt good to hear myself make that sound again. Apparently, we needed the laugh over his discomfort to break the tension and get the conversation flowing. He was still the same person I remembered from so many years ago, and right then, I needed all the friends I could get.

After we finished eating, Jared and I chatted while we waited for the valet to bring the car around. I felt relaxed after the bottle of wine and the exhausting day, and I realized maybe I'd let my guard down a little too much when a text set off my phone alert. When I looked at the screen, my hands shook so much I nearly dropped my phone.

It was a message from Aaron.

What I would give to be holding you right now.

CHAPTER SEVENTEEN

Realization

Aaron

I took Delilah's challenge to heart. A week ago, she asked how I planned to win Christa back, and that made me realize I needed a legitimate plan if I had any hope of succeeding. After my disastrous apology, it was clear I had to change my tactics completely to break through the walls she'd constructed around her heart.

She was still mine, and I'd make *her* remember before it was too late.

Part one of my "win Christa back" campaign was to send her short text messages to let her know I was thinking of her. I tried to figure out what to say as a follow-up to the first message, something more heartfelt, when my ringing doorbell stopped me.

When I opened the door, I couldn't decide if I was more disappointed that my visitor was *not*

Christa...or that it *was* Lance.

"What do you want?"

"Is that any way to greet your brother?" He brushed by me and into my condo, glancing around as if he was looking for someone.

"She's not here." I closed the door and walked into the room behind him. "Yet."

"You convinced her to take you back?"

Even though his reply rubbed me the wrong way, the inflection in his tone was sincere. The thing was, I wouldn't have to convince her to take me back had I not listened to him in the first place. I couldn't put the blame on him, no matter how much I wanted to do just that.

"No. She had a great argument for not accepting my apology."

"I'm very good at arguing and negotiating. Let me help."

"No fucking way. Why are you here anyway?"

"Come on, Aaron. I'm your brother, I can help you."

I hated to admit how stupid I was, but that was the truth. "She pointed out what an idiot I am. There were a few days missing, yes. But we'd been together a lot longer than that, so I shouldn't have handled it the way I did."

"You mean the way *we* handled it." Lance shook his head then found an interesting spot on the floor to stare at longer than normal. "I'm sorry you're going through a tough time. But if I had to do it all over again, I wouldn't change my initial reaction. My first thought is to protect you—always. Maybe I don't always respond in the best way, but you're always my first thought."

He walked to my kitchen table and picked up the packet the process server delivered. The older brother in him didn't hesitate to open the envelope and snoop. The lawyer in him needed to know every single detail, especially when he realized what he held. He took a seat then took his time reading every word at least three times.

He finally looked up at me. "When did this happen?"

"As soon as I got back from San Diego. The process server was waiting for me in the garage. Served me at my car."

"She wants an annulment. This is perfect." He had the nerve to sound excited. "It'll be like it never happened. She won't have any claim to anything you own. You are one lucky son of a bitch."

"You must be fucking kidding me. Did you not just offer to help *negotiate* to get her back? I'm not accepting an annulment. I'll fight tooth and nail to stop it."

"Aaron, come on. You can have the marriage annulled and still date her. It's not like you knew her long enough or well enough to get married anyway."

"Why are you here? You have about thirty seconds to tell me, and then I'm tossing you out on your ass."

"You're needed back at work. You've had your sabbatical, but now it's time to get back on track. Kylie was thrilled with the models you selected, and the results of their dry run are better than she expected. Word will spread fast, and more major designers will contact us to stay in league with Kylie."

"I've told you, I'm not staying. I'm done."

"You really mean it this time, don't you?" His brows furrowed, and he cocked his head to the side. He finally stopped calculating every move and countermove to take a good, long look at me.

"Yes." My fists went to my hips, and I stood tall. Determined.

"Can you at least work out a two-week notice and train one of our up-and-coming junior agents?"

It was the least I could do for the company we built from the ground up. "Two weeks, Lance. I'm not traveling, and I'm not staying any longer than that. If you ask me to do either of those things, you'll piss me off.”

“No travel and no extensions. You have my word.”

“Then you have mine. I’m yours for two weeks. After that, you buy my half of the company.”

“I’ll get started on the paperwork. So, you’ll be back in the office Monday morning?”

“Yeah, I’ll see you then.”

Lance left, and I glanced at the clock. It was too late to text her again and finish what I wanted to say, knowing how early she got up for work in the mornings. Instead, I sat at my laptop and did the next best thing—I arranged for special delivery sent directly to her shop the next day.

As I closed my laptop, a memory flashed in my mind, and I saw her as clearly as if she were standing in front of me right then. She was tossing a bouquet of flowers over her shoulder at our small reception party. Several other people we didn’t know were there, but they were all wearing black-tie attire, as if they were members of other wedding parties.

“The chapel held a joint reception for everyone who got married there that evening. We were laughing because our party of four was the smallest one they had all day.”

She threw a bouquet of Stargazer lilies, with dark pink centers and a bright white edge. Her favorite flower. The girl who caught the bouquet waggled her brows at her date, and then the rest of us pointed and laughed at his terrified expression.

I grabbed my phone and opened my contacts. I stared at her name with my thumb barely hovering over the button. Just a slight movement more and I'd hear her voice again.

But I'd hear her angry voice. The one that didn't want to hear from me. The tone that said all the things she couldn't, or wouldn't, because she was too good of a person to try to hurt me in that way.

"Motherfucker!" I dropped my phone on the couch and paced across my condo. From the door, across the width of my home, to the wall of windows overlooking the bay. Then back again.

Going nowhere fast.

Getting nowhere slow.

Jared

"Let me walk you in." I put the car into park and cut the engine outside Christa's apartment. "To make sure you get in there safe and sound."

"Jared, I've been walking inside my apartment alone for many years now, and I always make it in safe and sound. Tonight won't be any different. Thank you for dinner, and for the offer, but I'm dead on my feet and have a full day ahead of me tomorrow. Drive safely."

She jumped out of the car before I could even respond. She was quiet the entire ride back for some reason. She seemed more distracted and even a little jumpy, but she never said why. I chalked it up to the predicament that shithead of a husband had left her in. Her heart was broken, her pride was wounded, and her mind was twisted. Expecting to be more than a friend with a shoulder she occasionally cried on was a surefire way to set myself up for disappointment.

I watched until I saw lights in different rooms turning on and off in her apartment before I left. It was still early by my standards, and I wasn't ready to sit alone in my condo just yet.

"Sean, where the hell are you?"

"I'm at this terrible dive bar called Entranced. Have you ever heard of it?" The music blaring from inside the club pulsed through my car stereo speakers. The voices of the drunk girls urging him to rejoin their private party quickly followed.

"Dive bar? Try the most popular new nightclub in the city. Yeah, I may have heard of it once or twice."

"Then get your ass down here. There are two girls hanging all over me. Hot, willing, and ready. I'll share one with you, since I'm nice like that."

"I'm on my way. Don't you dare leave before I get there."

"The party is just getting started, brother. We've been waiting for you."

My foot pushed on the gas pedal a little harder, the speedometer needle moved to the right a little more, and my knuckles gripped the steering wheel a little tighter. Sean and his two companions were three sheets to the wind by the time I found them inside. In no time, I'd slammed multiple shots and was quickly closing ranks on them.

The scantily clad brunette at my side slid over a little closer to me, and I caught a trace of the sweet scent of her perfume. With every smile, she leaned toward me and moved nearer. She put her hand on my arm and threw her head back in laughter, using nonchalant ways of letting me know she was interested.

I wasn't quite as bashful and tentative as she was, though.

When she put her hand on me again, I wrapped my

fingers around hers and pulled her to me. She didn't resist, and I didn't delay. My eager mouth covered hers. My hungry lips claimed her soft ones. My tongue demanded access with a swipe across the part in her lips, and she willingly complied. She tasted sweet, like the Redheaded Slut shots she'd been downing.

The silky slide of her tongue across mine was an aphrodisiac itself. The slight moan that escaped her throat spurred me on. My fingers gripped her hair at the root, and I tilted her head, giving me better access to devour her like a fine delicacy.

Her fingers tightened on my shirt, her muscles tensed, and she pressed her breasts against me. My fervor was matched motion by motion. We lost ourselves in each other, the shots and beers we drank removed any inhibitions or second thoughts. All I could think about then was burying my cock balls deep in her pussy and hearing her scream my name.

"Maybe you two should get a room." Sean's voice pulled me from the Redheaded Slut-shot induced haze and back to the table in the nightclub.

My make-out partner looked up at me from under her lashes. "Maybe we should."

The suggestive undertone of her voice shot straight to my already hard cock, making it twitch behind my zipper. I stood and pulled her up with me. "We'll be back."

Couples had disappeared down the hallway behind the stage, so that was the direction we went. The hallway was long and dimly lit, with recessed doorways every ten feet or so. The dark alcoves provided the perfect spot for a club quickie, or a voyeur's wet dream since most of them were taken by couples in various states of sexploration.

We finally found one that was empty, and I claimed it by pushing...err...what's her name against the door. I closed in on her in a heartbeat; my body crushed against hers and our mouths clashed, needy with want. My hands roamed over her body, noting the weight of her breasts in my hands, the curve of her hips, and the bare skin of her ass thanks to her thong.

I pushed her short skirt up around her waist, her thong down toward her ankles, and freed my cock from the confines of my pants. Her soft hand wrapped around my girth, stroking back and forth, increasing her grip slightly with each pass. I drove my fingers deep inside her wet pussy, pumping in and out of her while she rode my hand, increasing her pleasure.

"Fuck me, Jared." Her words were breathy but high-pitched.

I was quick to oblige. Sheathed and hard as a hammer, I gave her what she wanted and then some.

With her back pressed against the door and her leg hooked over my arm, I pushed into her, driving to the hilt. Her body wrapped around me tightly, the friction producing the most intensive pleasurable pain. I reached down and lifted her other leg, using her weight as leverage as I pulled her down and pushed her up. The fast-paced frenzy drove her to the edge. Her cries of pleasure built until she screamed loudly, and I give up control immediately after.

After I lowered her legs to the floor, she quickly tugged her panties up and straightened her skirt. We separated awkwardly, each heading for the bathroom, and I began to plan my escape route. When she entered the ladies' room, I stepped into the men's and disposed of the condom, then quickly darted down the hall and keep moving until I was on the outside of the club. When I reached the line of cabs waiting out front, I texted Sean to let him know I was leaving. There was nothing worse than an awkward goodbye, especially when I didn't remember her name and I wasn't interested in a repeat.

"You are cold, man." Sean's reply pinged on my phone. I could hear the laughter in his voice despite the words he used.

"She can go home with you for round two." My reply got the point across—don't give her my contact information.

"Only if you twist my arm."

By the time I reached my condo, I already regretted what I'd done. Another one-night stand, another meaningless encounter. I was alone again, lying in my bed, thinking of the one I wanted more than anyone. The one who should be there with me—the one who should've always been with me, but I was too stupid to see it before it was too late.

My tossing and turning didn't stop all night, and by daylight, I was even more tired than when I got home the night before.

And I still needed to pick up my car I'd left outside the club.

The hot water in my shower helped revive me, or at least, made me feel alive again. I ran a towel over my hair and quickly dried off before throwing on an old pair of shorts and a T-shirt. It was my first Saturday off work since I started, and I planned to take full advantage of doing nothing at all.

All day.

I waited until the last possible minute to go get my car. Before I called a cab, I had an idea that could help improve my mood and help me reach my goal.

"Hello, Christa. How was your day?"

"Busy. I'm glad it's over. How was yours?"

"Very unproductive, exactly the way I planned. But I do need a favor, if you feel up to it. If not, I understand."

"Of course. What do you need?"

"A ride down to Entranced to pick up my car."

"Oh, umm, sure. I guess you went down there after you dropped me off last night?"

Shit.

"Yeah. My best friend from college called as I was driving home. He talked me into meeting him. I didn't want to take a chance on driving after I'd had a couple of drinks. Losing my license and losing my job costs more than the price of a cab ride home."

"Wise decision. So, you just need a ride downtown?"

"Yeah, but if you're busy or too tired, I understand. You've had a long day, and I don't want to impose."

"You're my friend, Jared. You could never impose on me. I'll be there in a few minutes."

"Thank you, Christa. You are the absolute best."

CHAPTER EIGHTEEN

Quarter After One

Christa

"He loves you, ya know?" Allie said from behind me. She wasn't exactly asking a question as much as she was pushing me to surrender to what my heart knew it wanted.

"I thought he did."

"Those flowers are gorgeous. I didn't even know Stargazer lilies were your favorite, and I've known you forever."

"You've known me just over two years."

"Feels like forever. Still, I spend nearly every day with you, and I didn't know that. He remembered after one conversation about them. What does the letter say?"

She had asked no less than ten times about the letter from Aaron that was waiting in my mailbox when I got home today. In return, I'd told her no less than ten times it was none of her business. As my best friend in the world, she rejected that response.

It was pointless to argue with her.

She grabbed the envelope from the table and took a seat, making herself at home as she read a very personal letter from my soon-to-be nonexistent husband. I didn't have to read over her shoulder...I knew every word by heart.

She read it aloud anyway.

My love –

I remember the day I found you. From behind the counter in your coffee shop, you put me under your spell, and my heart was forever yours.

I remember the day I lost you. When I left the office building, I thought that day was the worst day of my life. But I was wrong. Every day without you has been the worst day I've ever had. So, every single day is literally the worst day of my life.

To pass the time and to prove my love, I'll tell you every day one reason why I love you.

Day One: I love your ass. It makes me smile.

Forever yours,

Aaron

"Christa, how can this not melt that foot of ice around your heart?" Allie put the letter back in the envelope and stared at it for several seconds. "Do you have any idea what I'd give to have someone love me like this?"

"I don't believe him. Allie, how am I supposed to trust him again? He crushed me."

"He's trying to make up for it. Think of all the ways he can make it up to you for the rest of your life. Make-up sex. Make-up jewelry. Make-up vacations. A lifetime of groveling from a hot, sexy man who loves your ass. How can you possibly ask for more?"

I couldn't help but laugh at her—I knew she was joking. Partially, anyway. "Maybe you're right."

"Of course I'm right. I'm also right about not trusting this Jared guy with you. I'll go pick him up and take him to his car."

"You'd do that for me?"

"Of course. Now get ready for a night out of drunken debauchery. We're going out and staying out until dawn, or until one of us pukes then passes out. You haven't been properly introduced to the club scene. Whatever you're wearing when I return is what your ass is going out clubbing in, so you'd better make it something good."

Even though going out after a long day was officially the last thing I wanted to do, I had no doubt Allie would do exactly what she said. She'd drag me out of my apartment in my ratty old pajamas without a second thought. She left to play taxi for Jared while I jumped in the shower.

The hot water felt so good on my aching muscles I was tempted to stay in my locked bathroom and ignore Allie. But she was right. I did need a night out with her to let loose, to enjoy myself, to do things I'd never done before. However, I couldn't stop laughing to myself when I thought about the look on Jared's face when Allie arrived for him instead of me.

I should've had her text me a picture of his reaction.

For the first time in several weeks, my hair wasn't pulled up in a ponytail. My face was fully painted with all the makeup. My clothes made me feel sexy— or sexier. Let's not get too crazy. But our night out would be a night to remember. I could feel it.

I was slipping my feet into my shoes when I heard the front door open, followed by Allie's laughter carrying down the hallway. The sound of it—the unmistakable mischievous cackle—pulled a bubble of laughter from my own chest.

"What did you do to Jared?"

"Nothing permanent. Are you ready to go?"

"Yes, I'm ready." I stepped into the hall and met her.

"Whoa. You clean up nice. I may even be into you myself."

God, I loved her. I never would've made it through the previous several weeks without her beside me. My cheerleader. My confidante. The irritating thorn in my side.

"You can't afford me. I know how much you make."

"Yeah, my boss is a slave driver who pays me in scones and coffee."

"You could do worse. Where are you taking me?"

"The same place Jared left his car last night. I'm telling you, Christa, that boy is full of shit. He dropped you off and hit the hottest club in the city for a reason. He got laid last night."

"Did he tell you that?"

"Of course not. Mark my words, though. Now, let's see if we can do the same for you."

"No." My tone was instantly firm and resolute. "If you even try to hook me up with some guy, a dance, anything, I will leave you there alone. This is a girls' night, and I'm going with my girl, and I'm leaving there with my girl."

"Yeah, yeah, I hear you."

She ushered me to the door and to her car. Within minutes, we were outside the club, and I was instantly ready to leave.

"Look at that line. We'll never get in."

"Of course we will."

She took my hand in hers and pulled me toward the bouncer manning the door. He looked up at us, the serious expression on his face enough to stop me in my tracks, but not Allie.

Then his face split in two with a bright, handsome smile. "Hello, Allie. Who do you have with you?"

"This is my friend Christa. She needs to get shit-faced tonight. Christa, this is Rory Shields."

"You're Rory?" The inflection in my tone was impossible to miss. In my defense, that name was impossible to mistake.

"Yeah. Do I know you?" He narrowed his eyes, furrowed his brow, and studied my face intently.

"Not me. But I've heard all about you from Jen Miller."

"Oh, really?" His smile was even bigger at the mention of her name. Interesting. "You're friends with Jen?"

"Yes, she's one of my closest friends." My eyes darted between Rory and Allie. "How do you two know each other?"

"Rory is my cousin. You'll have to tell me everything Jen has said about him. Give me all the dirt."

I smirked at her. "I know he's good friends with Jared."

"Ugh." Allie rolled her eyes in disgust. "You could've left that part out. All right, Rory, we're going in to party now. Thanks for having our backs."

"If you drink, you'd better take a cab home, or I'll have your ass."

"I'm designated driver and party master tonight. Christa is the one who needs to get drunk."

Rory opened the velvet rope and allowed us to enter. The throngs of people waiting at the entrance grumbled, but he ignored them. Allie steered me through the packed club and stopped only for a moment until she spied an open table. She made a beeline directly for it, with me in close tow behind her, and we snagged it just in time. The waitress appeared almost as soon as we were seated, and Allie ordered for both of us.

Water for her. A continuous flow of Mind Eraser shots and beer chasers for me. Any thought that the energy we exerted with all the songs we danced to would counter the amount of alcohol I'd consumed flew out the door with all my cares. I was officially numb and carefree.

And I felt young and entitled to do something utterly stupid and immature for the first time in my life. But I was too drunk to care what anyone thought about it. Or maybe that was my excuse, since I was justifying it while drunk.

Either way...I had to know.

Aaron

My phone rang, forcing me to move my arm that was draped over my eyes and look at the clock. I'd had another sleepless night, but a phone call at a quarter after one in the morning was rarely a good sign. One look at the screen sent my blood racing and gave my heart palpitations. *Christa.*

I snatched my phone off the nightstand and bolted straight up in the bed. "Christa? Baby, are you okay?"

There was no response, but the call was still connected. I heard muffled noises at first then the line suddenly became clear. I imagined her phone rolling around in her huge bag, accidentally dialing my number, but she hadn't disconnected yet.

"Baby, please say something. I miss you so much. *I love you*, Christa. With everything I am, I love you." I begged her to answer me, just to say something. Anything.

"Aaron," she finally choked out. That was all the encouragement I needed.

"I'm on my way, baby." I didn't wait for her to object. I was taking a chance I might later regret. But I wasn't missing it for my life. I threw my shorts on and drove like a bat out of hell to get to her apartment as fast as I possibly could.

I called her back as I climbed the stairs two and three at a time to get to her door. She picked up the phone but didn't say anything.

"Baby, open the door. It's me," I told her before I knocked softly. I waited, my lungs burning from the breath held in my chest. Waiting to see if she'd actually let me in.

After a few anxious seconds, the lock turned, and I waited to see her beautiful face. The door slowly opened, and she stepped back with it. Then she motioned for me to enter with a slight nod of her head. Once I was well inside the room, she closed the door, walking slowly with it to keep her back toward me. She was freshly showered—her hair was still wet, and the sweet aroma of her bath gel was still strong. She wore a T-shirt that swallowed her whole, giving me a peek of her toned legs sticking out from underneath.

Not being able to see her face was killing me. She intentionally kept it hidden from me. I didn't move from my spot, giving her time to adjust to my being there with her again. I'd put her through hell, and I'd been through my own tour of duty in hell without her.

"Baby, are you all right?" I couldn't hide the concern for her in my voice. She was too quiet, and I was too impatient. All I wanted was a second chance. All I wanted was to be hers forever.

Christa turned and raised her eyes to mine. They were red-rimmed, bloodshot, and puffy from a deficit of sleep and an abundance of crying. All because of me. The second our eyes collided, she flew across the room and straight into my waiting arms. No longer able to resist, unable to take another second of not being able to touch each other, the consequences and regrets of tomorrow be damned. We were together, and that was all we needed to know.

My arms folded around her, crushing her small frame to me as I buried my face in her hair. Her scent stayed with me, taunting me, creating a void nothing and no one else would ever be able to fill. I went from ice-cold to scorching hot in a millisecond, and my arms wrapped under her ass and pulled her up, sliding her body against mine. Her legs automatically encircled my waist. Her mouth searched for mine, kissing along my jaw before finding my lips then moving along the other side. I carried her, kissing her neck and pulling her earlobe between my teeth, to her bedroom without asking permission. There was no doubt she wanted me as much as I wanted her.

There was so much I wanted to say, so much I needed to explain. But taking a chance on words right then was not a risk I was willing to take. I'd make her feel my love through my every touch. We reached her bed, and I gently set her down before removing her oversized T-shirt. Noting it was actually my shirt she wore gave me a glimmer of hope. I quickly shed my clothes as she watched, her eyes raking over me and silently calling me to her.

The moonlight shone directly through her bedroom window, casting its silvery light across her naked body. Her eyes glistened with unshed tears that she quickly blinked back. My hands reached out to her and cupped her face to kiss her deeply. I tasted the faint sweetness of alcohol. With my intensity increased, I poured every bit of my love into the kiss, willing her to feel it and take her fill of it. I gently pushed on her shoulders, silently instructing her to sit, and then I helped her move up to the head of the bed.

I started at her feet, kissing, licking, sucking, and nipping my way up and down each leg. I took my time loving her, worshiping her entire body, and pouring my whole heart into her. Then I worked my way back up her leg, stopping momentarily at her core to meet her gaze. My chest clenched at her expression. It was a mixture of the worst pain, the purest bliss, and the deepest love I'd ever seen. That expression would haunt me—later. I'd berate myself for causing her so much pain and confusion, but for as long as she'd let me stay, my sole focus was to make her feel better.

I dipped my head and sucked her clit into my mouth. She gasped and grasped my hair in her fingers. Intermittently, I sucked on it lightly then gently ran my tongue over, under, and around it repeatedly. I moved slowly at first, savoring her natural flavor and every sound of approval she made. The intensity inside her was building to massive levels. She was so close but not quite there yet—but she would be there many times before I was done.

"I fucking love how you taste. And the sounds you make. The way your tiny fists pull my hair just before you come. Your breathy voice when you scream my name." Her body melted under my touch, my words only adding to her need for more.

I increased the suction on her clit then scraped my

teeth across it. Her hips bucked upward involuntarily. Her grip on my hair increased, slightly tugging on it and pulling me closer to her at the same time. Her hungry moans were sexy enough to push me over the edge before she even touched me, but I retrained my focus on her pleasure.

I wrapped my arms under and around her legs and pulled her core to my mouth, and I hungrily lapped her up. After a quick dart of my tongue in and out of her pussy before rolling it inside her, she almost sat straight up from the intensity. When she fell back against the pillows, I continued assaulting all her senses. My hot, wet tongue found her nub once again before my lips closed around it and my finger thrust into her waiting entrance.

As I pushed it in, her moans became louder and her grip became tighter. I deliberately moved my finger in and out of her at a leisurely pace. The need to see her almost matched my need to have her, so I raised my eyes to watch her. Her neck was arched back, her eyes welded shut, and her mouth was agape, with her sexy moans involuntarily escaping at my ministrations. With an added second finger filling and stretching her, I increased the pressure and crooked them to catch the spot that sent her over the edge.

"Aaron," she screamed, and it was the sweetest music.

I pressed on until she rode the last wave of her orgasm and soaked my hand. When I pulled my fingers out of her, she opened her eyes in time to see me put them in my mouth and lick her essence off them. Her lips parted and her eyes widened. The pulse in her neck jumped in time with her pounding heart. She tried to pull me to her, but I gently nudged her back down, silently shaking my head side to side.

Her responding grumble made me smile against her skin as I continued licking, nipping, and sucking my way up her stomach and ribs until I reached her breasts. The stubble of my unshaven jaw rubbed against her soft skin, leaving light red abrasions like they were my own personal branding iron. My possessive side appreciated the fact that her skin held my mark. She was *mine*, after all, and I was determined to win her back. When I reached her breasts, I took one into my mouth, sucking and biting on her nipple while my hand kneaded her other breast. My thumb and middle finger closed around the taut peak of her nipple, and I continued my double assault on her. Her fingers gripped my shoulders and back, her nails dug into my skin in response to the powerful sensations.

"Aaron," she panted.

I raised my head to meet her eyes, yet I was afraid to speak the words that were on the tip of my tongue. Afraid the words would break the spell, and she'd tell me to leave. That she'd realize this wasn't just a dream she'd later wake up from and instantly regret her middle-of-the-night phone call.

"Aaron, if you don't take me *now*, I will leave and find someone else who will!"

Her words struck a chord in the hidden chasms of my mind. I knew her declaration was part bluff and all frustration, but that very thought had tormented me countless times every night. The thought spurred me to speak my mind, my response leaving no room for discussion or argument.

"The. Hell. You. Will. You are *mine*, Christa. For better or for worse. *Till death do us part.* And it'll be over my dead fucking body that any other man touches you—or it'll be *his* fucking death." I meant every word of it.

Her eyes widened in surprise, studying my face and partly losing the glazed look of desire. I sensed my fear was about to come true—she was on the verge of realizing our rendezvous was a huge mistake and making me leave. So I decided to finish what she asked me to start. I aligned the head of my cock at the entrance of her wet core then slowly pushed into her, giving her body time to adjust to my size.

Once I'd pushed in to the hilt, burying myself fully inside her, I curled my hips and thrust slightly harder into her. I straightened my arms and looked directly into her eyes, holding hers captive. The glazed look returned to her eyes, and her hands moved to my chest, gripping, holding, and stroking me as I thrust into her harder and harder.

When she closed her eyes, I immediately issued an order. "Open your eyes and look at me. See *me*, Christa. You were made for me and only me. You are like a finely tuned violin, custom-made to be played only by my hands. Your body wraps around and fits me perfectly. I know every sound you make, when your breathing changes, and only I can give you what your body craves. I am the only man who can answer its call. *You. Belong. To. Me.* And I belong to you." I kept my voice low and let it flow across the air between us. Her inner walls quivered and squeezed me as her body shuddered at my words.

I pulled her legs up, wrapped my arms behind her knees, and increased the angle and depth of my penetration. Christa grasped at the sheets, writhing beneath me in sheer ecstasy. Harder and harder, I thrust into her over and over until her orgasm completely took her over the edge. When she screamed out my name again, I felt her tightness squeezing around me, holding me inside her and milking me for everything I have. I gladly gave it to her, emptying myself deep inside her and groaning with complete satisfaction as I said, "You have all of me."

I lovingly and slowly placed kisses all over her face and neck, reveling in her taste and smell as long as I could. My body still covered hers, but I held my weight off her to avoid crushing her petite body. I was still buried deep inside her and couldn't bring myself to pull out, to feel that emptiness again. Whatever it took to win her back, I silently vowed I would do it. I didn't want to push her, but I'd never just back off and leave our fate to chance.

The realization of what just happened between us crept into her eyes. I steeled myself against what she might do or say next. Would she regret it? Would she tell me to leave? Or would she admit she loved me and wanted to be with me? The questions flew through my mind at a mile a minute as I searched her eyes for the answers.

"Don't." I lowered my head and whispered the command softly in her ear.

"Don't, what?" she whispered back.

"Don't worry about tomorrow. Stay right here—with me, *right now*."

"Okay." Her reply was unsure, but I'd take it. At least I had a brief shot at convincing her I was sorry. That I loved her. That I wanted our marriage, our life.

I reluctantly rolled off her and aligned our bodies, turning so that her back was to my front, and my arm was draped over her protectively. I pulled her as close to me as possible. After a couple of minutes, she couldn't stop her body from shaking or her tears from falling. Her sniffles killed me, because I knew I caused them.

"Talk to me, baby. What are you thinking?" My lips were against her neck, and her hair was fanned out on the pillow above her head, giving me full access to her sensitive skin. Placing light kisses along the back of her neck and shoulders, I hoped my touch helped her relax and talk to me.

She wiped her eyes and took a deep breath before speaking. "I'm thinking about how much I've missed you, Aaron."

"I've missed you, too, baby. So fucking much, you have no idea." But the fact that she admitted she missed me made my heart soar. "What else are you thinking?"

She hesitated a little longer than I was comfortable with, so I rose up on my elbow to see her face. She rolled over onto her back and met my gaze before she answered.

"I'm really trying to stay in the *now* for tonight, Aaron. I don't want to talk about the rest...yet."

CHAPTER NINETEEN

A Date at Court

Aaron

I knew I shouldn't have pushed. I should've taken what she was willing to give and not questioned her. But the part of me that desperately wanted to claim her as mine, and hear her say she was, refused to let our relationship stabilize naturally.

So I pushed.

She retreated.

Then when she felt cornered, she unleashed on me with both barrels.

"What am I thinking?" Her tone dripped with pain and anger. "I'm thinking about all the pictures and news clips I had to watch with barely clothed models hanging all over you. Then to hear the entertainment news talk about your relationship with those girls—but we both know what they meant by that, don't we?

"Add to that how you and your brother ambushed

me with divorce papers in his office. If none of that is enough to explain my hesitation, throw in how pathetic I am for calling you tonight, knowing everything I know, after everything you've done to me."

The more she ranted, the madder she became, and she eventually told me to leave, despite my pleas to hear me out. Despite my reassurances those models were no one to me and nothing happened. Despite my explanation of holding the model's hand in mine was only to keep her hands off me.

She said just looking at me hurt her too much. She said she couldn't let me go, but she couldn't stay with me either.

Rather than get arrested, I left. Slowly. Dejected. Disappointed.

But not defeated.

That was a week ago, but she still loved me. She wanted to be with me, but she was afraid to give her heart to me again. She wanted to forgive me, but her pride was in the way.

The thing was, when it came to her, I had no pride. Because without her, my chance of ever being happy again was slim to none. My text to her that day was simply to tell her what she meant to me.

"I'm sorry I pushed you when you weren't

ready. I only wanted to love you, but I hurt you instead. So I want you to know, nothing matters without you. My heart still beats in your chest. My love still flows through your veins. How do I know? Because I still feel you when you're not here. I love you, Christa."

I hit send and watched like a stalker until the "read" status showed underneath my message. She didn't reply, but I didn't expect to hear from her yet. We'd both been silent for the past week, and I hoped I'd given her time to decompress after our emotional night.

After I finished writing my next letter to her, I made the drive to my former office. It was time. It was past time, actually, and I was so looking forward to writing "the end" on that chapter of my life.

I strolled into Lance's office with a smile on my face. The fact that that day was the first time I'd genuinely smiled when showing up at my own business wasn't lost on me.

I smiled because it was officially my last day. Lance was buying out my half of the business by converting our privately-owned company to a publicly traded company. The faithful, high-performing employees would receive stock options as a retention incentive. I was happy for Lance, and I was happy for Rivers Forte. It would make the company stronger. Most of all, I was happy for me. I was finally stepping out from my brother's shadow—and from underneath his thumb.

"Aaron. How have you been?" Lance approached me and shook my hand. The way he looked at me was new—almost as if he was seeing me for the first time.

"I'm okay. I've started building plans for my next venture. I'm trying to win my wife back. Getting my life and priorities in order."

"First order of business, just sign a few papers, and I'll have the money wired into your account. You'll be free and clear of all agent duties for Rivers Forte."

"Music to my ears. Thank you, Lance. I appreciate everything you've done to make this happen."

He nodded, but the serious expression didn't leave his face. "Have a seat." He motioned toward a chair, then sat in the one next to me instead of behind his huge oak desk. "Years ago, I believed you needed me to take charge and tell you which direction to take. You were lost after the accident, and Mom, Dad, and I were afraid we'd lose you forever."

The mere mention of that time in my life was almost enough to send me back into a tailspin I wouldn't recover from. A few mere months ago, the memories of it would have consumed me. The guilt would've eaten me alive. The blow to my self-esteem would have negated all the accomplishments I'd made since then.

But not anymore.

"I did need your guidance then, there's no doubt. But I've realized I outgrew the need for your help a long time ago. I've kept the peace, but every time I've tried to make my own way, you throw that back up at me. And put me right back in my place.

"No more. It was a long time ago, and I'm not that same young man anymore. I'm grown. I'm making all new mistakes, but they're mine. My choices. My life. My decisions."

"You're right. You're exactly right, and I'm sorry. I know that doesn't make up for the shit I've put you through, but know everything I've ever done has been to help and support you. Even if I executed my actions poorly."

"Wow. What is becoming of Lance Rivers? You keep surprising me."

He laughed and shook his head. "I met someone. And she has turned my world upside down. Plus, she calls me out on my shit and makes me see the error of my ways."

"I am speechless. My brother is in love."

"Yeah, well, she helped me understand what Christa means to you. I want to help you save your marriage."

"I'm all ears."

"The hearing is in a couple of weeks now, Aaron. From what I read, they're pushing for it based on your medical condition at the time of the ceremony. They allege you weren't of sound mind at the time. With your concussion and subsequent amnesia diagnosis, the judge could grant it.

"Annulments are still very rare, regardless of what anyone says. I wouldn't have taken the case myself because the chance of winning is very low. I want to help make sure there's no chance in hell it'll be awarded."

"Tell me what you need."

"We need proof you knew what you were doing at the time vows were exchanged. Do you remember the ceremony yet?"

"Only bits and pieces of my memory have returned. But I have a packet at home that includes a DVD of our ceremony and a bazillion pictures we had made immediately afterward. The DVD clearly shows I was of sound mind and elated over our wedding. I recited my own vows."

"Perfect. Let's make a plan to keep her your wife for as long as possible, then. I want you to be prepared, though. When the judge denies this request, he will advise her she can file for a divorce, and her lawyer will strongly suggest she does it immediately. It'll still take six months before the divorce is final, though."

"So, I have six months to win her back or lose her forever."

Jared

I'd waited long enough. Today was the day. In a few short hours, her annulment would be granted, and we could finally be together. After all the years I've denied how much I wanted her, it was time I corrected that error.

I'd been sitting outside her café for the last twenty minutes, waiting for the early morning rush to clear out to give us more privacy and time to talk.

It was now or never.

"Christa, can you take a break? I need to speak with you."

"Sure, Jared. Coffee?"

"How can I turn down your delicious coffee?"

She made two cups and joined me at the table farthest away from the few patrons left.

"What's up?"

"This may come as a shock, and it's probably the absolute worst time to share this with you, but I have to."

"We're friends, Jared. You can talk to me about anything at any time. I'm not the only one who needs to bend someone's ear."

It was insane, what I was about to say. Yet I was determined to blurt it out anyway.

"I love you, Christa. I am so very in love with you and have been for so many years. I've never told you because I knew you'd wait for me, and I never wanted you to put your life on hold while I was off living mine. Now that I'm back, I want us to be more than friends."

I expected her to be speechless.

I didn't expect the expression of dismay that subsequently shrouded her face.

"Jared, I don't know what to say."

"Say you love me too."

"I do love you." She hesitated. That was never a good sign. "I love you as a friend, Jared. I'm not sure I'm capable of more."

"I'll wait for you to be ready. You've had a lot happen in a short time. I knew this was bad timing, but waiting and losing you forever to someone else is a worse alternative."

"Someone else?" she scoffed. "I can't even move past the man I'm married to, much less on to someone else."

"You're still in love with him? After everything he's done to you?"

She looked away. Not to avoid me, but deep in thought, reliving a memory.

"He wants me to give our marriage a chance."

"Have you been talking to him, Christa?" I thought my heart would burst through my throat. We were hours away from the annulment hearing, and I was only then learning they'd been conversing. No lawyer in his right mind would've taken her case knowing that. My win/loss ratio would take a substantial hit before I was even established.

"I haven't talked to him in a couple of weeks, but he texts me every day and sends me love letters."

"What happened two weeks ago?"

Her face flamed red, and that time she purposely avoided my gaze. This couldn't be good. I dropped my face into my hands and released a frustrated groan.

"Tell me you didn't, Christa."

She shrugged, still avoiding eye contact, and wrung her hands. "Allie took me out to Entranced and plied me full of alcohol. I had a weak moment and called him. He showed up at my apartment and…"

"And?" I demanded. I was her lawyer; I needed details. We were about to go to court.

"We slept together, then my temper got the best of me, and I made him leave."

"Christa, as your lawyer, I have to say your annulment will most definitely be denied. He's fighting it, and now he'll have a damn good case to prevent the court from ruling in your favor. It's rare enough as it is, but you've reconciled, for all intents and purposes. Changing your mind now discredits your unsound mind claim. We've already lost the case before we even stepped foot in the courthouse."

"I'm sorry, Jared. I didn't even think about how it would affect your career. Obviously, I didn't think about how it would affect anything. I'll understand if you want to drop my case."

"I can't just drop your case, Christa. It requires filing a motion with the court and getting approval."

"I see. Well, then, you're fired. You can bill me for

your time up until now."

"Christa. You know what they say about someone who represents herself."

"She has a fool for a client. I think I've already proven that more than once. I'm not taking you down with me."

"You'll still push for the annulment?"

"I have to. We made a huge mistake getting married so soon after meeting."

Sitting in the courtroom, watching Christa take the chair normally reserved for first counsel, unnerved me. I should have been beside her. Even though she didn't return my declaration of love, I was positive we still had a shot.

We all rose when the judge entered and took his seat. When we sat, I noticed her hands shaking before she clasped them in front of her. The judge looked at her and cast a hard glare.

"You fired your lawyer before your hearing today?"

"Yes, Your Honor."

"Care to explain why?"

"A disagreement on how to proceed with my request."

He quirked one eyebrow slightly, but enough to get his point across. He didn't approve of her representing herself either.

"You realize your husband is here with his attorney, and you have no legal counsel to guide you." He didn't ask a question—he made a very firm statement.

"Yes, Your Honor. I do realize that."

"Let's get started, then. Mrs. Rivers, please explain to the court why you think an annulment is warranted."

Regardless of how intimidated she was, Christa kept her head held high and her shoulders back as she stated her case. She started with the Monday morning after the wedding, the presentation of a divorce settlement, and Aaron's subsequent concussion and loss of memory diagnosis. The judge looked more convinced than I thought he would. But it wasn't over yet.

"Mr. Rivers, I understand your client contests the request to annul the marriage based on unsound mind at the time of their vows."

Lance Rivers stood to address the court. "That's correct, Your Honor. We have evidence to prove he was of sound mind and body during the vows. His medical issues came into being after the ceremony and consummation of their union."

Lance submitted a DVD for evidence, and the bailiff played it for all to see. There, on the screen in front of me, was the love of my life marrying another man. The love brimming in her eyes when she looked at him tore at my heart. The video left no doubt of Aaron's state of mind—he loved and cherished her, with or without the vows.

"As you can see from this video, and these wedding photographs taken immediately after the ceremony, my client was completely competent."

"At what point was his state of mind called into question?"

"As Mrs. Rivers testified—" Lance looked over at Christa, but I didn't see the cold, calculating man she described, "—when Mr. Rivers awoke Monday morning, his memories were temporarily compromised. After a thorough medical examination, we've determined he had a seizure due to post-traumatic brain injury. He's fortunate to have only lost one week of memories. However, those memories are returning intermittently. We're holding out hope they'll eventually return completely."

"Mr. Rivers," the judge addressed Aaron.

"Yes, sir," Aaron replied as he stood.

"Do you remember your wedding yet?"

"I remember parts of it. Christa walking down the aisle toward me and how I wanted her to hurry before she changed her mind and ran the other way. The reception hall where the other couples and their wedding parties waited for us, since we were the last ceremony of the day."

"You wanted her to hurry? Why is that?"

"Because I love her more than my own life, Your Honor. Because I want to spend the rest of my life with her. Because everything in the world means nothing without her."

Aaron was brave, I had to give him that. Although he spoke to the judge, his eyes were locked on to Christa's the entire time.

"Based on the evidence provided today, I'm ruling against your request for an annulment, Mrs. Rivers. This marriage was entered into knowingly and willingly by both parties. There's no evidence to substantiate Mr. Rivers was of unsound mind at any point before, during, or immediately after the ceremony. If you wish to pursue dissolving your marriage, you can file for a divorce and wait the required six months before it's granted."

With the ruling I expected handed down, Christa stood as the judge left the courtroom. Then she turned to face Aaron—and froze. Watching her watching him was painful because I felt their connection from where I sat. He wasn't giving up, he wasn't giving in, and I was the odd man out.

He was fighting to win her back, but not before I could win her over.

CHAPTER TWENTY

Best Friend Love

Christa

Divorce?

"Allie, I know this sounds crazy. I can't even explain my own thoughts and feelings. But I don't want to file for a divorce."

"Then don't. Stay with him."

"I mean, I don't want to be twenty-two, married, and divorced. The whole point of the annulment was to wipe it away as if it never happened."

"If there has ever been a time I wanted to grab you and shake some sense into you, right now is that moment. It doesn't matter if the judge calls you in the next thirty seconds and says he made a mistake and your marriage is annulled. You. Still. Married. Him.

"It won't wipe your feelings away. You won't

magically get a fresh start. Nothing will make you forget him or how much you miss him."

"What are you saying, Allie?" Her words cut me to the bone. She knew me too well.

"Walking away won't solve anything, Christa. You're in love with your husband. And from the looks of all the Stargazer lilies in your apartment and in the shop, he's in love with you too. He's at least trying to win you back. He's fighting for his marriage, no matter how some things look."

"What things?"

"Your infatuation with Jared, and his with you, for starters."

"I'm not infatuated with him!"

"Maybe not, but you don't do much to discourage him. Yet Aaron still tries to show you he's the better man. Remember Jared dropped you off and hit the club with his buddy. Don't think for a second that man went home alone."

I loved my best friend. Sometimes I wished she wasn't so blunt. Other times, like this, I was grateful she smacked me across the face with her words.

"You believe Aaron?"

"Absolutely. I've told you this. Jared already filed the divorce papers, didn't he?"

"He helped me with them. I couldn't ask him to do it after the mess I made of the annulment hearing."

"Maybe I'm going out on a limb here, but I think you sabotaged it on purpose."

I refused to get into this discussion with Allie. Because I wasn't convinced she wasn't right. I was more confused then than I'd ever been in my life.

"Do you know why you've mindfucked yourself so bad over this?"

My eyes closed, and my hand gripped the oven door handle until my knuckles were white. It was almost time to remove the day's bakery items, but all I could think about was what she'd say next. I knew what was coming.

"Why?" I managed to squeak out.

"Because that nutjob you called 'Mom' brainwashed you into thinking you don't deserve better. She was a sorry piece of shit who should've been sent away for child abuse and neglect. You don't have to think about her again."

"She knows."

"What?" Allie's surprised expression reminded me of a cartoon character. If her tongue could roll out like a red carpet, the look would be complete.

"She called last night. Out of the freaking blue.

Someone found the request for annulment and starting prying into my life. The gossip news producer found my mother and questioned her about me before showing up at my apartment last night. That's when precious mommy called—to ask for money."

"Did you tell her to go fuck herself?"

"Pretty much."

"I'm proud of you. Now, let me read the latest letter from your husband."

I didn't bother to hide them anymore. She found and read them anyway.

My love—

I remember the sparkle in your brown eyes when you walked down to the aisle toward me. I've watched the DVD of our wedding so many times, it should be worn out by now.

I remember when you first made an appearance in your wedding gown. Every other bride in the world paled in comparison to your beauty. I wanted you to hurry and say "I do" before you changed your mind. I wasn't worthy of you then, and I'm not now. But there's nothing I won't do to become the man you'd be proud to call your husband.

Day Thirty-Five: I love the sounds you make when I'm inside you.

Forever yours,

Aaron

"Christa, you bitch."

"I love you too, Allie."

"If you don't call him and at least talk to him, I'm taking him away from you."

"The hell you are." I rounded on her, my hands on my hips and my jaw set, ready to fight tooth and nail.

I was met by her knowing smirk.

"You bitch."

"Takes one to know one, my dear. Now, fucking call him before I do." She nudged me to the side so she could take the trays out of the oven. The ones I'd already forgotten and most likely had overcooked by that point. Then she left me alone in the kitchen while she filled the display case and our new bread baskets.

I glanced at the clock and shook my head at my own stupidity. I'd just filed divorce papers, and I was about to call my husband.

"Call him. He's not going to abandon you like your shitty parents did. He's been hanging on to you no matter how hard you try to get away. Get over your childhood abandonment issues."

"You really should have a talk show. You'd be awesome at solving people's deep-rooted mental problems."

"Yes, I'm a fucking spiritual guru. Now call him."

"Fine. After the morning slows down, I'll think about thinking about calling him."

The slew of profanities flowing from the front of the shop made me laugh. I was so glad my BFF was behind me no matter what. Even if she was threatening to kick my ass while she was back there.

When Allie turned the OPEN sign over and unlocked the door, customers started filing in and lining up. Jared was one of them, looking handsome in his expensive suit and tie, perfectly dressed for seeing his clientele today.

"Have you thought more about what I said?"

"Which part?" I stalled while making his coffee then gestured toward an open table.

We sat together, and I kept one eye on the counter and one on him.

"You've filed your divorce papers, right?"

"Right."

"Then it's time for you to move on. The best way for you to get past this is to move on with someone else."

"I'm not ready for that, Jared. I've never been so hurt. I don't know how to move past it."

"But we're perfect for each other, Christa. We've known each other practically all our lives. My family loves you. I love you. We should've taken this step years ago."

"Maybe. But we didn't. So now, we have to deal with where we are, and I'm not in a good place."

"I'll help you get there."

"Christa, can you help me get the sourdough out of the ovens?" Allie called from behind me, saving me once again.

"Sure. Enjoy your coffee, Jared. I need to get back to work."

"Okay, sweetheart. I'll call you later."

When I reached the kitchen, I looked at the ovens and back at Allie. "They're empty."

"Of course they're empty. What the hell are you doing?"

"I was telling him no."

"No. If you told him no, I would've heard you say 'No, Jared. My answer is no, and don't fucking ask me again.' Instead, I heard, 'I'm a weak little woman who can't make up my mind, so you do it for me, big strong man.' Made me sick to hear it."

"Wow. Why don't you tell me what you really think?"

"Don't think I'm not holding back, because I am. I'm the one who loves you, and I'm only trying to help you."

"I know you are. What would I do without you?"

"Let's find out. I'm going to leave you all alone now, and you call your husband."

"Allie," I started tentatively. She stopped at the tremor in my voice. "I don't even know what to say to him. How to even start to talk to him. About any of this."

She gave me a small, understanding smile. "Start with the letter he sent you. How it made you feel. Ask how he's doing, if his memory is improving. Tell him you just wanted to say, if he expects you to text him a picture of your ass, he'll have to send you a dick pic first."

Allie knew exactly how to calm my nerves and ease my anxiety.

I loved my best friend.

Since Allie had the front covered, I stepped out the back emergency exit and stared at Aaron's name on my phone. My thumb hovered over the button as an internal battle of wills waged. My head screamed not to trust him again, that I'd be a fool to forgive and forget.

My heart said I'd never find another man like him, that I'd regret not giving him another chance for the rest of my life. The dire warning crashed through my carefully constructed walls. Then a vision of him giving his heart to someone else nearly incited a panic attack and prompted me to act.

My thumb jerked, hitting the call button, and his phone barely had time to ring before he answered.

"Hello?"

"Hi, Aaron." It felt strange not to know what to say to my husband. "How are you?"

"I've had better days. How are you?" His usual warm, loving tone had disappeared. He sounded detached and cautious.

"Did something happen? Are you okay?" I was honestly concerned about him. He didn't sound like my Aaron.

"Oh, let's see," he began, and I closed my eyes just to listen to his voice. "The judge denied your request for an annulment a few days ago, but your lawyer is abnormally expedient.

"Your process server is especially efficient too. He's already been by to hand-deliver your divorce papers. I assume you've called to ask if I can send them back today so the next six months will fly by."

The palpable pain in his voice brought me to my knees. I had no idea he'd receive the papers today. Jared's assistant filled them out at the same time I filed for an annulment, just in case. When I filed the divorce papers, it simply felt like the next logical step.

Then I had to face how much that action hurt Aaron. He hurt me. I hurt him. He fought to hold on to me. I hurt him again. Every day for the last thirty-five days, I'd received a text from him with one reason why he loves me and one memory he has of me.

"Aaron," I replied, barely holding back the sob trying to break free.

"I understand, Christa. I had the best person in the world as my wife, and I fucked everything up, as usual. It's my calling card. I don't blame you at all.

"As for the papers, I'll have a courier deliver them to you as quickly as possible. One less thing for you to worry about."

"Aaron, wait."

"I really have to go, Christa. I'm in the middle of a

meeting," he interrupted me. "You take care of yourself." The gentle, loving inflection in his words automatically prompted the tears.

Then he disconnected.

Just like that, he was gone.

Aaron

"That was the hardest fucking thing I've ever had to do."

"I know it was, my boy. But it was necessary," Delilah replied. "Trust me. I'd never steer you wrong as long as you're doing right by my girl."

"How is that supposed to help me convince her not to go through with the divorce?"

"You've been chasing her. She's gotten a taste of how good it feels to be wanted, and believe me, she likes it.

"But she filed the papers anyway. Out of spite or pride doesn't matter—neither will do her any good in the long run. Now, she needs to understand how it feels to think she has truly lost you. She has to learn to appreciate you and your love for her."

"I don't like playing games. I'd rather just tell her exactly how I feel. Be honest and upfront."

"You already have, Aaron. Where has that gotten you? She has to realize what's at stake on her own."

"I'm not giving up on my plan, Delilah. I still have six months before the divorce is final."

"No, you won't give up at all. But it's time to reformulate your plan of attack. You're no longer the whipped dog, begging for table scraps, happy to get whatever she'll throw your way. You're going to make her remember the confident, cocky man who captivated her in the first place. You're going to make her want that man again."

"Yes, ma'am." My smile was genuine, and my confidence received a much-needed boost. "I'm ready to throw my wife over my shoulder and carry her back to my man-cave."

Delilah winked mischievously, sealing our conspiracy. "That's my boy."

CHAPTER TWENTY-ONE

Personal Delivery

Aaron

Instead of sending the divorce papers via a courier, I decided to deliver them personally. Besides, I needed coffee and croissants for breakfast. It was convenient since there was only one place in the world I'd go.

The Sweet Spot.

When the chimes over the door rang, announcing my entrance, Christa looked up to greet her customer. The sweet smile plastered on her face fell, and apprehension took its place. My presence there made her nervous.

Good.

At least she wasn't indifferent or mad. She was affected by me, and that meant her real feelings were still buried.

"Good morning." I approached the counter with my usual confident swagger. The half-smile playing on my lips wanted to break out into full seal-the-deal mode, but I withheld it. "I'll have a coffee, black, and a caramel croissant, please."

Christa's confused expression amused Allie, who nudged her way in to ring up the sale. After paying for my breakfast, like any other customer, I found an open table and sat where I could watch Christa work.

A couple of minutes later, Christa approached with my order, and I stood to take it from her. "Thank you. You didn't have to bring it to me. I could've grabbed it myself."

"You know me—service with a smile."

"I do know you. Very well." My eyes dropped to her mouth, then to her breasts, and feasted on the rest of her as if she was mine to devour. Because she was.

Her pink colored cheeks were a dead giveaway to her thoughts. She went to the same place I did with a slightly suggestive comment. Her heart remembered. Her body remembered. Now to convince her mind our marriage was what she wanted.

"What brings you in this morning?"

"Besides the best coffee and croissants known to man?" I winked, then softened my expression. "I've signed these. Thought I'd bring them back to you myself." I reached inside my jacket and produced our divorce papers.

Giving them to her killed me because a divorce was the last thing I wanted. But she was damned and determined to be damned and determined. The best way to convince her otherwise was if she worked through the motions for herself.

She reached for the papers, and her hand held on to them tightly as her eyes lifted to meet mine. Our locked gaze held us in place every bit as much as the tight grip she had on my hand. She didn't want to take the papers from me. She didn't want to let go of my hand.

So, I let go.

The emptiness I felt from instantly missing her touch made me grab the coffee cup before I did something stupid, like grab her instead.

"This coffee is so good. You're turning me into a junkie."

The quirk of her lips into a partial smile came and went so fast, I almost questioned if it was even there. One fist wrapped around the papers, curling them tightly while she wiped the other palm on her thigh.

"I'm glad you like it. I'll just go put these up."

A simple nod was my only reply before I tore into the

croissant I didn't even want. It was all I could do to force it down, knowing she was hurting, too. Knowing I only wanted to make everything right. Knowing she was still my wife, and that was all I wanted.

She walked away, and Allie approached me the second Christa was out of earshot. "Very smooth, slick. Want some help?"

"Absolutely. Has Jared made his move yet?"

"He tried, but I've actively worked against him. He's not for her."

"Does she agree?"

"I don't know, Aaron. She loves you, that much I know. But Jared is safe, or she thinks he is anyway. She's known him and his family for a long time. One thing she hasn't had in her life, but she desperately tries to find, is safety."

"You have a great point, and my plan fits perfectly with what she needs."

Allie leveled me with her serious expression. "Don't hurt her again. Ever. Or I'll cut your dick off and auction it on eBay."

"Fair enough." Christa emerged from the kitchen area, wiping her eyes. I inclined my head slightly toward her and said to Allie, "Time for step two."

Christa avoided looking at me as she stepped behind the counter. I slid out of my chair and sauntered toward my wife. "Delicious breakfast, as usual."

"I'm glad you liked it." She still refused to look up, and she kept her voice low. But I could see her fight against her quivering bottom lip.

"Let me take you out for a delicious dinner tonight. You work hard serving others all day. You deserve to be catered to after work."

She finally met my gaze. "But...you signed the papers. You want a divorce."

One side of my mouth lifted in a half smile. "Those two things are not mutually exclusive. I signed the divorce papers because I won't fight you on it. That doesn't mean I won't fight like hell *for* you until the last possible second."

Her lips parted, and an audible gasp escaped. She was speechless, but I was relentless.

"Christa? Dinner?"

"Uh. I guess that'd be okay."

"Good. I'll pick you up about seven, then."

"All right."

I turned to leave, walking away without a care in the world. When I reached the door, I looked over my shoulder at her and she was smiling.

Score one for Aaron.

Christa

I changed my clothes five times in fifteen minutes, and after I was finally dressed, I considered changing again. Nothing looked right. Nothing fit right. All my clothes should be burned so I could replace them with acceptable attire.

Aaron would be there in a few minutes, if not right then since he was normally early when we went out. My level of excitement over having a date with my husband, or soon-to-be ex-husband, should have been alarming. It should have raised some kind of red flag, signaling I was broken and needed serious therapy.

But I didn't have time to consider that since I was back inside my closet, searching for something appropriate to wear out to dinner. I chose a blush-colored casual shift dress with strappy wedge sandals. He knocked on my door just as I was adding the finishing touches of jewelry.

When I opened the door, it was all I could do to breathe. He was larger than life, filling the doorway and looking so handsome. Even in casual clothes, he was the sexiest man I'd ever seen.

His eyes raked over my body, touching me physically and making me yearn for him even more. "You look absolutely stunning, Christa." The smooth timbre of his voice glided over my nerves, igniting the passion deep in my core.

"Thank you, Aaron. You look very handsome yourself." My eyes had a mind of their own, because they drank him in from head to toe then back up again.

His confident smirk was intact after catching me checking him out. I drew my lips together, attempting to hide my guilty smile. Unsuccessfully.

He extended his arm toward me with a full smile. My God, that smile always slayed me. "Shall we?"

I grabbed my clutch then wrapped my hand around the bend of his arm and drew closer to him. The spicy-sweet blend of his cologne was intoxicating on its own. Mixed with Aaron's natural essence, being so close was almost cruel and unusual punishment.

He closed and locked the door, double-checking it latched completely before we left. "I have to make sure you're safe."

We moved toward the elevator, content in our silence, when none other than Jared stepped into our path.

The reaction I expected from Aaron didn't happen. I waited for his muscles to tense and his temper to flare, but he was relaxed. Jared, on the other hand, appeared as if he could chew nails like gum. His gaze landed on my hand wrapped around Aaron's arm then flew up to question me wordlessly.

Funny thing was, I didn't have an answer. Not one I could verbalize anyway. Why was I dressed up and going out on a date with Aaron? Because right then, there was nowhere else I'd have rather been and no one else I'd have rather been with.

Aaron extended his hand toward Jared, who still hadn't spoken. "Hi, Jared. How are you?"

"Fine."

Jared's response was terse, and he barely looked at Aaron when he accepted his proffered hand. His angry eyes were set on me. He'd never hurt me or even acted like he would, yet I found myself shrinking behind Aaron's arm.

Sensing my discomfort, Aaron shifted his weight to widen his stance and shield me even more. "Do you have business to conduct with Christa?"

"No," Jared replied to Aaron, then shifted his attention back to me. "I thought I'd drop by and ask if I could take you to dinner."

"Thank you for the thought, but we already have plans tonight." I waited uncomfortably as Jared processed my reply, but Aaron remained cool and collected.

"We'd better get going so we don't miss our reservations. Nice to see you again, Jared." Aaron tightened his arm against my hand and stepped around Jared to punch the elevator button.

Once inside, we turned to face the door, and Jared was still standing there. Not on the elevator with us, but in the hallway watching us.

"Going down?" Aaron asked calmly.

My heart was thumping wildly against my rib cage.

"I'll wait."

"Okay. Have a good night."

The doors closed, and I expected Aaron to question me about Jared's territorial behavior. But he didn't.

"My buddy owns the place I'm taking you to eat tonight. It's a little unorthodox, but I hope you enjoy it."

"He owns it? Is he the chef?"

"No, though he used to be. He said being the owner is more fun since he doesn't have the stress of cooking and managing the entire kitchen. He still walks around and talks to the customers about their experience, but any comments about the food aren't a direct insult to him anymore."

"What kind of restaurant is this?"

He smiled, and I felt my knees go weak and the butterflies flurry in my belly. His lips were perfect—not too thin, not too big. Perfect kisses. Perfect smiles. Perfect...naughty things I shouldn't have been thinking while we were alone in the elevator.

The bell dinged for the lobby, and Aaron stepped out, still holding on to my hand with his muscular arm.

"It's a murder mystery dinner theater."

I looked up at him in surprise. "I'm so excited. I've always wanted to go to one, but I've never taken the time—or had anyone to go with me."

"Well, now you have me, and I'm more than happy to go anywhere with you."

The rest of the night was like a dream. We talked, we laughed, we touched—lightly, but I felt the electricity flow through me every time. He opened doors for me, pulled out my chair. Everything he said and did was perfect, even when it wasn't.

Now he was walking me back to my apartment, and we were nearing my door.

I was in deep trouble.

"So, how was your date with your husband?" Allie waited all of two minutes after we opened the café before asking.

I'd been dying all night to talk about it with someone who understood my lunacy. "Allie, I think I may have made a mistake."

"By filing for a divorce? Yes, you did. I've told you that many times."

"No. By agreeing to go out with him. It's just too much."

"What's too much, exactly? Be more specific. In fact, be very specific."

"We had a great time together. He took me to a murder mystery dinner theater, and it was amazing. They pulled me up to be part of the show and gave me lines to read. Aaron took pictures of me as an actress." I laughed and shook my head at the memory.

"I'm not hearing a problem yet."

"That's the problem. Well, part of it anyway. He's perfect in almost every way."

"Christa, seriously?" She didn't even try to hide the disapproval in her tone.

"Hear me out. Against my better judgment, I took a chance on him before, and look what happened. We ended up married, and then he completely forgot about it. Now I'm pushing for the divorce he started.

"He has already crushed my heart, and I understand he's trying to make up for that now. But if he changes his mind again later, he'll destroy me. I've learned my lesson about taking chances. Only safe bets from now on."

Allie put her palms down on the kitchen island. Her shoulders sagged, and the crestfallen expression on her face was more than objection.

She was disappointed in me.

"You're taking a worse gamble with what you perceive as a sure thing."

I opened my mouth to ask her to explain, but she walked to the other end of the room to work with her back to me. I wasn't psychic, but I could read her like a book, and she was finished talking to me for the time being.

CHAPTER TWENTY-TWO

Unexpected Visitor

Christa

What I didn't get to tell Allie was what happened after the date. When he walked me to my door.

He checked the doorknob again, ensuring it was locked. Then asked if he could check the apartment before he left. He said he wouldn't be able to sleep if he didn't confirm no one was waiting for me inside.

I didn't bother to object again. His protective side was just one of his wonderful characteristics.

"All clear. Now I can sleep, knowing you're safe."

"And I can sleep, knowing you've checked every possible hiding place."

He stood at the door, looking too sexy for *my* own good. "Good night, my love. Get that fine ass of yours over here and lock the door behind me."

I walked across the room and leaned against the edge of the door. "Thank you for dinner and the mystery theater tonight. I had so much fun. I haven't laughed that much in forever."

"It was all my pleasure. I'd love to take you out again soon."

I couldn't help myself. I mean, he was right there. He was so damn sexy. He smelled so damn good. His smile was so inviting, the attraction was too strong, my willpower was too weak.

I stepped into him, wrapped my arms around his waist, and raised up on my tiptoes. My lips found his—and they tasted so good. My tongue swept across the part in his lips, and his mouth opened, inviting me in.

So, I took the chance.

I tried to take control of our embrace. I attempted to seduce him, to convince him to stay with me all night. But Aaron maintained control—in every sense of the word.

Every move I made to increase the fervor, he countered with measured discipline. When I tugged on him to pull him back inside my apartment, he didn't budge. When my hands roamed over the hard ridges of his muscles down to his pants, his big hands softly gripped mine and lovingly held them in place.

"Stay with me tonight." Looking back, I all but begged with the inflection in my voice.

"You have no idea how much I'd love to hold you all night, Christa. But it didn't turn out so well last time, so maybe we need more time learning all about each other."

With that, he kissed me softly again then turned and left. My body hummed with desire, and my frustration level was through the roof. Nothing satisfied the intense desire coursing through my body.

Before I fell asleep, doubt had seized control of my thoughts and convinced me of one thing. When he was in San Diego, he hooked up with one of the beautiful, sexy, successful models—and I didn't compare.

I knew if I tried to explain my irrational insecurities to Allie, she'd call me a pussy. *At least*. Then she'd go on a thirty-minute rant to outline all the ways I'm an idiot.

She'd try to convince me I was wrong about not taking a chance on Aaron. It wasn't that I was afraid she was wrong. I was afraid she'd be right. I was afraid I'd fall even more in love with him than I was right then.

I was afraid he'd leave me.

I was afraid. Period.

A knock on my door drew my attention, and my first thought was of Aaron. I'd already showered and was wearing my comfortable pajamas, but I couldn't help but hope it was him.

When I looked through the peephole, I saw an uncharacteristically disheveled Jared standing on the other side. A confrontation with him over Aaron was the last thing I wanted, but I'd rather get it over with than allow it to linger between us.

"Jared. What are you doing here?"

"Christa, we have to talk." The smell of alcohol hit me from the few words he spoke. He ran his hand through his hair, leaving it even messier than a moment before.

"Okay. Come on in."

He breezed past me and sat on the couch. No sooner did he sit, than he jumped right back up and paced as I walked toward him. When his eyes finally locked on mine, I noticed they were bloodshot and glassy.

"Jared, did you drive over here like this?"

"No, the taxi just dropped me off."

My brows drew downward before I even realized a *"what the fuck"* expression covered my face. "Why would you have a taxi drop you off here so late? And when you're drunk?"

"Christa, don't throw away our chance to be together. We've waited too long for this. I saw you with him last night. You're falling right into his trap again."

"You're not making any sense. He's not trapping me. For what? What do I have he'd possibly want to use me for?"

"He doesn't love you like I do. Dating him will only cause you more heartache. You have to cut the ties with him. We can be happy together."

"Jared, you and I are friends. That's all. At one time, I had a schoolgirl crush on you, but now you're more like a brother to me. I'm sorry, but I just don't feel the same."

"That's only because of him. Spend the night with me. Give me a chance."

"No, Jared. You're not spending the night. Let me call a cab for you."

"Kiss me. Kiss me, and tell me you feel nothing for me at all."

He took a step toward me, and I put both hands up in front of me, palms out. "Stop, Jared. Right now."

My phone pinged with a text at that exact second.

"Is that him?" Jared demanded.

Without turning my back on a drunk Jared, I stepped back a couple of steps and grabbed my phone.

Aaron: ***I miss you so much. I'd love to be there with you right now.***

For the first time in the last six weeks of messages, I sent a reply. ***Please come over. Now. Would feel safer.***

Aaron: ***I'm on my way. What happened?***

Me: ***Drunk friend won't leave.***

Aaron: ***Yes, he fucking will.***

"What did he say?" Jared was essentially standing over me. His eyes dropped to my phone, but I hoped his vision was too blurry to see anything.

"It was a private conversation, Jared. You need to leave now. I can't talk to you when you're drunk." I moved away from him again, refusing to be cornered anywhere in my apartment without an escape route.

"Why are you acting so strange? I'd never hurt you, you know that. Just kiss me, Christa. One little kiss, and I guarantee you'll forget all about what's his name."

"The fuck she will. Get the fuck away from my wife.

She said no, and she told you to leave." Aaron's deep voice resonated through the room, causing Jared's head to snap in his direction.

Relief covered me, because I knew I was safe. Even though I knew Jared would never physically hurt me, his words and demeanor made me feel very uncomfortable. Jared's head swung back around toward me, his expression one of disbelief.

"Don't look at her. I'm warning you one last time. Leave on your own two feet or flat on your back. Whatever you choose is fine with me, because you'll leave either way."

Jared replied with a disgusted snort and turned toward the door. Aaron moved over slightly to give him room to pass, but Jared purposely knocked into Aaron's shoulder on his way out. Except, Aaron didn't budge and Jared was on unsteady legs, so Jared bounced off the doorframe and stumbled before righting his balance.

Aaron smiled from ear to ear before his laughter broke free. "Nice try, prick."

He turned his gaze to me, and his expression turned to concern. "Are you okay now, baby?"

I nodded, but for some stupid reason, the tears started when he called me baby. I'd really missed hearing that. He crossed the room in three giant strides and drew me into his arms.

"Did he hurt you?"

I shook my head, because I couldn't speak.

"Just scared you?"

I nodded against his chest and buried my face tighter against him. He understood what I needed, because his arms curled tighter around me. This was my safe spot; my heart knew that was true. My mind played tricks on me, though.

"I've got you now. No one can hurt you. Or scare you. Or come near you." He rested his cheek against the top of my head, and I felt completely wrapped in love.

When my sniffling subsided, he gradually released his hold and took a half step backward. With his thumb and index finger on my chin, he tilted my face up to look at him. "How do you feel now?"

"Safe and protected," I blurted out before realizing it.

"Good." He leaned down and kissed me on the tip of my nose. When I scrunched up my face in confusion, he chuckled. "I can't kiss your lips and still be the good guy tonight. I know exactly what that motherfucker was thinking of doing to you because I've had the same thoughts. But I'll never give you a reason to look at me like that."

I shook my head lightly from side to side. "Thank you

for rushing over here so fast."

"I'm glad I was already nearby, leaving from a late meeting."

An instant pang of jealousy hit me. "A late meeting with a leggy model?"

"No leggy models tonight. But she is a very sly and demanding lady."

"Sorry I interrupted." Where was this jealousy coming from? I was the one who was pushing for a divorce, after all.

"You didn't, but it wouldn't have mattered who I was in a meeting with anyway. When you need me, I'll be here." He brushed his fingertips along my cheek, and chill bumps flared out across my body. "Since he's gone and you feel safe, I guess I should get going myself. Don't open the door for him again tonight, even if he says he's sober. He may be waiting for me to leave."

I honestly hadn't even thought of that.

"Do you have to get back to your client?"

He shook his head. "No, we're finished for the night." He paused and tilted his head to the side. "Are you afraid to be alone?"

I nodded. It was ridiculous, but I couldn't help it. After everything that had happened, I didn't want to be alone that night.

"I'll stay if you want me to," he offered. My knight in shining armor. Actually, my knight in a dark blue Armani suit, as the case may be.

"I'd feel so much better if you did."

"I'm yours all night, then." His voice dropped an octave. The sexy, silky timbre calmed my nerves and excited my senses. "I'll be right here on the couch."

Did someone just throw a bucket of ice-cold water on me?

Aaron

Christa didn't get much sleep last night. I heard her tossing and turning, punching her pillow, and huffing loudly. That also meant I didn't get much sleep. Knowing she was just a few feet away. In the bed. Most likely naked and waiting for me.

But I couldn't do exactly what I wanted to do. Storm

into her room, throw the covers off her luscious body, and do all kinds of wicked and naughty things to her until the neighbors complained about her screams.

That was exactly what she wanted me to do, of that I had no doubt. But she wanted that before and I gave it to her, then she regretted it. I hadn't forgotten how that hurt, even though I couldn't blame her after the way I'd hurt her.

Because of that fiasco, she had to be sure she wanted me. Not for just one night. Not just for the time being.

Forever.

When streaks of sun shone through the blinds, she got up and went straight to the shower. After I made her breakfast with coffee and left it on the table with the latest letter, I slipped out the door and locked it behind me. Then I sat in the parking lot and kept a watchful eye on her place for a while. When she emerged, slid into her car, and drove away, I made my way back to my condo.

My meeting last night was with Delilah. I changed up the rules again. Christa would still get the daily texts and the occasional letters, but she'd see less of me. Believe me, there was no doubt that would hurt me more than it would hurt her.

I hoped absence did make the heart grow fonder.

My whole world was riding on that cliché.

CHAPTER TWENTY-THREE

Change of Plans

Aaron

Everything that happened last night still weighed heavily on my mind first thing the next morning. I ran through the events one more time as I sat outside Christa's apartment, hanging around to make sure that dickhead didn't show back up for some reason.

My thoughts drifted back to the beginning of the evening, before Christa's encounter with Jared...

"Now that she's had another taste of the man in charge, it's time to take him away from her." Delilah pinned me with her steely-eyed gaze. She knew I didn't want to do this part of the plan.

"Delilah, what if this backfires on me?"

"It won't. If she doesn't miss you when you're gone, there's not much to fight for, Aaron."

I couldn't even consider that possibility, but I knew she was right. Christa had to want us as much as I did for our marriage to stand a chance.

"Okay. What are the rules?"

"You can only see her twice a week. Pick two days, stick to the plan, and make the time with her count."

I left Delilah's and headed home, wracking my brain to figure out how I'd make the time with Christa count. How I'd make her miss me so much that she couldn't stand to be away from me one more day. How our time apart would make her love me even more than she did then, even if she wouldn't admit it.

Since she was on my mind so strongly when I left Delilah's. I sent her a text the moment I stopped at the red light.

Red was all I saw when I read the text back from her saying a drunk friend refused to leave. Only one motherfucker would be so bold.

I thought it took all my self-control when I didn't break him in half at seeing him in her apartment, demanding a kiss. But I was wrong. The images of Christa in her bed alone, naked, and just as frustrated as I was took all my self-control and even some I didn't know how I had.

I watched her leave and decided I was putting the

plan for month two into play starting right then. Leaving before she saw me that morning wasn't originally part of my plan, but the timing couldn't have been better. Safe and secure in my arms the night before. Alone and hopefully missing me the next day.

God knew I missed her more every day.

The love letters and daily texts would continue, but the visits to her café wouldn't.

Not only was I depriving myself of Christa, but I'd also miss out on her tasty treats.

Damn it.

Delilah had better be right about this.

Back in my condo, I took a quick shower and gathered my equipment to spend my Sunday hiking in the park, far away from the city and cell towers.

And temptation.

Spending so much time with Delilah wasn't without benefits. She shared her wealth of knowledge and insight freely. Sometimes too much so, since she didn't hold back what she thought. Ever.

My assigned task for the day was to come up with the next step in my plan to get Christa back in case my absence didn't work in my favor. Delilah kept telling me not to view this in singular acts, but in the grand scheme. Stepping stones that led to the ultimate prize.

After a couple of hours of meandering through along the trails, I found the perfect spot and set up my tripod and camera. Since I'd left Rivers Forte, I'd taken time to pursue my passion—photography. My eclectic mix of urban grunge and natural beauty had caught the attention of a magazine editor I knew. I wasn't doing it for the money. As conceited as it sounded, I had more than enough of that.

My little hobby had become therapeutic. I looked for beauty in everything now, and I found it. Then I captured that beauty in my own way. The pictures reminded me not to be so hard on myself about my past mistakes. I was still a work in progress, and that was okay.

I spent the day leisurely strolling and snapping pictures, always with Christa on my mind, but still at peace alone. Dusk settled in by the time I returned to my car and stowed my equipment bag in the trunk. Once I reached a more populated area, I reluctantly powered on my phone to check for any messages from Christa.

I couldn't help but feel disappointed when I realized she hadn't tried to contact me all day.

Christa

Dear God, it had been a long day, and I didn't want a repeat of it ever.

First, I stepped out of the shower with every intention of having a long, sit-down talk with Aaron. But he was gone. A delicious plate of my favorite breakfast foods and a piping hot cup of coffee were the only evidence he'd even been there that morning.

As much as I wanted to talk to him about everything, I took his absence as a sign it wasn't time to have that conversation.

But no matter what the universe tried to tell me along the way, there was one conversation that couldn't wait one more minute. I quickly scarfed down my food and jetted over to Jared's place.

It was still early, and no doubt he'd be hungover from his binge the night before. But I didn't care. Headache or not. Crouched over the great porcelain throne or not. Apologetic or not. He was in for a giant piece of my mind.

I repeatedly banged on his door with my fist and

even kicked it a few times. When it swung open, I was ready to tear into him with my angry tirade, my finger already pointing in the general vicinity of his face. Instead of seeing Jared's face, I stared into the wide-eyed, bewildered face of a redhead who'd obviously just stumbled out of bed.

Her hair was a bird's nest of tangles. She wore Jared's shirt inside out. Even with my small stature, I must have looked somewhat intimidating because she instinctively took a step backward and glanced around the room nervously.

"Jared!" I screamed and stormed past her. "Get your ass out here."

"Listen, I'm sorry if you're his wife or whatever. He said he wasn't married." His overnight guest pulled at the T-shirt she wore, trying to cover herself more.

"I'm not, and he's not." I kept walking through his condo, yelling his name.

"Fuck, Christa. Can you lower your voice? I think the neighbors five floors up can hear you." Jared finally emerged from his bedroom, trying to tame his hair with his fingers.

"I don't give a fuck if the neighbors at the end of the block hear me." I crossed my arms over my chest and stared him down.

"Umm, excuse me. I'll just throw my clothes on and

leave you two to talk." The third wheel crept past us, and Jared's expression became instantly guilt-ridden.

"Let's go into the living room and talk, Christa." Jared extended one hand toward the area behind me, where I'd just come in. When I turned to walk ahead of him, he put his hand on my lower back.

I jumped to the side and turned toward him at the same time. "Don't. Touch. Me."

He held his hands up in mock surrender, and at least he had the decency to appear duly chastened. When we reached the living room, I sat in the chair, and he took the couch. I didn't want any chance of him sitting close to me after the previous night.

"I had our entire conversation planned out before I came over here, and it started with you explaining yourself for last night. But now, I've changed my mind. There's nothing you can say or do to explain away what you did."

"What did I do?" He appeared genuinely confused and concerned. "What are you talking about?"

"Look, I've already had one man play the amnesia card on me. I'm not falling for that bit from you."

"I'm serious, Christa. I have no idea what you're talking about."

"Maybe because you were way too drunk to be out

alone, much less coming to my apartment at that time of night."

"I went to your apartment last night?" He furrowed his brow and scraped his hands across his face. "Put a Bible in front of me, I will swear on a stack of them I don't remember that at all."

I recounted the entire scene, from the time he knocked on my door to when Aaron slept on my couch because I didn't want to be alone.

His slightly green complexion paled to nearly translucent white by the time I finished. His guest slid out the door at some point during our mostly one-sided conversation. When the door clicked shut, Jared didn't even look up to acknowledge her departure.

When he finally did raise his head, the ice around my heart melted a minuscule amount. Tears dropped from his eyes and ran down his cheeks. He didn't wipe them away, and the pain radiated from his eyes when he met my unaffected gaze.

"I'm so sorry. Normally, I'd say you were crazy for even thinking I'd do anything to hurt you— physically or emotionally. But apparently, I'd be wrong. The last thing I remember was meeting my buddy from school for a few drinks. A couple of beers turned into a lot of shots.

"How can I fix this? How can I fix us? We've been

friends forever. I can't lose you like this."

"Who was the girl here with you? What was her name?"

He wiped his face and stared at the floor for several seconds. "I don't know. I don't even remember where I met her or how we got here."

"Jared, I think you have a drinking problem, and you need to seek help for it. I watched my mother succumb to her addiction demons for years. You're headed down the same road, and you'll find out too late that the bridge is out."

He started to protest, saying he was simply having a good time with friends, then promptly stopped himself. "You're right. I never would've done the things you said I did if I hadn't been so fucked up. Knowing I hurt you like that tears me up inside." He paused and took a few seconds to look deeply into my eyes. "I love you. I hate myself for putting you in this position. This is a selfish question, so I'll apologize now for asking. Will you stand by me while I get help?"

"I will support you and cheer you on from the sidelines."

That was the best I could give him under the circumstances. I'd decided on the way to his condo our lifelong friendship had come to an end. But seeing him so broken tugged on my nostalgic heartstrings. If he genuinely sought help and completed a substance abuse program, we might be able to salvage our friendship.

He showered, and we went to his parents' house together—but in separate vehicles—to break the news to them. He had a loving and supportive family to help him through whatever he faced. I left them to talk about his options as a family. I had enough problems of my own to sort out.

By the time I finished running errands on my only day off, the sun had started to set. Then I was alone in my apartment and staring at my phone.

No call.

No text.

No word from Aaron all day.

Where could he be?

I remembered I never opened the letter he left beside my breakfast. In my hurry to tear Jared a new one, I'd completely neglected to read what Aaron had to say.

My love—

I remember the night I spent making love to your body before we actually had sex. The scent of your arousal. The softness of your skin. The taste of your kiss.

I remember everything about you. You have the biggest heart and give love without fear of rejection. You have the most beautiful soul and the most gorgeous personality. I hope you never change, regardless of what happens with us.

Day Sixty-Seven: I love how you lick your bottom lip when you want me but you're too embarrassed to tell me. It's sexy as fuck.

Forever yours,

Aaron

I sat at the table, reading and rereading the letter, soaking in every word. I felt his hands on me. I heard his breaths in my ear. I craved the way he licked and bit the tender skin on my neck.

My God, I missed my husband so much.

CHAPTER TWENTY-FOUR

Safe and Secure

Christa

The texts had slowed down considerably over the past three weeks, and I'd hardly seen Aaron at all in that time. While he used to send the texts daily and the intermittent letters, I was lucky to receive a couple texts per week. I hadn't received a letter in a while, and wondered if I would. He came into my café the same days every week. I wanted Allie to ask where he'd been, but she hadn't.

She called me out on it one morning.

"Not knowing where he's been is driving you crazy. You need to woman up and ask your husband what he's been filling his days with. Before someone else does." Her words struck a chord in me I'd not fully experienced before. It was a mixture of sheer panic, heartbreak, and jealousy.

"What makes you think I even care?" I threw back at

her.

She stopped wiping the empty table and speared me with her penetrating glare. "You may be able to bullshit some people, but not me, Christa Lanes-Rivers. So why don't you try leveling with me, and with yourself, instead of running from your feelings?

"Yes, Aaron fucked up your relationship. But you've done your fair share to keep it fucked up. Make up your mind if you want him around and quit stringing him along. Because you're not being fair to him, just like Jared wasn't fair to you when he was away at college. And, you're being an immature little bitch about it."

Ouch.

What hurt even worse than her words was knowing I couldn't argue. I hadn't given Aaron the same respect I'd expected from Jared. Only Aaron deserved more because at least he tried to reconcile with me.

Or he *was* trying, at least. Had he given up on my stupid ass?

He should come in that morning, if he continued the same schedule he had over the past few weeks. I arrived extra early that morning to cook, finding myself eager to make something special for his breakfast. Like I did when we first met.

That day seemed so long ago now. Looking back hurt because I realized something that morning, when I burned my arm removing the trays from the oven. As much as the day he presented me with a divorce settlement devastated me, learning about his medical condition must have had a similar impact on him.

Yet, he never gave up on me, no matter how hard I tried to push him away. Regardless of how stubborn and resistant I'd been to his attempts, he'd been true to his word. He'd told and shown me repeatedly he loved me.

I could only hope and pray I hadn't waited too long.

Every time the bell chimed with a new customer, I was disturbingly excited and hopeful I'd see Aaron walking in. Then when I realized he wasn't there yet, my spirits fell a little more. He was usually there by 7:00 a.m., so at 9:45, I was convinced he'd moved on without me.

"Good morning." I knew that smooth, masculine voice. The one that wrapped around me like a warm blanket on a cold night. The one I needed to hear and feel. The one I loved.

I turned to face him, my heart catching in my throat. "Good morning. I'd nearly given up on you." My words held a double meaning, and I wondered if he'd pick up on it.

"You were expecting me?" He sounded surprised—and hopeful. I'd been so wrapped up in my own hurt, I hadn't stopped to consider how badly I'd hurt him over the past several weeks.

"I hoped I'd see you today. You've probably already had breakfast somewhere else. Can I get you some coffee?"

"Actually, I'm starving. I was out all night and didn't get home until just before sunrise this morning. I'd love to stay in bed all day, but sleep will have to wait."

He was out all night? Had he met someone else?

"You said you hoped I'd be here this morning. Is there something we need to talk about?"

After he spoke again, I realized I'd been standing there staring at him with my mouth open. Attractive, Christa. Real slick.

"Yes, if you have time to talk. We can have breakfast together and talk if you'd like."

"Sure. Whatever's easiest for you is fine with me. I'll have whatever you're having." He pulled his wallet out and handed me a $20 bill. "I'll even buy your breakfast for you."

Just like with every other time he tried to pay, I took his money and put it underneath the cash drawer. He had no idea, but it was important to me.

"Pick a table with a view for us. I'll be right back."

That smile. He flashed that smile at me, and my heart ran wild. Before the flush on my cheeks gave my thoughts away, I turned and rushed to the kitchen to grab our plates from the warming drawer.

On my way back, I noticed he picked the table directly in front of the hall that led to the kitchen rather than the one in front of the picture window. "This is your table with a view?"

"Yep. A view of your nice ass walking away from me and your beautiful face walking toward me. No table anywhere provides a better view than this one."

My plan to hide the blush covering my face and neck was pointless, so I smiled and shook my head at him. He stood and took the plates from me. "You love to embarrass me. Let me grab our coffees so I can at least hide my face behind the cup."

His laughter followed me to the carafe, and a sense of loss hit me from nowhere. I hadn't heard that laugh in so long, and I'd missed it so much. With an internal pep talk and a focused effort to avoid appearing sad, I returned to him with two steaming cups. I was überconscious of his eyes tracking my every move.

"What's this? A new menu item? It looks delicious." He was so relaxed, not at all the bundle of nervous energy I was.

"It's not on the menu," I admitted. "I made it just for you."

He looked up from his plate with only a tiny glimmer of hope in his expression, and I realized I caused the doubts he had about us. With my indecisive behavior and mixed signals. "You did?"

Anyone would only try for so long before accepting the inevitable. Most guys would've given up long ago. Was that where he was?

"Yes. Allie said something that really hurt me, because it's true. I've held on to you while I pushed you away. With one breath, I tell you I want you around, and in the next, I tell you to leave me alone. I haven't been fair to you in all this, and I'm so sorry. I can't apologize enough.

"Allie said I need to make up my mind about you, one way or the other. She's absolutely right. For both of our sakes, and sanity, we have to talk about what we honestly want. Without letting our pride or stubbornness get in the way."

"Sounds good. Ladies first. Tell me what you want."

His reply stunned me silent for a second. After my long-winded speech, I expected more of a reaction. Maybe I also hoped he'd be the first to declare his undying love for me, making my confession easier to relay.

Woman up, I heard Allie chide me in my head. She bossed me around even when she wasn't around.

After I took a deep breath to calm my nerves, I decided to just tell him. No holds barred. No fear of rejection. We both deserved complete honesty, especially now that I was finally facing my true feelings.

"I'm scared, Aaron. Underneath this *'I can handle everything because I'm tough'* act, everything scares me. When I first saw you, I was captured by your handsomeness, but even more than that, by your confidence. Then when you were interested in me, I couldn't believe it. You chose *me*, of all people.

"I never took chances. I played everything safe. But with you, that was the first time I listened to that voice that asked, 'what's the worst that can happen?'

"For a while, we were perfect. Everything just seemed to fall into place, like we were meant to be. Then I found out exactly what the worst thing that could happen was, and losing you nearly destroyed me."

I stopped to take a breath and gave him a chance to speak, because I had so much more to say. But he was silent. He was listening intently, but silently.

"I never talk about my family for a reason. I've told you some of it, at a surface level only, though. My mom is an alcoholic and a drug addict, has been my whole life. She was abusive—physically and mentally. When she wasn't berating me, she neglected me.

"My father is equally a winner. He knew what she was doing to me, and he left us anyway. I'm grown, so I'm not blaming my behavior on my parents. But the deep-seated insecurities resurface occasionally. If my own father didn't think I was worth the trouble, why would any other man?"

"And then, when your best friend didn't bother to keep in touch with you, it only exacerbated those insecurities. Right?"

"Right," I whispered, grateful he understood. "I made excuses for my father at first. Then I made excuses for Jared. But I was wrong about both of them. So when I felt betrayed by you, something inside me broke, and I couldn't let myself give you another chance.

"If I played it safe before, I've completely closed myself off to everything now. If I gave you another chance, and you hurt me again, I'd never recover from it."

"So that's it, then? That's your decision? You've decided to live the rest of your life alone and afraid?" His elbows were on the table, his body leaned in toward me, and he was completely attuned to me. As he spoke, he leaned back, withdrawing from me, and crossed his arms over his chest, shutting me out.

"It *was* my decision," I clarified. "At first. Until reality slapped me across the face. By hurting you, I'm hurting myself over and over again. By cutting you out of my life, I'm cutting my heart out of my chest. When you're all I think about and all I want, I'm depriving us both of happiness by holding on to my stupid fears. I'm so sorry for blaming you for everything that's wrong between us. My heart knows what my pride has tried to fight. I love you, Aaron. I always have, and I always will. And..." I swallowed the lump of emotion clogging my throat. "I miss my husband."

His silence concerned me, but his refusal to look at me downright terrified me. Had I wasted too much time sorting through my feelings?

When he finally made eye contact with me, the happiness I hoped to see on his face after my declaration of love was nowhere to be found. His pensive expression was understandable; he was absorbing everything I'd finally admitted. I could even empathize if he wasn't yet fully convinced that I was committed to him and our marriage. But there was a deep sadness I saw and felt in his eyes, and I didn't know how to interpret it.

The little girl inside me was frightened and told me to get up and walk away. Accept it was over right then before I invested more of myself in a one-sided love affair. My automatic shields wanted to go up, protecting me from further heartache and

embarrassment…from   rejection…from
abandonment.

But I fought against her with every beat of my heart. Because my heart was sitting across the table from me, and I was not ready to give up on my happily ever after yet. Rather than assume I knew what he was thinking and cause more trouble, I took Allie's advice to woman up. At least I'd know without a shadow of a doubt where we stood when I heard it from him.

"Talk to me, Aaron. This is a time for brutal honesty. Tell me what's on your mind, regardless of how hard it is to say, or even if you think you'll hurt me."

CHAPTER TWENTY-FIVE

Absence Makes the Heart Grow Fonder

Aaron

Listening to Christa open up about her childhood and how the hurtful events of her past affected her today made me want to protect and shelter her even more than I already did. What her parents put her through, how they treated her, pissed me the fuck off. I wanted to punch that dickhead Jared in the face for treating her like a second-rate friend for so long, when she'd been nothing but good to him.

Then there was me. What I did to her. How I contributed to all these feelings. My actions were the final blow that pushed her over the edge into not believing in anyone anymore. But she didn't know about the schemes I'd concocted to win her back. The games, the intentional mindfucks for someone who already battled enough tormentors in her own mind.

Let's not forget I hadn't told her about my own utter

failures in life. How could my confidence attract her when I faked every second of it?

When I told her everything, would I lose her for good?

With all my heart, I knew I didn't deserve her. But I couldn't delay the inevitable any longer.

"Thank you for sharing your life with me." I meant those words in every conceivable way they could be perceived. "There are a few things I need to tell you before you decide if you want to be married to me or not. I'll abide by whatever you want."

She nodded, her eyes shimmering with unshed tears and her chin quivering slightly. But she held on to her stubborn pride, swallowed hard, and gave me all her attention.

"I'm sure if you've questioned my relationship with Lance once, you've questioned it a hundred times. He's my brother and he loves me, that much I know, even if his actions appear otherwise.

"When I was a sophomore in college, I knew it all. Young, stupid, and more interested in partying than anything else. I'd just turned twenty, so in hindsight, maybe I should've cut myself some slack. But my parents and my brother didn't, so why should I, right? A couple of my fraternity brothers had arranged for an off-campus party to celebrate...something, I don't even know what. It was probably just an excuse to get drunk and have a good time, but I eagerly participated.

"I'd been seeing this girl for a few weeks and had finally convinced her to have sex. She was a virgin, I was her first, she was in love with me. For the record, I did care about her, but I wasn't in love with her. I was a horny twenty-year-old sophomore who was just having a good time.

"So, I go with my buddies to the off-campus party, at someone's place in the city. We're all drunk, doing stupid macho stuff guys razz each other to do or risk being called a pussy for the rest of college. When this girl I didn't know propositioned me in front of my buddies, I didn't say no. How could I? They'd never let me live it down.

"That's what I told myself anyway. Truth was, I didn't want to be tied down when other girls were willingly throwing themselves at me. The girl I'd been seeing, Stephanie, shows up at the party, looking for me, and finds me with the other girl whose name I never even asked. Stephanie runs out of the house screaming and crying, causing a huge scene that embarrassed me in front of all my friends. All the shocked faces were staring at me. The same people who'd encouraged me when the girl came on to me looked at me like I was a piece of trash.

"I chased Stephanie outside, where more people were milling about, and they had a front row seat to our huge fight on the sidewalk. Stephanie turned to leave, she was done with me, but I didn't want to end things on that note. So, I grabbed her arm and tried to get her to just talk to me. The more I tried, the more she fought me.

"She pulled free from my grip and stumbled backward. I thought she'd caught herself for a second, but the heel of her shoe got stuck in a crack. Everything happened in slow motion from that point. I guess to make sure it's forever burned into my memory.

"She hopped on one foot for a second, trying to keep her balance and get her high heel free. Then her foot came out of her shoe, and she stumbled backward again. Only this time, she stepped off the curb and into the path of an oncoming car. She died on the way to the hospital."

I recited the entire memory without looking at Christa. I was still so ashamed of my part in Stephanie's demise, I couldn't bear to think about that night. But Christa deserved to know everything about me before she decided to spend her life with me.

"I'm so sorry that happened and you had to witness that tragedy, Aaron. But I don't understand why you think it's your fault. It was a terrible accident, and my heart breaks for Stephanie and for her family. But it also breaks for you."

"The rumors started almost instantly when word spread she'd died after we fought. Some said they witnessed it, that I pushed her in front of that car. They'd seen me grab her arm, trying to talk to her and calm her down. But with her shrieking at me on a busy sidewalk, that's not at all how they viewed the events.

"An inquiry into her death meant the police had to investigate every aspect of what happened. They don't share details of an ongoing investigation. When you're at a college where it seems everyone knows everyone, absence of information ensures rumors, conjecture, and outright lies become the gospel.

"My parents and my brother stepped in and took control because I just shut down. I couldn't go anywhere without people pointing and whispering about me. By the time the police concluded their investigation and released the security video that captured our entire ordeal, my reputation was already ruined. I transferred to a different college and gave my family complete control of my life. Where I went to school, what I majored in, starting the company with Lance. They became my coping mechanism so I didn't have to make any important decisions."

"That explains why you didn't speak up in Lance's office."

"It's why I didn't question him when I woke up with a wedding ring on and a wife who had moved in with me, but no memory of any of it. He assumed I'd fucked up again, and he went into overprotective big brother mode. It's what he's done for years."

She leaned against the back of the chair, stared at the uneaten food on her plate, and chewed on her bottom lip. That was the first defining moment of where our future went. She was replaying that day in her mind with new eyes. Seeing my failures as a man, as a husband, in a new light.

"There's more. Should I go on?"

She nodded but didn't look at me.

"I quit my job with Rivers Forte and sold my half of the company. When I realized what I'd done—to you, to me, to us—I finally woke up to what my life has been for the last seven years. That's not the life I want, so I've started my own business doing something I love to do.

"Before I tell you the next part, I want to stress something first. Everything I've done or said or written has been one hundred percent true. I love you, Christa, more than anyone or anything in my life. The texts, the letters, coming here, not coming here—it's all been part of a scheme to get you back. First, I was around all the time, hoping you'd change your mind. Then I stayed away, hoping you'd miss me enough to want me again.

"If confessing to all this means I've lost you because you can't trust me again, I'll understand. I'll never be happy without you, but I won't trick you into thinking you want and need me."

She looked up at me with a small, sad smile. "I knew what you were doing, Aaron."

"You did?" I picked my bottom jaw up off the floor.

"Delilah is my friend, too. She told me not to give in too easily. She strongly suggested I make you work for it to teach you a lesson."

"That sneaky, little old lady." I was shell-shocked. She hoodwinked me into thinking she was only giving me relationship advice.

Christa laughed openly now. "She is that, but she has a heart of gold. She thinks the world of you and tells me every chance she gets."

We finally looked at each other—really looked at the other—for the first time in a long time. There was still so much I didn't know about her, and so much she didn't know about me—the odds felt insurmountable. We hadn't even delved into the whole family dynamics and how that situation would affect us in the future.

I wrapped my fingers around her hand and lifted it to my lips, placing a soft kiss on her knuckles. "We both still have a lot of soul-searching to do before we make a life-changing decision. As much as I'd love to take your declaration of love as a rock-solid promise we'll be together, the better course would be for us to take the next few months to get to know each other better. Maybe we can start dating again.

"So, wifey, can I take you out to eat sometime? Maybe to a movie. A romantic walk along the water. A thrilling hike in the park. An adventurous weekend away."

"I'll have to ask my husband if he approves of me dating you." She laced her fingers with mine and squeezed. "But I think he'll be okay with it."

"Are you free tomorrow night? There's something I want to show you."

"I am, and I'm looking forward to it. Will you text me? And tell me what to wear?"

"Text you what to wear?"

"No. I miss getting text messages from you every day, and I need you to tell me what to wear tomorrow night."

I fucking loved her. With a few simple words, she made me feel invincible again.

"Yes, to both requests. Feel free to reply to my texts at any time of the day or night."

"Speaking of, why were you out until sunrise?"

"That's part of what I want to show you. You'll have to wait until our date." I winked then kissed her palm, flattened her hand against my face, and inhaled her scent.

"I'm glad you came in today." She reached across the table and grasped my other hand. That was the first gesture she'd made to touch and connect with me in months.

"So am I. Just so you know, I'm reverting to my previous schedule of daily visits to your establishment. I've had enough of making you miss me."

"You've missed me too much to do it any longer is what you're actually saying."

"Absofuckinglutely."

I tugged slightly on her hands, and she eagerly complied and met me halfway across the table for a real kiss. I took it, but it only ignited my desire for her even more. "I'll still text you later, but there's something I need to tell you while I'm here."

"Should I be afraid? I mean, what other secrets could you possibly have?"

I smiled, broadly and deviously. "I've missed kissing your lips."

Her perplexed look amused me. "You just kissed me. But just so you know, I've missed kissing your lips, too."

"I wasn't talking about the lips on your face."

There was the bright-red blush I wanted to see. She dropped her face into the crook of her arm since I was still holding firmly on to her hands, and her shoulders bounced from laughter. "I should've known there was a catch to that innocent remark."

"Can I call you between text messages?" I asked, still laughing over her red face.

"Absofuckinglutely," she replied, mimicking and surprising me. "In fact, you can use FaceTime instead of a regular call."

I could have been wrong, but I sensed I'd awoken a closet freak who intended to get the best of me.

Challenge accepted.

"Anything you say, my love."

With that settled, I reluctantly left her to prepare for the lunch crowd while I worked on my own new business. But only after I coaxed a not-suitable-for-work kiss out of her.

CHAPTER TWENTY-SIX

Dating My Spouse

Christa

By the time I trudged down the hall to my apartment, I was beyond tired. Allie'd had the day off, and I spent a long time talking to Aaron, so playing catch-up took a toll on me.

When I unlocked the door, the room was filled with lit candles. Music was playing softly from my bedroom. I followed the path made by hundreds of red rose petals to my master bathroom, where more candles, a bubble bath, and a bath pillow awaited. On the ledge around the tub was a bottle of Moscato D'Asti in a wine chiller, and a glass already poured, waiting for me. An iPad sat at the other end of the tub.

My heart swelled with love. I couldn't believe he went to all that trouble for me. The water was still piping hot, so he must've left just before I arrived. Since I wasn't one to pass up a good, long soak in a hot, sudsy bath, I quickly shed my clothes and sank down into the water.

After a couple of minutes, the iPad began ringing, and I couldn't help but giggle. The display screen read "Your Husband."

When it connected, Aaron's handsome face filled the screen. "Hello, gorgeous. How's my wife enjoying her bubble bath and chilled bubbly?"

"It's pure heaven, Aaron. I can't believe you did this for me, and I don't know how you pulled it off. But my aching feet and legs agree we should do this more often."

That time when he smiled, I saw the love in his eyes again, and I felt the response in my heart. We were taking it slow and getting to know each other, but all I could think about was declaring my love for him.

"I've told you before, I plan on spoiling you much more than this. If you'll just let me. You know, you're welcome to come to my place and soak in my tub whenever you want. I'll even turn the water jets on and massage your legs."

"You'll let the water jets massage my legs?"

"No, my love. That pleasure is all mine."

I sat up and moved closer to the screen. The bubbles slid down my skin, and his gaze followed until the clump of suds moved past my bare breasts.

"The pleasure is all yours?" I challenged.

"Allow me to rephrase my answer. It's my pleasure to massage your legs, but you can have all the pleasure you want."

I crossed my arms nonchalantly under my wet breasts, purposely pushing them up. "You're such a good husband. Always thinking of your wife. It's too bad you're not here for me to take you up on that offer right now."

His sexy growl came through the speakers and echoed off the walls, sending a lightning bolt straight between my legs.

"You don't play fair, Christa."

"All is fair in love and war, my hubby." I took a sip of the chilled wine, closed my eyes, and moaned appreciatively as I swallowed it. "That is so good."

"Fucking hell. I knew this would backfire on me."

"Don't try to play games with me, love." He was all but panting into the camera, watching me with rapt attention. "Do you have a bubble bath planned for our date tomorrow night?"

"I do now."

The rest of our video chat was filled with playful banter, sexy innuendo, and fun flirting. We couldn't go back to square one like strangers, and I wouldn't want to try. But we could get back what we had and then make it even better.

I firmly believed we could do it.

Maybe I was becoming an optimist.

While I was positive Aaron would've been game, I didn't take our flirting to voyeurism for a specific reason I hadn't shared with him yet—I was packing an overnight bag to stay at his condo the following night.

The one night I stayed there before wasn't long enough to soak in his jetted tub, so I was counting on an extra-long bath, and I wouldn't be alone.

Just as I was getting ready for bed, my phone sounded with an incoming text. Giddy with excitement, I rushed to see what he sent, then almost dropped it from surprise.

The man was trying to kill me.

He sent me a dick pic with the message, "Someone is thinking about you."

How the hell was I supposed to fall asleep after seeing that? If I couldn't sleep, he wouldn't get to sleep either. So I slipped out of my pajamas, crawled into bed, and recorded a short video of my fingers sliding into my pussy. Then I returned the favor by sending it to him with the message, "Someone is thinking about you, too. I'll give you one guess who."

I started to doubt myself, wondering if I'd sent it to the wrong person when I didn't receive a reply for several minutes. Relief and amusement washed over me when I got his reply.

Aaron: ***"Fucking hell. I'm going to take a cold shower. Again."***

Me: ***"I miss you, too."***

Aaron: ***"I love you, baby."***

Me: ***"I love you, too. Good night."***

Aaron: ***"Sweet dreams. You'll be in mine. And they'll be wet."***

When I arrived at the shop, Allie was already in the kitchen pulling the first batch of pastries out of the oven. While whistling.

I stopped in the kitchen doorway and stared at her in disbelief. Allie was actually cheerful in the morning, and the sun wasn't even up yet.

"All right, spill it."

She jumped and yelped while whirling around, ready

to fight the intruder. "You're a fucking ninja, Christa. Warn somebody when you steal up behind them before dawn."

"I didn't steal up behind you. I unlocked the door, came in to the chimes ringing, locked the door again, and walked back here. Your whistling was too loud, I guess."

"Whatever."

That was a telltale sign if I'd ever seen one. When Allie gave up a chance at retaliation, it was because she was hiding something.

"Who is he?"

"Who is who?"

"The man who has you singing and carrying on like a canary."

"I'm doing no such thing. So, how'd it go with you and Aaron yesterday? Did you two kiss and make up?"

"How did you know?" Then it hit me. "You let him into my apartment."

"Maybe. Somebody had to. You need to get laid so you'll chill the fuck out."

"Were you secretly born a guy?" I asked jokingly as I tied my apron behind my waist.

"Very funny. Just because my lady balls are bigger than most men's testicles proves nothing. Now answer me."

"We kissed. We decided to take it slow and get to know each other before making any decisions. We had a long talk and realized there's a lot we haven't shared."

She stared at me for several seconds, her mouth agape and a disgusted scowl on her face. "You two need to borrow my lady balls and stop pussyfooting around. Jump in headfirst without checking the water beforehand. You think it'll hurt any less if you lose each other after taking it slow? No, you'll have more regrets and more 'what-if' questions."

"Interesting theory."

"Theory, my ass. It's called life, sweetheart. And you need to start living yours before it passes you by."

Three hours later, everything was ready, and we had a few minutes to catch our breath before the Saturday morning crowd arrived. The first person to walk through the door was Aaron, and my heart quickened at the sight of him.

"Are you here to borrow my balls?" Allie asked then took a sip of coffee, as if she just asked about the weather.

"Umm..." Aaron began to answer then paused.

"What?"

"Ignore her. She was out in the forest last night, sacrificing innocent animals, so she's in an especially good mood today." Aaron's gaze shifted between Allie and me, clearly confused after stepping into this crazy conversation. "Are you ready for coffee and breakfast?"

"I am so ready." He looked relieved at the abrupt change in subject. "I'm also ready for our date tonight. Can we start early?"

"Sure. What time did you have in mind?"

He looked at his watch. "How about 7:10 a.m.?"

I glanced at the clock. "You're giving me a whole two minutes to get ready? That's so generous of you." Aaron leaned down and kissed me. Thoroughly. Deeply. Panty-meltingly.

"You two are sick and sweet," Allie grumbled. "She can leave at two o'clock today, and I'll cover the store alone until closing."

"Allie, you're the best. After Christa." Aaron lifted his cup. "To Allie, for saving the day."

"Yeah, yeah. My standing threat is still valid."

"No need to worry. I'll take good care of her." Aaron turned to me and waggled his eyebrows.

We had breakfast together, with me jumping up between bites to help fill the many to-go orders. "Okay, where were we?"

"I was just about to ask how your catering plans are shaping up. Any progress on that front?"

"You know, that was originally my goal, but I've changed my mind. I really enjoy what I'm doing now. I love baking new treats, trying new recipes, and having the final say in how creative I want to be. I'm considering expanding this business rather than morphing it into something else entirely."

"I hope that expansion includes hiring more help so you and Allie can take off at the same time in the future."

"That is priority number one on my list."

"Glad to hear that. Okay, I'm off to work now."

"You work on Saturdays?" I cut my eyes sideways at him.

"I do now. I'll pick you up at your apartment at three. Is that enough time?" He stood and pulled me into his arms, effectively changing the subject.

"Plenty. I can hardly wait." I rose on my tiptoes to kiss him goodbye.

His fingers weaved through my hair, gripped it at my scalp, and tilted my head to the side. Then he deepened the kiss, his tongue sliding along mine. He was making a promise of more to come and curling my toes with anticipation.

I didn't want to spoil his big plans for us tonight, but I hoped he wasn't taking me to a movie. We'd end up calling Allie to bail us out of jail.

By 1:59, I'd finished everything I could possibly do to help Allie with closing time chores. I rushed home to shower and change clothes. Aaron sent a text saying to wear something "nice and sexy, with fuck-me-hard-all-night-long heels." I was glad we were on the same page with that, at least.

When he arrived, my overnight bag was packed, my expected heels were strapped securely on my feet, and I was more than ready to spend the rest of the day and night with him.

I opened the door for him, and he looked down at my small bag. He fought the cocky grin that threatened to break free.

"Are you planning to spend the night with me?"

"Yes, I am." My voice was steady and unwavering, daring him to deny me.

"Mrs. Rivers, I'm appalled at you. You must think I put out on the first date."

"You do, and you will again tonight."

He threw his head back, roaring with laughter, and swept me up in his arms. "For you—anything you want. I'm your genie, and you have an unlimited number of wishes."

"Careful. You'll spoil me, showering me with so much love like this. I'll start to expect the same special treatment every day."

"Is that your first official wish?"

With all sincerity, I answered him. "It's the only wish that matters to me."

"Your wish is granted. From this moment until I die, I will spoil you with more love every day."

He took my overnight bag from my hand and checked the weight in his. "You didn't pack much. Is that because you expect to be naked most of the time?"

I actually did, but that wasn't why I didn't pack more. "I just put enough for one night in there. I'll have to be at work early Monday morning, and I didn't want to be that presumptuous."

"How about you add a few more outfits to this bag, and let's play it by ear? I can take you to the café early whenever you need. It's not like I won't be there eventually anyway."

"If you're sure?"

"I'm positive. You can bring your whole closet, and it wouldn't bother me one bit."

"A few outfits for now will do." I was secretly thrilled he said that, but I was trying not to hit the throttle too hard.

After I rummaged through my clothes and threw a few in to cover anything we may do the next day, we climbed into his car and came to a stop in front of the Museum of Modern Art.

"I didn't know you were an art fan. I don't think they normally have valets out here. It looks like they're having a gallery showing tonight."

"They are, but you get to see it first."

"How exciting! How did you arrange that?"

"I've told you before—it's good to have friends in high places."

The valet took Aaron's keys, and we walked into the museum hand in hand. Once we reached the third floor, Aaron gestured for me to enter the exhibit area first.

The first photograph we saw was amazing. The detail the photographer caught in the landscape made me feel like I was there with him. Aaron asked my thoughts of each one and listened to my replies, but he didn't add his own commentary.

Every picture was better than the last, and my excitement of discovering the next one in the series was hard to contain. When we turned the corner to find the centerpiece of the exhibit, I couldn't breathe.

I couldn't move. I was rooted to the floor in front of the enormous photograph.

Of our field in the woods.

Of our trail.

With our picnic basket and blanket in the exact spot where we spent the day.

But this photograph was taken at night, under a full moon.

"This is where I was when I didn't get home until dawn. The centerpiece of the exhibit had to be perfect, and I worked night and day to make it exactly what I needed. I was afraid it wouldn't make it in time for opening night with the rest of the exhibit. But now I'm convinced you're my lucky charm. It was after our talk that morning when I learned the printer could meet my specifications on such short notice."

I looked closer at the name of the photograph.

Completely Captivated.

"You took all these?" I whispered, afraid to break the

spell of perfection around me.

"Yes, this is my new job. My passion is photography. I love being behind the lens and capturing the beauty in normally mundane subjects."

"No wonder I love this entire exhibit so much. You're a part of every subject in here. I can tell they hold significance to you in the way you present them."

"That's because every single picture in here was taken with you in mind. Something that reminded me of you. Something I thought you would like. Something I wanted to show you, or somewhere I wanted to take you."

"What did you name the entire exhibit?"

"Love of a Lifetime."

CHAPTER TWENTY-SEVEN

Meet the Family

Aaron

I watched her with purpose and intention—to read her body language for what she wasn't verbalizing. She was shocked, there was no doubt about that, but she was having a hard time finding the words to convey what she was thinking without giving too much away.

"Say whatever's on your mind. I want to hear it. Don't keep your thoughts from me."

"I'm thinking...I'm blown away. I didn't even know you enjoyed photography, much less that you're such a natural at it."

"I took a few classes in college, but I learned a lot from the photographers I've worked with over the years. All those model photo shoots I had to endure paid off."

She looked back at the picture of our special place and stared at it for several more seconds. I could almost see the entire scene replaying through her eyes as she relived it.

"I remember." My voice was low, meant only for her ears.

Her eyes rose to meet mine. "I remember that day too."

"I don't mean that day in our field. I remember, Christa. I remember everything."

I brushed her long blond hair behind her ear, grazing her cheek with the pad of my thumb. "We were in the suite, and you wanted to surprise me. You locked the bathroom door so I couldn't peek in and ruin my special gift, and we laughed through the door about you barring yourself in the bathroom to get away from me on our wedding night.

"While I waited for you, I turned the music on, letting it play softly in the background. Then I lit a few candles and waited on the bed until you unlocked the door."

Her eyes grew bigger with every word before sparkling with tears. Her lips parted, and she inhaled sharply but didn't release her held breath right away.

"When you opened that door, all I could think about was devouring every inch of you. Slowly. All night long. Over and over again. You were in all white—your lacy lingerie, white fuck-me-now heels, and your wedding veil. But your lips were a shade of deep red wine, and I had an immediate visual of them wrapped around my cock."

That admission had one side of her mouth quirking up, though she tried to hide her smile. I shrugged one shoulder. It was true. What could I say?

"I don't even remember getting off the bed, but that's not because of my head injury. I think I instantaneously transported across the room to your side. But you were in my arms then, and that's all that mattered. You were mine.

"I led you to the bed and told you I wanted our first time to be face-to-face. But after that, I was up for whatever adventurous position you wanted to try."

She looked up at the ceiling, fluttered her eyelashes, and ran her finger under her eyes to catch the tears before they had a chance to fall.

"Your next words nearly made me drop to my knees. You were mortified to confess you were a virgin, thought I'd want you less. You were afraid you wouldn't satisfy me in bed. What you didn't know then, and what you don't realize now, is there's nothing you could say or do that would ever make me want you less. In fact, I was fairly certain I'd spontaneously combust from how badly I burned for you.

"The first time we made love was the best experience of my life. Until the second time, then the third, and... You get the point. It's you, Christa. Only you fulfill every need I have, every desire of my heart. If I can't have you, I won't have anyone."

"Do you mean that, Aaron?" Her question was sincere, but I had a feeling her words held a deeper meaning.

"On my life, Christa. There hasn't been anyone else in my life or in my bed since the day I met you. I'll never leave you. I'll never stop loving you."

She was no longer holding her breath. Her chest heaved heavily as uncontrollable emotions rolled through her. I sensed her inner turmoil, and I recognized the second she stopped fighting it.

She stepped forward, grabbed the lapels of my jacket, and molded her body to mine. I wasn't stupid—I wasn't about to question her rash decision. Every hurdle we crossed only brought her closer to stopping the divorce altogether.

Even in her heels, she wasn't tall enough to claim my mouth. But I was more than willing to oblige her. Once our lips met, everything around us faded to black, and only she and I existed in the world.

Her taste. Her scent. How she felt. The sounds she made. When she let go and gave me complete control of her pleasure. She was still mine. She'd always be mine. She just needed time to realize it.

"Aaron," she whispered between kisses. "Where?"

I slid my hand around hers and pulled her with me, checking doors for an empty office we could put to good use. The third door we came to was unlocked and appeared to be unused from the neatness of the desk. After I ushered her inside, I glanced up and down the hall before slipping in and locking the door behind me.

She moved over to the desk and looked over her shoulder with a devilish grin. She shimmied her dress up her legs and revealed her bare ass.

"You're not wearing any panties. Fuck me."

"Funny, those words were just on the tip of my tongue." She bent at the waist, resting her forearms on the desk, and widened her stance. "Are you going to stand there staring at my fine ass, or are you going to come take care of your wife?"

My dick was harder than a diamond right then. "I'm fucking taking care of my wife. Right now." One step later and I'd reached her. My pants and boxer briefs were shed in the blink of an eye. Positioned at her wet entrance, my hips surged forward to the hilt. My growl and her moan sounded simultaneously. My fingers dug into her hips, an unintentional punishment that felt too good to release. I pulled back, and each forward push moved the desk a little more. Our combined grunts and groans filled the room, spurring us on until the pressure built to uncontrollable levels. She cried out, my name falling from her fuckable lips, as her muscles tightened around me, milking every last drop.

"Fuck, Christa. That was so fucking hot."

"Aaron, I think you're becoming a bad influence on me."

"If this is my bad influence, I approve and will up the ante."

Thankfully, we'd found an office with its own bathroom, and the probability it belonged to a museum executive hit me. We quickly cleaned up and straightened our clothes together, but I couldn't leave without one last kiss. We managed to sneak out of the office and back to the gallery floor.

The official kickoff wasn't for another couple of hours, but I wanted this time alone with my wife first. Having her eyes be the first to see the photographs was important to me, because I wanted her to be first in everything in my life. After she knew they were all mine, she wanted to walk back through the exhibit and view them with a new understanding.

She spent time staring at each photo, absorbing the meaning behind them, as she worked her way through the room. By the time she made it back around, guests for the opening night gala began to arrive. She was relaxed and happy, at ease by my side as I introduced her to everyone as my wife.

Then Lance stepped onto the floor, and I felt her stiffen beside me. I stopped speaking midsentence and looked down at her.

"Christa, is something the matter?"

She shot daggers at him with her eyes. *If looks could kill*, I thought to myself.

"Lance, hold my purse for a minute," a familiar voice demanded. I watched in astonishment as he complied. Willingly.

"Is that—"

"No. It's not possible." Christa shook her head but kept her eyes glued to the scene unfolding directly in front of us.

Allie held on to Lance's arm for balance while she adjusted the strap on her shoe. Then she took her clutch from him and wrapped her hand around the bend of his arm when they started walking toward us.

Lance's eyes were glued to Allie, while Christa's could've become flamethrowers at any second. My brother was so beguiled by the beauty on his arm, he had no idea of the wrath he was walking straight into.

Until it was too late.

He turned his head just in time to meet my gaze, happiness written all over his face. Then his expression fell when he saw Christa's icy glare.

"Lance. Allie. I'm...stunned...to see you two together." My shock was impossible to hide, so I chose not to try.

"Lance and I have been in negotiations. He's finally beginning to see the error of his ways and the benefits of mine." Allie's smile resembled a fiendish cat that had just pounced on its prey. "Lance, don't you have something to say to my best friend?"

"Yes, I do. Christa, I've talked to Aaron and Allie, but I haven't apologized to you. My primary concern was for Aaron and his safety, but that's no excuse for how I treated you. I hope you can accept my sincere apology."

"I appreciate how protective you've been over Aaron." Her words may have been gracious, but her straight spine and stiff jaw said otherwise.

Christa

"Will you two excuse us for a moment? I need to speak with my best friend alone." Allie released Lance and took my arm instead, leading me away from our dates and out of earshot.

"Want to tell me what the hell you're doing with him? Of all the men you could've picked in the world, you had to choose the biggest dickhead you could find?" I nearly raised my finger to point at the demon spawn beside Aaron, but I caught myself just in time.

Allie's smirk almost made me laugh. Almost. "Do I need a reason other than that?"

"You are infuriating. You make me mad and laugh at the same time. Now, stop it. You know what I meant. He's the worst man in the world."

"He's not, once you get to know him. He's been thoroughly chastised and punished for what he did to you. He's genuinely sorry, and he'll never do anything like that again. Especially not while I'm around. Give him a chance—for me?"

She knew I couldn't resist her when she asked nicely.

"I'll try. No promises, though."

She kissed me on the cheek and smiled so much I was sure her cheeks must hurt. "That means yes in Christa-speak."

"I'm obviously way too predictable," I grumbled as we walked back toward the guys. "Maybe I should shake things up, cause a scene or something."

"Not tonight. May be best to save that for a more private moment with Aaron." Allie swung her arm around my shoulders and squeezed.

"I'm only refraining because this is the opening night of Aaron's exhibit, and I don't want to ruin it for him."

A group of people had gathered around Aaron, asking questions about his work. From a few feet away, I watched as he animatedly explained each picture. His enthusiasm spread to the people around him, and murmurs of buying his work soon followed. Every time he explained the photograph's focal point, he sought me out. Our eyes met, forming an invisible connection that kept us tethered to the ground while our hearts soared in the clouds. He was telling and showing me how I'd always been his focal point.

With the growing crowd around him, I moved around the room to give him space to mingle. The beacon drawing me back in was the centerpiece, our field of wildflowers hidden in the forest. Our blanket and our picnic basket in the exact spot as when we enjoyed that day away from the hustle and bustle of life.

"This picture is simply gorgeous, isn't it?"

I turned to reply to the woman who'd joined me.

"Yes, it is. I love them all, but this one is my favorite."

"I may be slightly biased since I'm the artist's mother, but I love them all too. They're pure genius."

"You're Aaron's mother?" Other than repeating back what she'd just said to me, I was speechless. How did I even begin to introduce myself?

"Yes, I am. My name is Leigh Anne. How do you know him?"

"Mom, this is Christa, his wife," Lance said as he and Allie stepped up behind me. "I'm sorry I couldn't get over here in time to make proper introductions."

"You are our Christa?" A beaming smile covered her face, and she thrust her drink into Lance's hand before wrapping her arms around me. "Sweetheart, it's so good to finally meet you. I've heard so much about you, and I hoped you'd be here."

She didn't give me any choice but to hug her in return, because she obviously was not releasing me soon. "The exhibit was all a surprise to me, so I had no idea any of this was happening. It's great to meet you, too."

I know I sounded like an idiot, but I was more than a little flabbergasted.

She leaned back, and her hands rested on my biceps, still holding on to me. "You're even more beautiful than I've heard. It's not like Lance to describe two women as the most beautiful women he's ever seen, both in the same week. But that's exactly what he said when he told me about you and Allie."

Lance's face had turned multiple shades of red when I glanced over my shoulder at him. Leigh Anne kissed me on both cheeks then grabbed my hand to pull me along with her. "Honey, you'll never guess who I just met." We stopped at a handsome man, but there was no doubt as to who he was. Lance and Aaron were cloned replicas of him. "Brian, this is your daughter-in-law."

His surprised expression quickly turned endearing when he smiled at me. I could see where Aaron got the sparkle in his eye when he looked at me. Brian had the same sparkle when he looked at Leigh Anne.

"Christa, I can't believe we didn't know you'd be here, but I'm so glad to finally meet you. With everything Aaron told us about you, I feel like I've known you for a long time."

"It's very nice to meet you, Mr. Rivers."

"You can call me Dad. You're one of my kids now. We haven't even officially welcomed you into the family yet, but we'll rectify that very soon."

I almost choked, not only because I'd wanted someone to step in and be my father for so long, but because there was no hint of hesitation in his voice. He was welcoming me into his family, seemingly treating me as one of his own, and there were no strings attached.

Were other families always this open and affectionate?

"Christa?" a voice I would have recognized anywhere called out from behind me, and I turned to face her.

"Jen! I haven't seen you in forever. What are you doing here?"

"Apparently, this exhibit is *the* place to be tonight." She looked over at the centerpiece then back at me. "These photos have a lot of feeling in them, some very deep meaning behind them."

"They do," I replied, surprised at her keen eye for art. "How's Jared doing?"

"He's doing really well. His employer has been very supportive since he sought help before he lost control."

I nodded, keeping that night in my apartment to myself. He'd tell them the details when he was ready. "I'm glad to hear that. I hope everything works out for him."

"Speaking of working out, are you and Aaron back together?"

"They sure are," Leigh Anne replied before I could and introduced herself to Jen. "I'm already planning family vacations with my favorite daughter-in-law. I've been in a family full of testosterone for so long, I'm just grateful to finally have another woman in the mix."

"Congratulations, Christa. I'm happy if you are."

I felt the weight of Aaron's stare on my skin, so I searched the room until I found him. Our connection was strong, but I was afraid we were moving too fast. I'd just met his parents, and his mom was planning family vacations. His brother had apologized, but I wasn't quite over my anger at him. Aaron and I seemed to be both moving at light speed and standing still.

When I looked at him, when I was with him, I couldn't imagine being anywhere else.

When we were apart, I struggled with the whole forgive and forget concept.

Something had to give.

CHAPTER TWENTY-EIGHT

Always on My Mind

Christa

Spending the weekend with Aaron was even better than I'd anticipated. After his exhibit opening, we went back to his condo. I thought the painful memories would hit me when I walked in, but I was surprised I felt at home there. It was late when we arrived, and Aaron was exhausted from being in the spotlight all night, but that didn't stop him from revering every inch of my body until just before sunrise. Then we collapsed, spent and sated from feasting on each other.

I awoke Sunday morning to find Aaron resuming his focus from just a few hours before, though I had no objections. As promised, we soaked in his jetted tub together, spending every moment talking—when we weren't making love. We learned more about each other during those hours alone than in the rest of the time we'd been together combined. I wouldn't trade any of the time we spent together. We *needed* it.

Also as promised, Aaron brought me to work that morning, helped me get everything arranged to start cooking for the day, then left to finish his work in progress. I had been a bundle of nervous energy since he walked out the door, but I didn't know why. With my earbuds in and the music blaring, I baked, cleaned, and prepared food like a madwoman. By the time I'd run out of chores to accomplish, I already had the lunch sandwiches made, the soups ready to start, the kitchen completely cleaned, and not much left for Allie to do when she came in later today.

The long line of early morning customers occupied my time and my mind, keeping my thoughts from wandering too far off target. But the ominous foreshadowing I'd felt growing around me all morning never fully went away. The knot in the pit of my stomach warned me to beware.

But beware of what?

Allie and I were cleaning out the display case at the end of the day when the chimes alerted us of another customer. When I stood to offer a greeting, my voice was frozen in my throat.

"Hi, Christa." The door closed behind him as he stood rooted in place.

Allie grabbed my hand, her gaze cutting between

him and me. "Christa, are you okay? Who is he?"

"I'm her father," he replied, his eyes dropping to the floor. At least he had the decency to look ashamed of even referring to himself that way.

"What?" Allie demanded and stepped between us, as if she was my human shield.

"I know I gave up my rights to be your father years ago, but we really need to talk. Please, Christa. It's important."

"Make it quick. I have plans tonight." I took a seat and gestured for him to do the same. He sat across from me and fidgeted with the centerpiece on the table for a few seconds before he spoke.

"How long has it been since you talked to your mother?"

That wasn't how I thought he'd start the conversation, but I assumed he was leading up to something. "She called a few weeks ago, looking for money. The only time I hear from her is when she wants something. Why?"

"The sheriff's deputy showed up at my place today. Christa, there's no easy way to say this. She was found dead in her apartment. It'll be several weeks before the official toxicology report is back, but for now, it appears to be an overdose. I'm so sorry to have to tell you, to be the one who brings you the bad news." He stopped and looked at me, thinking I'd fall apart and he'd be there to put me back together. The hero. The ultimate father figure.

But I felt nothing.

The day I turned to him for any kind of comfort would be the day hell froze over.

He was still waiting for a reaction from me. "Had you stuck around, you'd understand why this news doesn't surprise me. Is that all you wanted to tell me?"

"Umm... Yes, I guess," he stammered. "Here's the key to her apartment. I'll let you go through her things for anything you want to keep. Whatever you leave behind, I'll make sure it's taken care of."

"Fine. You've done your duty and conveyed the news. Now, if you don't mind, we're trying to close the shop for the night." I stood and moved toward the door, ready to lock it once he was out.

"Can I come back soon? Just to see you, so we can talk?" He walked toward me, his eyes pleading for me to say yes.

But I couldn't.

"I don't think that's a good idea. Whatever you had to say to me should've been said years ago."

"I'm sorry," he mumbled then turned and walked

out, his shoulders drooping and his head hanging low.

I couldn't help but watch him walk away, down the sidewalk to his car. Part of me wanted to follow him, to see if he had a new family who'd had all his attention for the years he'd been out of my life. The years I spent under my mother's abusive thumb. Instead, I turned away from the door to finish working as soon as humanly possible, only to be stopped by Allie's intense stare.

"What?"

"Nothing. Oh, wait, there was something. What was it again? Now I remember. Your father just walked in here and said your mother died!" Her bellow echoed off the walls of this small café, making me cringe.

"I know he did, Allie."

"Then he said he wants to see you again."

"Again, I know, Allie. Let's just finish up so we can get out of here."

"I understand you need time to process this. If you need me for anything, all you have to do is call me, and I'll be there. If you need to talk, cry. Even if you need an alibi or someone with a good shovel. I'm your girl."

"You're always my girl." I threw my arms around her

neck and hugged her like the sister I never had. "You always know exactly what to say. But I need some time alone with this one. I'm not sure what I'm supposed to feel, or even how I truly feel."

She nodded in understanding then we finished the final chores and left the shop, the weight crushing my chest becoming more unbearable with every step. I just needed to make it home and deal with my issues alone. When I walked into my apartment, I realized I didn't even remember the drive home. Then an overwhelming feeling of being alone hit me, and my apartment no longer felt like home.

Aaron wasn't there.

On cue, my phone began ringing, his assigned ringtone filling the dead air in my living room. "Hello?" I found the phone and answered before it rolled to voice mail, thankful to hear from him in the very moment I needed him.

"What's wrong, Christa?"

"How do you know something's wrong?"

"Because I know you better than you think, sweetheart. Because I know that tone in your voice, and I can hear it in your one-word answer. Do you want me to be there with you?"

"More than anything, Aaron."

There was a knock on my door, and I couldn't stop

the smile in spite of the growing ache in my chest. I took a second to look through the peephole first, and then I jerked it open as soon as I saw his handsome face on the other side. That smug smile, the one that melted my heart and my panties, covered his face, and I collapsed into his arms. He walked me backward into my apartment while my face was still buried in his chest, inhaling the spicy scent of his cologne that both excited and calmed me.

"Talk to me," he murmured into my ear. "Tell me what's wrong."

Over the next several minutes, I gave him a play-by-play of my father showing up out of the blue, my mother's death, my lack of reaction, and my near breakdown once I reached my apartment. Through it all, his muscular arms held me, his strength carried me, and his love sustained me.

He didn't leave me to bear the burden alone.

"I'll go with you to her apartment. You shouldn't do it alone."

I raised my face to look at him, and my heart swelled with love for him. "You're spoiling me."

"Every chance I get."

He ordered a pizza while running a hot bath for me, and this time he used scented bath oils instead of bubbles. I sank down into the steaming water, and all my anxiety melted away. The lavender and vanilla scent was soothing and calmed my frayed nerves. Or maybe it was the man kneeling beside my tub. The one who was bathing me in his love every bit as much as with the water. Any other time, the way he touched me would be sensual, erotic, electrifying. But I was so attuned to his moods, I knew sex was the furthest thing from his mind. His sole focus was on me and what I needed to get through that terrible time.

When the pizza arrived, he left me long enough to grab the pie and pay the delivery guy. Then he was back at my side with an outstretched bath towel, waiting for me to step into his loving embrace. He was breaking down every wall I'd so carefully constructed around my heart and my life, with one act of love at a time.

Once I was dried off and my short robe was tied on, he led me to the kitchen and took care of the entire meal. Then he carried me to my bed and held me all night. When the morning sun streamed through the blinds, I awoke in the same position I fell asleep—my head resting on his shoulder, his arm wrapped around me protectively, and his hand holding mine.

"Thank you," I whispered, not expecting a reply.

"I love you. You never have to thank me for loving you," he whispered back, and I squeezed him closer to me.

"Can we go get this over with now? I don't want to spend my entire day off dreading it."

"Absolutely. We can get up and go right now if you want to. I'm yours all day."

"Only for today?"

"Yes, only today. All day, for every today, till death do us part."

We were both quiet while we dressed. I suspected Aaron was giving me a little space to get my head in the right place before going back to my former home. He took my hand as we left my apartment and headed toward his car. I gave him the address, and we were on our way, while I chewed my fingernails and lip the entire drive.

When we pulled up to the run-down one-story building, my stomach clenched, and I was glad I decided against having breakfast first. I thought I'd lose it right about then. Aaron squeezed my hand in support, then lifted it to his mouth and placed soft kisses along my knuckles.

"I'm here for you, whatever you need. I can go in and do this for you if you want me to. You don't even have to step foot inside. We can leave. I'll throw the car in reverse, and we can forget this whole plan. Or, we can walk in there together, face this together, and put it behind us—together."

"I love you for offering to take me away, but this is something I need to do. There's no way I'm doing it without you, though. So, together it is."

"Every step of the way."

Inside the dilapidated apartment, memories I'd pushed aside assaulted me from every direction, flying at me at the speed of light. Compartmentalize. Dodge. Deflect. One step at a time. That was how I'd make it through that ordeal, but only with him at my side. I walked through the few sparsely furnished rooms, looking at what was left of my mother's entire life. Aaron stayed one step behind me, sharing his strength with me as I went. A deep sense of regret and loss hit me when I realized something staggering.

There wasn't one thing there I wanted to keep as a reminder. Nothing held sentimental value to me. Not one personal item was attached to a pleasant memory.

A small stack of papers on the kitchen table caught my eye on my way out, and I stopped to look through them. Holding those papers in my hand and reading the words on the pages hit me nearly as hard as receiving the divorce papers from Aaron did. I collapsed into the chair. My hands shook uncontrollably, and my breath seized in my chest.

"What is it, Christa? What does it say?"

"She was filling out the paperwork to enter a rehab facility. The date on here is when she called me, asking for money. I turned her down flat. I didn't even ask her what she wanted the money for. Oh, Aaron, she wanted help to clean up her life, and I dismissed her. This is all my fault. She overdosed because of me."

"It's not your fault. She made her own choices, and she chose to use drugs your entire life. Hell, probably *her* entire life. That's not on you."

"But if I'd just helped her when she asked..."

"You had no way of knowing she wanted the money for treatment. She may have wanted it for something else entirely. You can't blame yourself when her entire life has been the same problems repeated."

The paperwork for a detox facility was the only memento I wanted from my dead mother. I asked Aaron to take me away from that place, and I left the key on the table before locking the door and closing it behind me. Then there was no way back inside. The door was forever shut behind me, closing in the past. The past hurts. The past ghosts. The past fears.

I was quiet in the car while I stared at the paperwork, the date in her handwriting attempting to taunt me one last time. But the lessons I'd learned from Aaron over those last five months wouldn't allow the doubts to take over again. He showed me how to value myself. He taught me how to love. He helped me overcome what I thought were insurmountable odds.

"Aaron?"

"Yes, my love?"

His reply was so open, so honest. Whatever I asked for in that very minute, he would've gone to the ends of the earth to make a reality for me. He put my needs first. Before his own. Before anyone else's. He was my better half, though he'd argue with me if I said that to him.

"Do you know why I kept these papers?"

"Honestly, I hope it's for a better reason than to beat yourself up over what you told me about them."

"All my life, my mother put drugs and alcohol ahead of me. Getting high and partying were more important than her only child. There were times I wouldn't eat for days because she was too strung out to make sure her child was nourished. She always put me last, without fail.

"Over the past five months, you've always put me first. You haven't just broken down walls to get in, you made me want to tear them down myself and forget they were ever there. You've shown me more love in this short time than she did my entire life. Her last act in this world was to selfishly overdose on the drugs she loved more than her child and leave me to deal with the aftermath of her choices again.

"I took these papers as a reminder of how precious our time together is, how short life is, and how it can all be taken away in the blink of an eye. They're important to me because I don't want to waste one more second fearing what the future may hold because of what my past held. And I don't want to spend one more night apart from you or take baby steps in our relationship while I make up my mind. If I lost you tomorrow, my biggest regret would be the time I've wasted not showing you how much I love you every single minute of every single day.

"I'm ready to be your full-time wife. I'll move in with you this very minute. I'll check every fear and doubt at the door and make sure our life together is incredible—if you still want me to."

"I've waited to hear those words from you every day and night for months. You're all I want, Christa. You're everything I could ever want. I'll send movers to your apartment to pack your things and deliver them to my place. I'm afraid you'll come to your senses and change your mind if you have to be there when your apartment is empty. But if it makes you feel better, we can go house hunting and find a new place that's ours."

I had to laugh at that, because he knew I'd feel sorry for my tiny, empty apartment. "House hunting? Does that include furniture and interior décor shopping?"

"Anything you want."

I leaned across the center console and kissed him. He turned his head slightly, trying to keep his eyes on the road while I kissed his cheek, his lips, and his neck. "I love you so very much, Aaron. I don't care where we live or what we have. As long as I'm with you, that's enough for me."

CHAPTER TWENTY-NINE

Endings—and New Beginnings

Aaron

"I still don't know how you convinced me to go along with this. Or why. Or why I'm even going through with it." Christa stomped through the condo, ranting in my general direction, though she was still getting dressed.

"Because you need it, sweetheart. I know you say you don't, and you're extremely adamant about it, but I was with you that day. You can't hide your feelings anymore." I helped her into her long wool coat and used that as an excuse to wrap my arms around her. "I thought you trusted me."

"I do," she conceded. "You're the best man I know, Aaron."

"I'll be with you. Every step of the way."

She tried to stall as long as she could, but eventually

she caved and got in the car. I'd talked her into having a memorial service for her mother. It'd be a small gathering, and she'd likely be the only one there who even knew the woman. In the few days after her death, the state had held her body until they ruled out any foul play. Every day of waiting in limbo affected Christa more than she wanted to admit.

But I knew her. I saw through her bravado. I felt her.

The click of her heels echoed down the vacant hall of the funeral home, and I expected to find we were alone in the sanctuary. My entire family was there, including my brother, with Allie on his arm. Jared and his family were also there. Though I wasn't thrilled with his presence, I was grateful for how his family supported my wife.

She introduced me to the entire Miller family as her husband, and I was positive I was a couple of feet taller than when we walked in. She spent time talking to everyone to avoid approaching the casket. Not that I blamed her, but I could feel her anxiety ratcheting up inside her with every tick of the clock. When she'd made her rounds and her avoidance became obvious, she dropped her purse in a chair and squeezed my hand in her dainty one.

"Stay with me, Aaron."

"Forever."

We approached the casket together, and she

remained stock-still while staring at her mother. "She's lost so much weight since the last time I saw her. Aaron, the what-if's flying through my mind are killing me."

"You couldn't have saved her." Another man's voice interrupted our conversation, and both of our heads snapped toward his direction. Christa stepped backward into me, her back against my chest, and I instinctively wrapped my arm around her.

"Who are you?" I demanded.

"My name is Chris Lanes. I'm Christa's father."

She molded into me more. My other arm wrapped around her, protecting her, shielding her. "I'm here," I murmured into her ear. "No one can hurt you while I'm here." Her nod was almost imperceptible, but I felt it. I felt her relax under my guard. I looked back up at Chris. "What did you mean when you said she couldn't have saved her mother?"

"Janice was never what you'd call stable, but she became worse over the last several months. She was mixing several kinds of drugs—crack, meth, heroin— you name it, she was addicted to it all. She'd called me, too, asking for money several weeks ago. I went to see her and took an application for a detox facility with me. The deal was I'd give her the money she asked for if after she completed the full program. I even offered to pay for it, if she'd just get clean.

"Even I couldn't save her, Christa. If she wouldn't do it for you, me, or the money I'd promised her, she wouldn't get clean for anything. You can't blame yourself or think you let her down in any way. You didn't, and if you'd given her anything, she'd just keep coming back for more and break your heart every time. Her addiction was too much for her to stop."

"You still loved her," Christa whispered, the pain in her voice palpable. "After all these years, you still loved her."

"I love her still. I'll never stop loving her. She wasn't always what you remember. She was the love of my life, and she captured my heart the day we met. She never gave it back."

"Why did you leave me?"

"I started using with her. It took a while, but I eventually saw how my life was spiraling out of control. She and I had a long talk about getting help, and she convinced me to check in to the hospital first so she could stay with you. When they were processing my paperwork, it triggered some outstanding warrants I had. So, the court ordered me to complete a one-year inpatient rehab stint or face up to seven years in prison. By the time I graduated from the program, Janice had taken out a restraining order against me and was in the process of having my parental rights taken away. I stopped that part, but I still couldn't come near her or you."

"How could she do all of that if she was abusing drugs and had no money to spend on a lawyer?"

"Her dealer had her selling for him. The longer she kept me away, the more control he had over her. It was a vicious cycle I never could break. I'm just so sorry you were caught in the middle of it, Christa. I tried to see you, I even tried to get custody of you, but nothing worked. My past never seemed to stay behind me."

"I know what you mean," Christa replied pensively. "Can you...come by the café sometime? I'd like to have a cup of coffee and chat with you."

His smile split his face in two, and the nearly broken man I saw a second before instantly transformed into a hopeful one. That was what my girl did to a mere mortal man. That was what she did to me.

I extended my hand toward him while keeping my other one wrapped securely around my wife. "I'm Aaron Rivers, her husband. It's good to finally meet you, though I'm sorry it's under these circumstances."

"Aaron, if you've earned Christa's love and respect, I have no doubt you're a good man. What you've done for Janice is more proof."

Friends and family gathered around us, and Chris

did his best to remember all the names thrown at him. He was especially grateful to the Miller family for taking care of his daughter when he couldn't be there for her. He and my father had an instant connection and were acting as if they were long-lost brothers before the funeral service was over.

After the burial, Christa and I were in the car, heading back to our condo, when she turned in her seat to face me. "Aaron?"

"Yeah, babe?"

"Why did you never give up on me? If you'd tried to push me away as hard as I did you, I don't know that I would've kept trying. I would've thought, if he wanted me in his life, I'd be in it. I wouldn't have to keep fighting for a spot. But you never gave up. Why?"

"You should never give up on someone you love. If you love them, they deserve a second chance, regardless of how many second chances they've already used. If I'd walked away without fighting for you until my very last breath, I would've regretted it for the rest of my life. I'd already learned my lesson about regrets, and you weren't going to be a repeat."

"There's something I need to do tomorrow morning. Will you come with me?"

"Of course."

"You're not going to ask what I need to do before committing?"

"No, because it doesn't matter. I'm in this for life. There is no you, no me—there's only 'we' now. We are one, so what makes you happy makes me happy. It's as simple as that."

She was deep in thought for the rest of the ride, no doubt reflecting on the emotionally draining day she'd had. When we walked into the condo, we headed straight to the bedroom and changed into our pajamas. I took a seat on the couch in front of the fireplace, and she immediately crawled into my lap. My arms circled around her, and I buried my face in her neck.

"I wrote down every text you sent me, and I kept every letter you sent me. I reread all of them every day. I'd wait for your text to come in and stare at it for the longest time, willing you to appear out of nowhere. Now you're here with me, and I'm never letting you go again."

I leaned down and gently kissed her. She knew how deep my love for her ran. She knew there was nothing I wouldn't do for her. Saying the words again was pointless. My actions proved it time and time again.

"I watched my father today when he wasn't looking. He stared at her lying in that casket like he wanted to crawl in there with her. After all this time, after everything she did to him, he still loves her. He'd rather die with her than live without her."

"I know exactly how he feels."

"I do too. That's what I was thinking about on the way home. So, from this second until the end of our life—notice I said life and not lives—we have no time for holding back. Every second of every day will be the best we've ever known. Even through hard times, even through all the fights where I'm right and you're wrong. Nothing can steal our happiness or take away our love. Promise?"

"Cross my heart."

Soon after we settled into a comfortable silence wrapped in each other's arms, she fell asleep, exhausted from the trying day. I stood with her in my arms, carried her to the bedroom, and undressed her for bed, all while resisting the urge to wake her with my tongue on her clit and my mouth devouring her pussy. As much as I needed to feel her body wrapped around mine, she needed to rest and recuperate.

But tomorrow. Tomorrow, she was all mine.

I slid in behind her, my skin against hers, and wrapped my arm around her. Sleep took over before I even realized how tired I was. When I awoke, it was to the most incredible feeling in the world. My morning wood was being put to good use by a warm, wet mouth hidden under the covers. I could barely open my eyes, but my body knew exactly what it wanted. And my cock was saying to take her right then before he exploded.

I reached under the covers to pull her up to ride me, but she resisted. "Baby, I've been holding back while we've been dealing with life. But right now, your mouth feels so fucking good, if you don't stop, I won't be able to stop."

Damn if she didn't work me harder, her actions showing me what she wanted. My hips bucked involuntarily, matching the rhythm of her mouth and hand working in tandem. My head fell to the pillow, my eyes rolled into the back of my head, and I took a flying leap over the edge while she swallowed every drop. My cock grew even harder when she crawled up my body and straddled me. Then she lowered herself down on me while I watched my dick disappear into her, one inch at a time.

Her hips undulated, first rocking back and forth, then up and down, while her fingers dug into my chest. My hands slid up her legs, clenched her hips, and helped guide her movements. As she came down, my hips surged upward, and her soft moans turned to feral screams. Sweat-slickened, her body glided against mine when she leaned over, her chest against mine. The sensation was too fucking much to handle, and I barely held on until she came one last time.

She collapsed on top of me, our bodies still joined as one in every possible way. If she moved in the slightest bit, I'd be ready to go again, though I wasn't sure she would be by the way she panted in my ear. Fuck, everything she did was so damn sexy.

"I have a surprise for you today."

"More than waking me up with the best damn blow job in the world?"

She giggled, and the ripples through her body hit mine. My cock began to harden inside her again, and then I thrust my hips upward. She sucked in a sharp breath and began to move with me. So, I rolled her over and fucked her with everything I had one more time. When we were both spent and breathing heavily, she gave me a lazy grin.

"I still have another surprise for you today. Do you think we can make it to the shower?"

I cut my eyes at her and raised one eyebrow in mock challenge. "Do you doubt my stamina? Do I need to prove it to you again?"

"No!" she yelled and laughed at the same time. "I believe you, I believe you. We have to leave the condo soon, though, so we'll have time for everything afterward."

"Get your fine ass up and shower, then. You have until the count of three, or I'm rolling over and fucking you again."

She found a sudden burst of energy and sprang out of bed. "If you do, we'll never get out of here!"

Showered, dressed, and in the car, she insisted on driving so I wouldn't know where we were going until we got there. She was so excited over the surprise, I couldn't deny her the pleasure of keeping it secret for a few minutes longer. When we pulled up outside the courthouse, I turned and gave her a puzzled expression.

"I thought we'd go in together and formally withdraw the divorce petition. There are some papers I have to fill out to stop the proceedings, and I want you to be there with me. It's symbolic of our new start."

"I'd love to, Christa." With my hands on her face, I pulled close to her and gave her the hottest, most X-rated kiss I could possibly give with our clothes on. "Mrs. Rivers."

"Forever," she replied earnestly.

With the papers completed, signed, and recorded, the sense of relief I felt was incredible. The last six months had been the longest of my life, every minute hanging on her decision to stay or go.

She looked up at me as we exited the building, love beaming from her eyes. I reached into my pocket and retrieved the small velvet bag that hadn't left my person since that day in Lance's office. When I stopped walking, she looked at me questioningly. Then I knelt on one knee and slid the rings back onto her finger. Where they'd always belonged. Where they'd always stay.

I raised my eyes to meet hers, and tears of happiness shimmered like diamonds. She smiled as I stood, still holding her hand in mine. "With this ring, I'm not only giving you all my love, but every part of me. Mind. Body. Heart. Making you fall in love with me all over again every single day will become my life's ambition.

"If the day ever comes when you give these rings back to me, I'll know you're throwing my love away, tossing us aside. I'd never be able to love anyone again after that. Hold on to us no matter what the future throws at us. Our love, our marriage, and our life together are all that matter. Never give up on me, Christa, and I'll make you the happiest woman who ever lived."

Tears rolled down her cheeks as she took my hand in hers, fingering the wedding band that hadn't left my hand since the night I put it on in Vegas. Even sitting in Lance's office, a strong foreboding and sense of profound loss wouldn't let me take it off.

"Before I met you, I never believed in love. I thought it was a fairy tale I'd only read about and could never happen to me. You took everything I held true and ruined it in the best way. The love you've freely given me opened my eyes, my mind, and my heart. The fears that held me captive disappeared when I found you.

"With this ring, I'm forever yours. I promise to love you more every day. To walk by your side, even when no one else will. To stand behind you and help you achieve your dreams. To be whatever you need when you need me the most. I'll never give up on you. I'll never stop loving you. If the day ever comes when you're no longer with me, I'll never love another. I've found the other half of my soul in you and only you."

"The wedding vows you wrote for me," I replied, equally shocked and thrilled.

"I still mean every word of them." She rose up on her toes and kissed me, sealing our commitment yet again.

"You've completely captivated me, Christa."

EPILOGUE

Delilah

Love is a funny thing, isn't it? People could be so fickle, never knowing which paths their lives should take. Sometimes they just needed a good, swift kick in the ass to make them see. Like my sweet Christa and her handsome man, Aaron. Now that their future was finally on the right road, it was time to turn my sights on another who had lost her way.

I stepped into the café, and the chimes over the door alerted her to my presence. Christa and Aaron were finally on their two-week honeymoon in Maui. Aaron tried to talk her into going somewhere more "exotic," but she was adamant to see Hawaii. Their absence left one person there to deal with me.

"Christa isn't back yet," Allie said, effectively dismissing me when she turned her back to me.

No matter. I didn't become the woman I was by

backing down from insignificant challenges. "I'm not here for Christa today, and you damn well know it, young lady."

She turned slowly but deliberately, cutting her hostile eyes at me. "I've tolerated your presence for Christa's sake, because she loves you and because I know you've been secretly helping her. She told me she refused the money you've been saving for her since she and Aaron have enough to make the world go 'round a few more times. But she doesn't know everything about you. She didn't grow up under your thumb, always made to feel irrelevant and like an outcast. Until Christa gets back, you can get your coffee somewhere else."

"You tasted happiness long enough for Christa to realize she'd found hers. Then you dumped that poor man, Lance, the minute Christa stopped her divorce. That man loves you, and it's time for you to stop running and *allow* him to love you."

"It's time for you to leave, Nana. You have no say over how I live my life anymore." Allie put her fists on her hips, drew in a deep breath, and glared at me.

I'd seen that stance many times before. Ever since she was a headstrong little girl, she used that posture to signal her stubborn streak. She wouldn't listen to me then, not in that state. It'd take more finagling to make her see the light.

Game on, little girl. Game on.

"Okay," I replied, infusing my tone with as much sadness as I could. "I'll go. I'm sorry you hate me so much. I love you, my little spitfire. I've always loved you with all of my heart."

My walk back to the door was unhurried and measured. She'd seldom seen me sad and never saw me broken, so that version of me was no doubt confusing. I wanted to give her plenty of time seeing me in that state before I was out of sight. It would help us both later, when I implemented my plan for Allie and Lance.

Until then, buttercups. Until then...

ACKNOWLEDGEMENTS

This part is the hardest part of the book to write because I don't want to leave anyone out or make anyone feel unappreciated. I am so grateful for everyone who supports me in this endeavor. Singling people out for their specific support is my way of saying an extra special THANK YOU for their unwavering help.

First and foremost, I want to thank my Lord and Savior for His continued forgiveness of a sinner.

To my husband: I love you. Thank you for putting up with the late nights, long weekends, and the less-than-stellar kept house. Writing the book didn't help much with any of that, either. ☺

To my reader group: You are the best. Thank you for being my beta readers, my sounding boards, my biggest supporters, and the all-around best people in the world. Love all of you!

Michelle Dare, you have talked me off the ledge too many times to count. I don't know what I'd do without you. You're one of my closest friends and one of the few people I actually do trust. Love you, my friend!

My Beta Readers, thank you for all the time you spend reading my books and giving feedback. But more than that, thank you for all the laughs in our secret group, for the friendships we've made, and the good times we've had. You're all forever in my heart.

Lisa Hollett, you're both my editor and my friend. I appreciate your feedback and witty banter...along with all the drinks, meals, and crazy conversations we've had!

The NCC Authors, you always have my back and are willing to try whatever crazy idea I suggest. You're the best group of ladies and I love all of you!

My FTN girls, thank you for the laughs, the safe space to vent, and the friendships formed in there. Lisa Paul, I freaking love you especially. If I didn't have to work all day, I have no doubt we'd spend hours on the phone, just talking and laughing, and loving every minute of it! Ilsa Madden-Mills, you are such a wonderful person! Mucho, mucho love for all y'all! ☺

Bloggers, thank you so much for everything you do to support my books and tell your readers about them. You make this dream possible and I'll never forget that.

Readers, without your support and willingness to take a chance on a new author, none of us would have a reason to do this. These characters live and breathe in our imagination and they come to life through you, through your love for them, and through your word of mouth. Thank you for reading authors everywhere, but a special thanks from this author for your support.

ABOUT THE AUTHOR

A.D. Justice is happily married to her husband of more than twenty-five years. They have two sons together and enjoy a wide variety of outdoor activities. A.D. has a full-time job by day, with a BS degree in Organizational Management and an MBA in Health Care Administration. Writing gives her the outlet she needs to live in the fantasy world that is a constant in her mind.

Thank you for reading and supporting A.D.'s books. Please take a moment to leave a review of this work.

Connect with her online:

Facebook: https://www.facebook.com/adjusticeauthor

Twitter: https://twitter.com/ADJustice1

Web: www.authoradjustice.com

Email: adjustice@outlook.com

Newsletter:
http://www.subscribepage.com/adjustice